Silver Moon

by Catherine Lundoff

Crave: Tales of Lust, Love and Longing (2007)

Night's Kiss (2009)

A Day at the Inn, A Night at the Palace and Other Stories (2011)

as editor

Haunted Hearths and Sapphic Shades: Lesbian Ghost Stories (2008)

Hellebore and Rue: Tales of Queer Women and Magic (2011)
[with JoSelle Vanderhooft]

Silver Moon

A WOMEN OF WOLF'S POINT NOVEL

Catherine Lundoff

MAPLE SHADE, NEW JERSEY

Published in 2012 by Lethe Press, Inc.
118 Heritage Avenue ♦ Maple Shade, NJ 08052-3018
www.lethepressbooks.com ♦ lethepress@aol.com
ISBN: 1-59021-379-3
ISBN-13: 978-1-59021-379-7

This novel is a work of fiction. Names, characters, places, and incidents are products of the author's imagination or are used fictitiously.

Set in Jenson and Ugly Qua.
Interior design: Alex Jeffers.
Cover design: Fred Tovich.

LIBRARY OF CONGRESS CATALOGING-IN-PUBLICATION DATA

Lundoff, Catherine, 1963-
 Silver moon / Catherine Lundoff.
  p. cm. -- (Women of Wolf's Point)
 ISBN 978-1-59021-379-7 (pbk. : alk. paper)
 1. Lesbians--Fiction. 2. Werewolves--Fiction. I. Title.
 PS3612.U54S55 2012
 813'.6--dc23

                    2012009886

Dedicated to Jana, who has always wanted me to finish a novel, and to Steve Berman of Lethe Press, who wanted me to finish this one. With many thanks to Connie Wilkins and Haddayr Copley-Woods, who provided invaluable feedback when it was most needed.

Chapter 1

Her first hot flash came on suddenly and unexpectedly, super-heating Becca Thornton's body from head to toe until she was drenched with sweat. It propelled her off the couch and into the bathroom to splash cold water on her face. As the water dripped down her cheeks, she glanced at her tomato-like complexion and bit off a shriek.

There had been something new in her reflection, a flickering of golden eyes and fur, visible for the blink of an eye. Something feral and wild strained its way toward the surface behind her otherwise utterly normal features. *What the hell?* She closed her eyes, shutting out the hallucination or whatever it was.

Everything slowed down for a minute, as if this new wildness that lurked inside her was being locked back in its cage. When she looked again, there was nothing new and terrifying to be seen. Her own face, round and furless, stared back at her, light brown eyes startled but perfectly ordinary. It was a face like that of any other woman of a certain age in a one-horse town like Wolf's Point. For a moment, she wondered if this gradual softening and rounding of features, this planing away of the sharp edges, was what they all had in common.

But the thought was overwhelmed by a second, milder flash. Becca lurched outside and dropped onto her porch swing, the fan in her hand trying to supplement the tiny morning breeze. She rocked slowly back and forth and cursed turning fifty, but silently so that the neighbors wouldn't notice. Here in Wolf's Point they noticed quite a bit, from what she'd gathered.

Across the street, her neighbor Erin walked out on her porch and Becca gave her a half-hearted wave. Just her luck, Erin waved back, then started over. This wasn't going to help cool her down much, that was for sure.

Silver Moon

Erin wasn't like the rest of the townsfolk, at least as far as Becca was concerned. She'd only been Becca's neighbor for about a year, which made her a little exotic by itself. Most of the other neighbors had been there forever. While Becca hadn't asked, she assumed that like her, Erin had married into Wolf's Point. Then lost her husband somewhere along the way and bought a house on a quiet street outside the downtown hub. Wasn't that what single women of a certain age did with themselves once their husbands were gone, one way or another?

But regardless of how she came to be there, just talking to Erin made Becca feel different, kind of shy and squirmy inside. It was weird; she hadn't had trouble talking to anyone or even speaking in front of an audience for ages now. Everyone said she was the best speaker at the Wolf's Point Women's Club. After all, she'd been doing that kind of stuff since Ed dumped her two years ago.

That, of course, sent her overheated brain spiraling off into thoughts about her ex. She and Ed had met at a bank in the city where she worked as a teller and he was trying to get a loan. After they got married, they'd moved around the country while he worked at too many sales jobs for her to remember and she worked at whatever was available. It had been a mostly good fifteen years, though she had missed settling down and really building a home, maybe raising a family.

Then they moved to Wolf's Point and everything changed. Ed decided his life was incomplete unless he got himself a twenty-something blonde and a sports car and that, as they said, was that. She wondered if it made him feel any younger. *Good luck to him and his trophy bimbo*, she thought contemptuously and smiled at how little the thought seemed to bother her anymore. It felt good to be leaving him like so much baggage on the side of the road, just like he'd done to her.

Erin arrived on the heels of the smile. "Hey there. Pretty hot out this morning, huh?" She grinned her slow lazy smile that always made Becca think about cowboys. Cowgirls. Whatever. Maybe it was her neighbor's long lean body or her short-cropped graying hair. Or the slow way she talked, like she'd just ridden in off the range. It wasn't too much of a leap to picture her on horseback.

Becca dragged her mind back to the present and gave herself a stern mental admonition to stop daydreaming. "Yep. And I'm even hotter on top of that." She rolled her eyes and fanned faster, like that was going to help. It wasn't quite what she meant to say but she figured it would pass without comment.

It didn't. Erin raised an eyebrow and cocked her head to one side like a big dog. "No question about that. Or am I missing something?"

Becca felt a flush paint her cheeks and nearly hid her face in her fan just like an old-time court lady. But, of course, Erin hadn't meant anything by it. Not like there was anything to mean for that matter. Who'd say something like that about her middle-aged dumpy self anymore?

"I'm…extra warm today. I seem to be coming up on the change," she mumbled finally when she realized Erin was still waiting for an answer. She could almost hear the word spelled with an invisible capital letter "C."

Erin's grin turned a little strange, as if her face was somehow longer than it should be. Becca blinked and tried to convince herself it was just a trick of the morning light. Her neighbor's face seemed normal enough when she looked back up: broad cheeks, silver-gray eyes, cheerful grin exposing slightly crooked teeth.

"Well," Erin said at last, "this calls for a celebration. We usually hold a little party down at the Club when that time of life comes around for one of our members."

"News to me. No one ever said anything about it before. This one of those Red Hat things?" Becca scowled. Why would Erin know something like this when she didn't? After all, she'd been a member for two whole years, for God's sake, a whole year longer than Erin. She was even in the running to be Club Secretary in the next election if all went well. But she'd be damned if she was putting on a red hat and a feather boa, no matter how much fun everyone else said it was.

Erin grinned a little wider as if she was imagining Becca in the hat and the boa. Becca wondered what else she was wearing in the other woman's imagination and flushed even more. Now where had that notion come from? This day got any weirder and she was going to need to go over to the clinic for a checkup.

Erin's voice cut into her thoughts, "Nope. Can you really see me in a red hat, much less a boa?" Becca glanced at her scruffy plaid shirt and jeans and shook her head. Erin went on talking, "We just get together, have some cake and a margarita or two and talk about some of the things that made life easier when we first started going through that time of life. Don't spread the word too far though; we're trying to keep the youngsters out until they're old enough to relate." She winked, a slow sensuous gesture that made Becca smile despite herself. Erin continued, "Your schedule pretty open Friday night? We like to run a little late on these things."

Becca raised an eyebrow but nodded anyway. She was trying to picture the older members of their little club staying awake past nine and so far it wasn't working. But maybe she didn't know them as well as she thought she did. Erin made another comment or two about stopping by to pick her up on Friday, then took off.

Becca made herself not watch her walk away, the fact that she wanted to do just that surprising her more than anything else that had happened so far this morning. Instead, she got ready for work and headed into downtown on foot.

Her walk down 5th to Main St. always gave her a terrific view of the mountains that surrounded Wolf's Point on three sides, their peaks looming over the tiny houses below. Becca paused a moment to let a breeze cool her cheeks and take a deep breath. Any time she wondered why she'd stayed on here after she and Ed split up, all she had to do was look at the mountains. This was her place now, the home she'd always wanted.

She made a quick stop beforehand at the store for lunch and to check out the magazine rack. There had to be something out there about dealing with menopause. Besides, the less thinking she did about Erin Adams and her mysterious groups, the better.

But the grocery story didn't yield much in the way of information unless Becca wanted sensual feasts to keep her man's interest. *Well, that ship sailed a while back,* she thought as she looked over the glossy covers.

And then, it was like she was someone else. Her lip curled over one incisor and she almost growled.

The sensation made her gasp and rub her face to get it back to normal. She took a quick look around, hoping no one else had noticed anything unusual. She needn't have worried. Becca Thornton at fifty might as well have been invisible. Carts went around her, younger women picked up the romance novels, men old and young picked up the sports and car magazines, and not one of them noticed anything different about her.

For a moment, that bothered her almost as much as the strange feelings, then she shrugged. It was just as well, given how strange she was feeling today. She glanced at the wall clock. It was almost time for her shift at the hardware store, that time of life or not. She paid for her sandwich and apple and headed out into the sunny street.

Peterson's Hardware was just two blocks away so she ate her lunch on the way. Not for the first time, she found herself being grateful that Wolf's Point still had a hardware store. And a downtown with a grocery store. Odd how the big chain stores were never able to get a foothold around here. Why, the nearest big box was over two hundred miles away. The end result was that Pete didn't have much competition and she got paid more than she would have at another kind of store. Just one of Wolf's Point's many good features, she reminded herself.

The blocks between the grocery and hardware stores were filled with pedestrians. There was a good flow of tourists in town and the crowds filled Main Street with energy and a sense of possibility. Sometimes, Becca thought that it felt like there was a kind of magic at work here, something that protected Wolf's Point from the worst of the outside world and only let in the good.

The notion made her smile as she walked up past the lawnmowers and grills that decorated the sidewalk in front of Peterson's. Then she swung the door open and her mood shifted. Erin and her buddy Molly Kirk and Shelly Peterson were all leaning on the counter, their heads close together like they were sharing secrets.

She wondered what they had to whisper about. Maybe about what she said to Erin? Erin wouldn't tell anyone about that, would she? And Shelly wasn't one for gossip. She watched her boss' brown-skinned, hawk-nosed profile tilt back in a quiet laugh that shook the long black braid that ran down her narrow back.

In contrast, Molly was a big, round, pale-skinned woman with a gap-toothed grin that lit up her face like Christmas. Watching her turn that grin on Erin sent a spike through Becca's innards before she could make herself think logically. What the hell was wrong with her? She had nothing against Molly Kirk and no reason to think any of them meant her ill.

But despite her intentions, she swung back and forth between jealousy and paranoia for a long couple of seconds, refusing to acknowledge that she felt either emotion. Finally, she made herself smile instead of giving her fears free rein. "Hi!"

The three turned and grinned at her, breaking her thoughts up into little jagged shards. She had a disturbing impression of glowing eyes and lolling tongues and she shook her head to clear it. Evidently her change of life was going to be more bizarre than anyone else's. Somehow, that figured, but at least it gave her thoughts some context. Now all she had to do was get a handle on her imagination.

That was the moment when Pete Peterson himself ambled down the nail aisle looking like a Viking god misplaced from some legend. He nodded a greeting when he saw her. "There's a guy over in the paint section who wants your help, Becca," he rumbled. "Ladies," he added, a second nod to the women at the counter, before walking away into the plumbing and electrical supplies section.

Silver Moon

Becca made herself not watch him walk away either. Peter was a fine big figure of a man, just the kind she would've gone for when she was younger. But he was married, and besides, he just didn't make her feel all squirmy inside like…

"Hey Becca, I'll stop by when you're done with your shift," Erin's voice purred in the vicinity of her ear, sending a flush through Becca's cheeks that she couldn't control. She nodded and bolted for the paint section, resolving not to think about anything except hardware for the rest of the day.

After Erin and Molly left, there was a succession of customers picking up paint or supplies or agonizing about color choices. Just enough to put Erin out of her mind. Almost, anyway. She settled into the rhythm of her work and restocked supplies once the first wave of customers came and went.

Then, when that got too slow, Shelly came by wanting some help with the window display. While they worked on that, they made small talk about the town and the store, about what would look good in the windows and about the forthcoming Wolf's Point Days sidewalk sale. Becca thought for the hundredth time in two years about how amazingly lucky she'd been to get this job. There was something about talking to Shelly that made every word seem significant, even if it wasn't about very much.

Before she knew it, it was the end of her day and there was Erin waiting outside, her long form leaning up against a lamppost outside like something out of a noir film. All she needed was a fedora and a smoke. Becca squirmed, fantasizing about ducking out the back door for a minute, but there were Pete and Shelly herding her out the front door.

"You gals have a nice evening," Pete winked at Erin.

Just like we were on a date or something! Becca bit the words back before they could cross her lips. No point in planting that particular seed where it didn't need to start growing. Those kinds of rumors could wreak some serious havoc on her nonexistent dating prospects. She bit back a snort and made herself smile up at Erin. "You didn't have to stop by to meet me, you know. I'm used to walking home alone in the evening."

Erin grinned back at her. "But tonight the moon's almost full and the mountains look even more gorgeous than usual. I thought you might want to take the long way home and check out the scenic route. I even brought tea." She held out a shiny little coffee mug and a small white paper bag. "And chocolate."

"You do think of everything." Becca helped herself to a small piece of the chocolate and gulped down the tea before handing the bag and the cup back. Erin turned away to tuck them back in her pack just as the moon caught Becca's eye.

She found herself staring up at it like she'd never seen it before. Had it always been so white, so compelling? It pulled at the tides in her blood, rustling under her skin until she was so jumpy she wanted to run and howl. She forced her tone to sound casual. "Let's walk then."

They moved briskly, Becca surprising herself by keeping up with Erin's long strides. There was a breeze blowing tonight, coming in from out of town somewhere. It was full of tantalizing scents, ones that Becca had never noticed before. The wind's fingers twisted their way through her hair, lifting it out of the scrunchy that tried to restrain it until she gave up and yanked it off. She felt like anything might happen tonight. The thought thrummed through her like a drumbeat.

"Do you run?" Erin's voice growled from somewhere above her and she shivered as if she was shaking off an old skin. For an answer, she swung her bag back out of the way. Then she lunged forward into a lope that came easily to her. It wasn't too fast but it was certainly more of a run than she'd attempted in years. She tried not to think about how much her calves would hurt later.

Erin effortlessly kept pace with her as they charged from downtown onto the more deserted side streets, heading for the river. The bag banging against Becca's back was a minor irritation, one she could ignore in her newly discovered speed and stamina. She sucked in the wind like a drink and imagined for a moment that the two of them were chasing something, something they had to catch. Her white tennis shoes twinkled below her against the dark pavement as they surged out onto the bridge.

The river rapids thundered beneath its rusting metal trusses and Erin caught Becca's arm to slow her down and draw her to the rail. Together, they panted out into the moonlit dark in companionable silence. Becca grinned down at the water, its rushing length matching her mood. "Maybe this will be the year that I finally go on that whitewater trip Ed was always going on about."

"Sounds like a great idea." Erin said enthusiastically. And just like that, Becca knew who she wanted to go with. She'd been alone too long; it was time that she started making some new friends. She glanced sidelong at Erin, watching her nostrils flare in the breeze. The slight elongation of her face that Becca had seen earlier was back, as was the silver tint in her eyes.

But now it felt right, like it was the way she should look. She grinned back at Becca, and even the length and sharpness of her teeth seemed to

Silver Moon

suit her face better than they had back in town. "Thanks for running with me. I needed that."

"Rough day crunching the numbers?" Becca remembered that Erin was an accountant, but she always had problems reconciling it with what she'd seen of her neighbor. She seemed like she should be herding cattle or something, lariat in hand.

"Always." Erin threw back her head, tilting her nose up at the moon. For a second, Becca wondered if she was going to howl at it. They both looked up, silent again for a moment.

Then Becca glanced down at the water and her hands on the railing. Had her fingers always been so long, the backs of her hands so dark, almost as if they were covered with…black fur?

"Have some more tea," Erin nudged her hard, as if determined to interrupt her thoughts, and thrust the thermos into Becca's hands.

When Becca looked at her fingers again a couple of seconds later, they looked normal. "So when you were going through menopause, did you think you were seeing a lot of crazy things, stuff you knew couldn't be happening?" She asked at last. She tried to make her tone casual, as if she was just making conversation.

"You kidding?" Erin laughed heartily. "I thought I was seeing Elvis down at the diner every time I had a hot flash!" She seemed to catch a bit of Becca's mood then and reached out to pat her shoulder reassuringly. "You'll be fine. It just takes a little adjustment."

Seeing Elvis wouldn't be so bad, Becca thought. It was the rest of it that was kind of disturbing. That was when she noticed the van traveling slowly down the highway that ran past the end of the bridge. Not that there was much to notice about it—it was white with a logo on the side that she couldn't read from where they stood and that was about it. But there was something about the tinted windows and the way it paused as it passed the bridge, almost like the driver was watching them, sizing them up, that made it sinister.

It made the back of her neck tingle and her knees quiver a little like she wanted to chase the van or run away or something. She could feel Erin stiffen at her side and when she looked up, she could see the other woman's lips curled back in a snarl. Her incisors looked impossibly long in the moonlight. "The bastards are back!" Erin spat, glaring ferociously at the van as it disappeared around a curve.

"Huh? What bastards? You know who it was driving that thing?" Becca was alert now, sensing some kind of danger though she didn't know what it could be.

Erin took a deep breath and seemed to force herself to relax a little. "Just some guys out to cause trouble. They've been around here before and a few of us had to let them know they weren't welcome. Looks like we'll be doing that again." Erin sent another glare in the direction the van had gone. "Well, come on. I think we better get you home."

Becca's lips parted as a horde of questions tried to force their way out. Why did Erin know all these things about Wolf's Point that she didn't? Secret rituals, vigilante justice—what was next? Monsters in the woods? But she glanced at her companion and closed her mouth, swallowing the questions back down. Erin's mind was elsewhere and whatever she was thinking about was serious. Her own curiosity could wait a day or two. She just hoped it wouldn't be longer than that.

Silver Moon

Becca tried to forget about the van and Erin's reaction during the gaping chasm of time that lay between her and Friday. She'd never known two days to pass so slowly, not even after her divorce, when it felt like time stood still. It didn't help her impatience and trepidation that Erin wasn't around and that Shelly wasn't saying much about anything at all.

It wasn't like Becca wasn't being direct, even more so than usual. They were restocking the shelves the next morning when she asked, "Hey Shelly, you know anything about some guys in a white van causing trouble around here? Erin and I saw them last night and she seemed kind of upset."

Shelly raised one dark eyebrow and gave her a sidelong glance. "Yeah, Erin mentioned that those clowns were back. They're just some jerks who like to get drunk in the woods. Every now and then one of them decides he's a wolf hunter. Erin'll let the rangers know and they'll run them off." Shelly looked like she thought that settled it and it might have except that Becca remembered that the rangers hadn't figured into anything that Erin had actually said.

She tried again and got nowhere. She couldn't dig up much on the Women's Club Friday night event either. Shelly practically grunted, "Margaritas, cake, talking, one or two other things. Nothing to worry about, we just need to see what happens. We've all been there, at least all of us who'll be there on Friday evening." And that and an enigmatic and distracted smile were all Becca could get out of her.

It didn't help Becca's state of mind that, silent treatment or not, Shelly seemed to be watching her with an odd expression every time she looked up. Almost like she thought she might go postal or something. Her nerves twitched until Becca thought she'd climb out of her own skin.

She even thought about calling Ed. Of course, they hadn't spoken in months and it wasn't like they were friends or anything like that. It was hard to get over being dumped for a woman half her age, after all, plus it wasn't like their communication had been that great before they split. But at least she knew what she was dealing with when it came to him.

He'd tell her she was just imagining things, like he always did. Then he'd rag on her about her weight and how she'd let herself go. Then maybe after that, he'd offer to come by and work on the house. And she'd get pissed off at him and stop talking to him again for a few more months. It was the same pattern they'd had for a couple of years and it was crappy, but at least it was something that felt normal.

But she really didn't want the same old, same old, not this time. She realized that. It was all different now. Now there were moonlit nights and runs through the trees and winds full of scents she'd never noticed before. And an intriguing neighbor she wanted to get to know better. Calling Ed dropped off the list of possibilities.

She thought briefly about calling someone else, family or friends, but she didn't have much family left, not that she was close to, anyway. This wasn't the sort of thing her cousins in Mountainview would get. That much she was sure about. As for friends, most of those would be there on Friday night so she could talk to them then.

Instead, she'd tried to fill the time by stopping by the clinic to see if they could figure out what was wrong with her. She was helpfully informed that "It was just that time of life, dear," which she supposed was meant to be comforting. Even going online at the library didn't tell her anything that described what she was feeling.

So when she got tired of thinking about her health, she found herself looking up Wolf's Point to see what else she didn't know about the town's history. There was, it turned out, quite a bit. The first white settlers, fur traders and miners, for the most part, called the valley "Mountainview." They assumed the land was unpopulated until they met the local Indian population. Or vice versa, depending on whose point of view you were reading.

After that, the details got murky. The local tribe called themselves something that the white settlers understood as "The Sisters of the Wolf." That part made no sense to Becca. What did the guys call themselves?

Aside from that one mention, there were a couple of sidebars on skirmishes between the two peoples, followed by the sudden and remarkable onset of peace. Wolf's Point's early inhabitants settled in and merged so thoroughly with each other that Becca couldn't find anything more about

Catherine Lundoff   12

the original tribe. That seemed kind of weird. Why wouldn't there be more of a record of what happened to them? Maybe the original Native folks in the area had been wiped out or sent to a reservation somewhere else. Or maybe they were still here.

She made a note to herself to ask around and kept reading. Elsewhere on the site, there were a few links leading to different references about people looking or acting like wolves. These were an odd mix of European and Native American stories and she had some trouble seeing what the connection was. She wondered what all the people who had come to the valley had in common, other than an unhealthy fascination with predators.

She did find out that the first mayor was a woman, which was pretty much unheard of in the late 1800s. In fact, if the site was correct, this happened a good ten years before the history books mentioned a woman getting elected to mayor anywhere in the U.S.

For an encore, shortly after she took office, the town council passed their first resolution: no one could hunt a wolf within the confines of the valley. Then they changed the town name to "Wolf's Point."

Becca felt something, not quite a chill, more like a shiver, run down her back, followed by a familiar flash of heat. Why was this so important that it was the first thing they decided? And why was she reacting to it? It wasn't like she was planning on going wolf hunting any time soon.

There were wolf packs in the mountains still, but most of the local wolves lived on the Wolf Preserve just outside town. She'd gone on the Preserve's Wolf Call right after she moved to town. She and Ed spent two nights camping out, listening to the wolves howl and tracking them through the woods. They'd been beautiful to watch and listen to and their howls haunted her dreams for weeks afterwards. But that was it. She didn't own any kitschy wolf-print sweatshirts or have any little paw prints tattooed on her ankles, like some of the women in town.

Then she poked around some more and noticed that the original ordinance was still in place. What was even more interesting, the towns around Wolf's Point abided by it too. She wondered how anyone enforced that. Sure, the rangers did their best but it was hard to protect the wolves off the Preserve and not everyone in the valley thought they were as beautiful as she did.

It was right after that when she made an even stranger discovery. Her search turned up a link for a site called "The Slayer's Nest." When she opened it, there was a call for volunteers, "warriors," no less, to go to Wolf's Point. Her Wolf's Point. It didn't say why. The site's overall look: animated flaming torches and blood-red lettering, didn't make her want to sign up

Silver Moon

for membership. There was also a logo: a wooden stake crossed with a gray bullet, surrounded by an open wolf's jaws. The front fangs were broken.

She bit back a snarl, her shoulders rising and skin hot with an oncoming flash, and she looked away from the screen for a few minutes while she forced air into her lungs. This was crazy. Why was she overreacting like this? It was probably just one of those role-playing games she'd heard about. But why come to Wolf's Point?

She couldn't figure it out from the public parts of the site and you had to sign up to get on their mailing list. Somehow, that wasn't very appealing. Still it was all enough to tell her that there was more to her town than met the eye, at least as far as outsiders were concerned.

She worried at her thoughts like a dog with a bone as she walked home to a solitary dinner. That night, she dreamt she was a wolf. She was running with a pack of other wolves that was tearing through the forest chasing something she couldn't see. The air whipped through her fur and her paws blurred beneath her as she sped up for the sheer joy of running, of chasing her prey. A larger wolf ranged alongside her and flashed her a panting doggy grin. Its eyes glinted silver and familiar and she barked a greeting at it. Together they jumped a stream and scrambled up some rocks.

Then she could see what they were chasing. She woke up with a yell, one foot landing on the floor next to her bed as her body jerked its way upward in shock. Trembling, she reached for the lamp on the nightstand and flooded the room with light. She pulled her foot back up and sat curled around her knees for what seemed like hours, her head held carefully in her hands until her breathing slowed and she stopped shaking.

That was when she realized that she couldn't remember exactly what she'd seen just before she woke up. Becca cursed her subconscious in a very unladylike way. Then she got up to get a glass of water. She wandered into the living room to drink it while she zoned out and stared down the deserted street.

Or at least it seemed deserted until she looked into the shadows. There were big dogs out there, five or six of them, traveling in a group. In the darkness, they all looked pretty wolflike, but she knew that was ridiculous. Wolves wouldn't be running through town like that, so it had to be dogs. She learned that much from the Wolf Call. Whatever they were, they seemed to be headed for the river and she watched, baffled, as the small pack vanished into the trees at the end of the street.

A part of her howled to go outside and follow them. She jerked away from the insanity of that notion, pushing it back down inside until she couldn't hear its crazy little voice. Instead, she dragged one reluctant foot

Catherine Lundoff

after another back to her bedroom and read until she was too sleepy to keep her eyes open or dream about wolves or anything else.

Silver Moon

Chapter 3

The morning arrived way too soon after she finally dropped off. When she couldn't pretend to sleep any more, Becca got up, glaring quietly at the light streaming in through the curtains. It was early enough for a walk, even after shower and breakfast. Unfortunately. But that might be enough to wake her up before work.

The decision was made for her and she wandered out of her house, still yawning. She found herself following the same route to the river that the dogs had taken the night before. Or morning before. She groaned out loud at the thought and kept walking.

The river gorge was beautiful in the early morning light. The trees, aspen and birch for the most part, rustled in the morning breeze and she started to relax for the first time since her dream. She perched on a large rock and watched the water go by, letting the newly risen sun sink into her bones.

The scrape of shoe against stone made her jump from her reverie, all senses on the alert. The woman who stood on the other bank watching her wasn't a local, at least as far as Becca knew. She was short and broad-shouldered and had a long, jagged scar on one brown cheek, visible even under the shadows from the trees. Her short-cropped hair was dark and wavy against her scalp and her eyes were hard. She didn't smile in response to Becca's nod.

Becca found herself getting more than a little angry. What was with people these days anyway? Who did this stranger think she was? Stupid tourists, traipsing all over the place with their white vans and their attitudes. She could feel her lip curl back over her teeth and it was all she could do not to growl at the other woman.

Silver Moon

They stared at each other for a few more seconds until Becca finally cleared her throat and demanded, "Yes? Do you need something?"

The other woman stepped forward into the sunlight, her lips curling in a smile that didn't reach her eyes. "Just out for a walk. I was camping downstream and this looked like a nice spot for a swim." She gestured at the pool with one broad hand.

Somehow, Becca didn't believe her. But then, what difference did it make? What kind of harm could she possibly do? She met the woman's eyes again and felt a little shiver run through her. There was some kind of challenge there, along with something that felt just a bit familiar. But that made no sense; she was sure she'd never seen this woman before. She blinked and glanced away for a second to clear her head and the sensation went away.

Then the woman stretched gracefully, her wide shoulders shifting like a wrestler's. "You ever see any wolves in these woods?" Her tone was casual but something in it caught Becca's attention, jolting her body awake and taut, like a wire.

But she took a deep breath to steady herself, trying to feel her way to a casual response; somehow she didn't want this stranger knowing what she was thinking. It felt like a test of some sort. "Yep, they're mostly down in the Preserve. It's illegal to hunt them around here, you know."

The woman smiled again. "I look like a wolf hunter to you? I take photos but I don't like to be surprised by my subjects. I just wanted to know how safe it was out here."

Becca found herself choosing her words with care again before she spoke. After all, it wasn't like nothing ever happened in Wolf's Point. No point in being too trusting about strangers. Or letting them think that they were all welcome, even the bad ones. There had been that young man killed out in the quarry a few years back. But then they'd caught the guy who did that, something about a fight over a truck.

Then there had been the couple who had tried to set up a meth lab just outside town—blown sky high the two of them were. But the coroner had ruled that an accident. Meth was flammable stuff, or so she'd heard. Good thing no one else was tempted to try it, at least that she'd heard.

Her thoughts wandered around until she wondered why she was thinking about making the town sound more dangerous than it was. It wasn't like she had any business running the tourists off. Even the annoying ones. She wondered if this was the onset of her crotchety old lady years. That was enough to make her choke out, "It's pretty safe around here."

Then something made her add, "Most folks who find it otherwise bring their own trouble with them." Her words surprised her, like they'd come from someone else.

The other woman raised an eyebrow and held up her hands to show they were empty. "Not looking for any trouble. Just heard this was a nice safe place to camp for a woman on her own."

Becca flinched. Her imagination was running away from her along with her hormones. Here she was projecting her nightmares and bad mood on some poor stranger. "I'm sorry. I had a bad night and you startled me, that's all. The wolves have never attacked anyone as far as I know and yes, this is a safe place to camp. If you want to go into town, we've got a pretty good deli and the pie at Millie's is the best for miles around. If you're up for a hike, Jenner's Falls is a few miles upstream. It's really gorgeous this time of year." She glanced down at her watch. "I need to head back and get to work. Have a nice stay."

The woman bared her teeth in acknowledgement and nodded. "Thanks. You have a good day."

Becca headed back up through the trees, but just before she went over the ridge, she glanced back. The woman was still looking after her but now she had company. There was a man, big and blond with a long, angular face, standing next to her on the riverbank. The woman seemed to know him. That was odd; why had the woman said she was alone if there was someone else with her?

Overcome by curiosity, she ducked behind a tree and watched them through a screen of leaves for a couple of minutes. The man was talking, gesturing, but she was too far away to hear what he was saying. Then he turned and she thought she saw a familiar logo on the back of his black jacket.

She remembered the website she'd seen and her pulse started to race. Her hands were shaking as she argued with herself: there was nothing to worry about and she was overreacting. The second and third repetitions didn't work either. This woman and her companion just…smelled wrong. Now where had that come from?

She took a couple of deep breaths to clear her head. Whoever these people were, even if they were just role-playing, someone should know about them and keep an eye on them. Becca headed for town at a trot. She had to tell some authority figure, warn them to look out for these strangers.

She raced toward the sheriff's office, her steps slowing to a walk as she paused to catch her breath on the outskirts of town. Odd how she felt so

Silver Moon

invincible running with Erin the other night and now she could barely do more than a brisk walk.

"You're in a hurry this morning." A familiar voice made her whirl around, pulse racing and cheeks flushing.

Erin was walking up the street toward her, looking concerned. Becca tried to sort through the jumble of her thoughts. What was she going to tell the sheriff anyway? Maybe she'd better practice the story first, make sure she was making sense to someone besides herself. "I saw some campers up in the woods. They didn't do anything but they gave me the creeps. One of them was asking about the wolves." She rubbed her arms anxiously and scowled.

Erin's face hardened and her jaw set. "You don't say?" She spoke softly, belying the menace in her expression. "What made you think there was something odd about that?"

"I don't know, really. The woman I talked to was asking about the wolves in the woods and said she was camping alone. Then this guy showed up after I walked away and he had on this jacket with a weird logo on it. I saw something like it on a website I looked at. But it's probably just some role-playing thing…no big deal." Becca shrugged, trying to shed the twisting feeling in her gut.

Here she was, trying to downplay something even though she knew that something about it was wrong. It felt like that right before she found out that Ed had a girlfriend. *You'd think I'd have learned to trust that feeling by now.*

But she could see Erin wasn't paying attention to her last few words. Instead the larger woman was frowning back at the woods. Then she caught Becca's shoulder in a light squeeze. "You going to let the sheriff know? Maybe one of his deputies or the rangers can check them out."

Becca nodded, relieved that someone else shared her fears. "Something just doesn't feel right."

Erin glanced away and nodded. "All right. I've got some things to take care of but I'll mention this to a few other folks too. The more people keeping an eye on them, the better. I'll see you tonight."

Tonight? Becca couldn't believe that she'd forgotten that it was finally Friday. "I'll be ready." She smiled, hoping that Erin couldn't see how nervous she was.

Erin winked and nodded. "I'll pick you up around nine." Then she loped off down the street toward downtown like something was chasing her. Becca walked after her and wondered just what was really going on around here. And why she'd ever thought that Wolf's Point was a boring little town.

Catherine Lundoff

Chapter 4

When she told Sheriff Henderson about the two strangers by
the creek, Becca tried to make her tone casual but concerned. Just the facts,
ma'am. But she could see that he wasn't really paying attention; there was
lots of nodding, but not much eye contact. Occasional grunts sounded like
agreement, but probably weren't.

He said the right thing though, "Sure thing, Miz Thornton. I'll have
Lizzie stop by and check it out." He jerked his head at the deputy sitting
behind him.

Deputy Lizzie Blackhawk was typing something into a computer, her
expression impassive. She glanced up at the sheriff's comment and gave
Becca a long unreadable stare. Then she raised one dark eyebrow and nodded before returning to the computer.

Oh well, Becca thought. *I've done what I can.* That didn't make it any less
disappointing. But since Lizzie was Shelly's cousin, maybe Shelly could en-
courage her to follow up a bit sooner rather than later. Or not at all.

She kept telling herself that during her shift at the hardware store, but
her nerves were on edge, fraying her concentration. She would have talked
to Shelly about the strangers but she wasn't around. Pete said her mom
wasn't doing well and Shelly was at her place helping out. Whatever it was,
his tone made it sound serious, and Becca was a little ashamed of her petty
fears.

It didn't seem like a good idea to share her worries about the campers
with Pete, though she really wasn't sure why. It seemed like there was
no point in planting the suggestion that she was getting loopy and cranky
in her old age. Instead, she fretted until her whole body felt like it was
strummed to the breaking point, accompanied by the occasional hot flash.

Silver Moon

By the time she left work, she was a wreck. She dashed home and took a shower, then inhaled dinner in what seemed like five minutes. After that, she stared into her closet for what seemed like an hour. What did you wear to a mystery event you were attending with a woman you wanted to impress, even though you knew there was no good reason for you to feel that way? Her thoughts whirled and she wished she was out in the woods, running in the moonlight, letting the wind whistle through her hair. *Now where had that come from?*

Becca shook her head and grabbed a matching dark blue top and slacks instead of her usual jeans. Nothing too fancy, but loose enough that she would be reasonably comfortable in it, hot flashes, nerves and all. Once she put it on, she realized it brought out the color of her eyes. She put her hair up in a clip and studied herself in the mirror, wondering whether makeup would help. Her skin was breaking out again. *Damn.* It was like being a teenager all over again, and that hadn't been that much fun the first time.

The doorbell interrupted her and she dashed out to let Erin in. "You ready?" Erin grinned down at her, a disturbing light in her silver-tinted eyes. "My, you look good enough to eat."

Becca shivered all over and fumbled for a response. "Um…thanks. Guess we'd better get going," was all that came to mind and voicebox. She grabbed her purse and pushed past Erin in her rush to avoid making eye contact. Erin led the way to her car without further comment.

The whole drive out to the Wolf's Point Women's Club was like that, at least from Becca's point of view. Erin chatted away about town gossip and projects she was doing around her house like nothing was wrong. Becca stared out the window and mumbled responses.

It was as if she could feel something huge and important hanging over them. Whatever it was felt like it was inside her too, coursing through her body with every thump of her heart until her skin felt like it was all that stood between her and some huge and monstrous transformation. Stagefright had never felt like this before. She rolled down the passenger window to get some air on her overheated face.

It didn't help. Becca almost bolted from the car when they got to the club. The woods on either side of the little red brick building beckoned, the inviting darkness under the trees called and the moon—when had she become such a nature freak? Sure, walks in the woods were fine in their place but in the dark? Though, come to think of it, it wasn't that dark even though the sun was down. She could see almost every twig in the darkness under the trees. Her fingers tightened on the car door as she struggled to keep herself from running into the woods.

"Later." Erin's voice came from way too close and Becca shuddered at the promise in her voice even as she turned and reluctantly followed her neighbor into the building.

She tried to analyze that feeling of dread as she walked into the club. Mostly she just thought that she wasn't ready for dealing with "The Change" with a bunch of women she clearly didn't know that well. That must be it. Night had just come on and she wanted its darkness to hide all these stupid thoughts and emotions. It was too weird to share. Somehow, the words to ask Erin if it had been like this for her wouldn't come to her lips and she was left mute and quivering.

Once inside, things felt even worse. It was like she'd never seen the place before, though that was a ridiculous notion since she'd been coming here for ages. It was just that she'd never noticed the way it smelled like pine or the little creaks and groans that the wooden walls made around them. Tonight there was something new and sinister about the shadows, the lit candles on the tables, the expressions on the faces of her own neighbors that made it new and even a little terrifying. Why weren't the lights on? The candles gave the place a spooky look.

Even Shelly seemed mysterious and scary tonight. She gave Becca what seemed like a long-toothed smile, predatory though clearly intended to be welcoming.

As Erin had promised, there was a cake and a couple of pitchers of what looked like margaritas on the table, along with some cans of soda, but Becca no longer felt like it was a simple celebration. The atmosphere was charged and while she was thinking about it, where was everyone else? The club had more members than this, and while she could hear movement in the next room, only Erin, Molly and Shelly were in the front room. Erin poured her a margarita and she gulped down half of it before she realized what she was doing.

Shelly sat on one of the padded benches and pulled her down to sit next to her. "Look, Becca, we weren't sure about what was going to happen tonight until a little while ago. Sometimes the change comes on really suddenly and we don't have a lot of time to prepare. It brings on new feelings and…transformations, physical and emotional. I know you're going through a tough time and I'm sorry that we haven't talked about it. Between my mom's illness and the Nest coming back here, I haven't been paying as much attention and preparing you the way I should have."

Becca wondered if she looked as puzzled as she felt. What was "The Nest"? Did Shelly mean the "warriors" from the website? If they included that couple by the river, that would make sense, given the logo and her

Silver Moon

general bad feeling about them. What didn't make sense was why Shelly would care about them. Did they pose some kind of threat?

Before she could ask, the front door opened and other women began trickling in by twos and threes. Shelly sighed and patted Becca's shoulder. "Don't worry about a thing. We all went through it our first time too. It'll be hard to get used to at first but we'll help you." She stood and walked away to greet the others, leaving Becca staring after her in complete bewilderment.

It looked like Shelly standing up was some kind of signal. Molly came over and ushered Becca into the other room and into a large cushioned chair surrounded by a circle of other chairs.

All the other women followed them in. Becca sat down nervously, the silence in the room making her twitchier by the minute. "So am I being initiated or something..." her voice trailed off. Erin gave her a reassuring smile that made her think of a wolf's grin and it was all Becca could do not to run for the door.

She made herself look around as the others, all twenty or so of them, sat down. She recognized women she had seen around town, even though not all of them lived in Wolf's Point proper. There was Mrs. Hui, whose family ran Wolf's Point's only Chinese restaurant and Carly Simpson, the Baptist pastor's wife. Her neighbor from around the corner, Gladys Sherman, nodded from her seat. Adelía Rodríguez from the gas station on Central gave her a shy smile.

She didn't know the others by name but all were women of a "certain age," as those stupid magazines put it, none under forty-five or so but all hale and hearty. There was something else that they had in common, too, though she couldn't quite put her finger on what it was.

Erin set up a large mirror across from her so she could watch her own frowning, searching face and stiff body. This senseless gesture annoyed her and she found herself snarling a little in response. There, just for a moment, was the face that had terrified her the other day in her bathroom mirror and she flinched away, shivering. Surely she didn't look like that all the time now, did she?

Despite her fears, she could feel that same wildness building in her. Something was clawing its way to the surface inside her, racing beneath her skin and preparing to break through. She wanted to run and hunt and feel the wind outside. It made her impatient and her feet and hands tapped the floor and the chair in time to her pulse.

As if Becca's mood was contagious, Shelly glanced out the window, then cleared her throat and stood. She held a long red taper in her hand, the flame dancing on an air current as it crossed the room. Distracted from her troubled thoughts, Becca imagined that her boss looked like an old-time shaman in a painting, standing there with her long black hair flowing over her shoulders and her dark eyes looking out on forever. She had never seemed so beautiful or so much a complete stranger.

Shelly cleared her throat and said, "I think we're ready to begin. The moon is starting to rise and we'll need to be ready. Thank you all for coming to welcome our member Becca Thornton as she enters the Change that has taken each of us in our time. Let us help Becca embrace her own transformation and join with us to make the Pack stronger." She waved the candle in a strange pattern and sprinkled some substance on the floor as she walked forward and circled Becca's chair.

What the hell was this? What was "the Pack"? Becca's thoughts were frantic now, her skin burning. She could feel the sweat trickling down her back and sides under her shirt, her heart racing so fast that she trembled with each beat. Her whole body felt odd, out of place, as if it belonged to someone else. Everything was too long, too short, too stretched. Too furry. *Furry?*

That was the realization that put her over the edge. She closed her eyes against the sudden wrenching pain that shot through her, starting at her feet and working its way up. It was like being pulled in fifteen directions and unable to respond to any of them. Her hair was standing on end and she felt her hands tighten on the chair. From somewhere close by, there was the sound of tearing and rending, of wood snapping. Something very scary was going on.

The thought drove her to her feet, eyes open now, and body tensed to flee. Her movement showed in the mirror and she glanced at it, then froze. Her face was long, her eyes golden. Her hair seemed to be working its way down her forehead in a "V." She was crouched over, huge and menacing. Her hands were far longer than they should have been, with fingers whose nails looked like claws. They were also covered with a light brown fuzz. The arms of the chair she'd been sitting in were matchsticks now, the stuffing trickling down to mound on the floor.

Becca Thornton opened her mouth to scream, but what came out was more like a cross between a howl and a yelp. She jumped forward, trying to get away from the monster in the mirror and found herself bouncing back from the surrounding air as if she'd hit a wall. She spun around the chair searching for a way out, clawing at nothing with hands that were no longer hers.

Silver Moon

Erin stood and walked up to the invisible barrier, whatever it was. She met Becca's eyes and held them with a silver-eyed stare as she unbuttoned her shirt and pants. She undressed carefully and calmly, as if being naked before the Wolf's Point Women's Club was the most normal thing in the world. Becca whimpered as she watched. Watching Erin's lean form emerge from her clothes made Becca's throat dry, made her heart beat even faster.

In that moment, she almost knew what she wanted from her neighbor. Almost, but it was all too much to think about right now.

And her thoughts changed as Erin began to transform. Her change was quick and fluid, beginning with the stretching of her face and her hands and ending with the growth of her fur. Within moments, Becca was staring at a large gray wolf with Erin's eyes. That was when she knew she was going insane. She had to be.

Or had they all known all along what was going to happen and just kept it secret? A sense of betrayal so deep it made her bones ache washed over her; how could her friends and neighbors have kept this from her?

Shelly's voice broke into her thoughts, forced her to hear something besides her own screaming brain. "Wolf's Point has always held its own magic, from time immemorial. In each generation, a group of women past childbearing age become its vessels and in turn, the protectors of this land and its people. We embrace the spirit form of the earliest inhabitants, taking on their skins and their strengths. We embrace the forms and rituals of the settlers who came after the First Ones. We are at once old and new. You are called to join us, Becca Thornton. The magic in your blood marks you as one of us. Do you hear its summons?"

Becca could feel her jaw drop. What was this, some episode of *Buffy* she'd never seen before? Sure, she heard a call all right, and it was telling her to run away from these crazy women and their wolves and their magic tricks. Telling her to run into the woods, to feel the moon's song in her blood, the wind in her fur, to chase down her prey and...*oh, shit*. She stared at Shelly for a long couple of minutes, all the while feeling shifts in her body that shouldn't, couldn't have been there.

The other women were changing around Shelly now and that wasn't helping. Becca could smell them all, for one thing, now that her senses were suddenly much more acute. And she could hear things, things that couldn't possibly be close enough to hear, like traffic on the highway and noises from town.

Meanwhile, Shelly kept on looking at her, clearly waiting for an answer. What the hell was she supposed to say? And how was she supposed to say it with her mouth like this? She wrestled with her tongue and fangs, making a whole series of weird noises in the process. Finally, she forced her long lips into something resembling human speech. "Do I have a choice?"

Shelly's lips quirked in something like a smile, but wasn't quite. "Not a good one. Sorry, Becca. The magic chooses its own; we don't control it."

That was when the final wave washed through Becca. She dropped to her hands and knees and retched as the rags of her blouse fell from her shoulders. She clawed frantically at the remains of her pants and her underwear, yanking them off as the rest of the fur sprouted from her newly bare skin. Her jaws stretched open in a scream that became a howl.

It was a sound of primal rage and terror, of wild magic turned loose. She rocked on her paws as the strange force filled her, changing her brain as well as her body. She was wolf-Becca now, a weird new combination of herself and something far wilder and more primitive.

She circled the chair once again and sat down in front of the mirror. A medium-sized gray wolf stared back her, moving when she did, completely still when she was. She picked up a front paw and looked down her muzzle at it. *If this is a magic trick, it's a damn good one*, she thought, strangely detached from what had just happened.

When she looked back up, Shelly had transformed into a brown wolf, a bit bigger than she was. The wolf that was Shelly paced over to the circle that kept Becca trapped. She looked at Becca inquiringly and gave a sort of bark that managed to be a question. After a long moment, Becca nodded her head, part of her knowing it to be a weirdly human gesture for a wolf. Shelly scraped back the circle, erasing it with her paw until there was enough room for her to step outside.

It felt to Becca as if she'd just been released from a cage. She stumbled forward as her back legs adjusted to walking in concert with her front paws. Her vision had changed along with everything else and she found herself watching the movements of the other wolves avidly. Shelly barked to get their attention and they all followed her to the door. In wolf form, it was clear that she was alpha to the rest of the pack. *That figures*, Becca thought muzzily with the small part of her brain not completely wolf.

The door opened and the wolves trotted out into the moonlit night, Becca along with them. They seemed to have a destination in mind and wherever it was, they were in a hurry to get there. Soon they were all racing behind Shelly through the woods. Becca gave herself up to the sheer joy of running as the scents of the night filled her muzzle and the wind sweeping down from the foothills dragged itself through her thick fur like a brush.

She wondered why they were quiet as they ran and the howl that she wanted to let loose surged up her throat. But Erin nipped her lightly, making her stumble on her still unsteady paws and she caught the warning look in the other wolf's eyes. They needed to travel silently to their destination, whatever it was.

That didn't make sense. There were no hunters in these woods, after all. Then she remembered the woman and her companion by the river and a tiny growl formed in her throat. For a few long moments, she lost herself in the wolf as she raced along behind the others.

Her detachment vanished when they splashed through the river shallows before picking their way across on the wet rocks. Surely there was only one reason for them to be down at the river tonight? They reached the far shore and the other wolves vanished with the exception of Erin who led her into the darkest bushes along the riverbank. Becca found herself nudged until she sat on her haunches and Erin settled in beside her.

Becca stirred restlessly until Erin leaned against her in the darkness, offering comfort and warmth. Then Becca settled down and began to listen to the night. She heard the rustling of small prey in the bushes and salivated at the thought of food. At least until the shreds of her horrified human self squelched that idea.

She could hear the stealthy movement of the Pack between the trees. Some were sitting still while others seemed to be spreading out, sneaking through the brush. It puzzled her, wolf and human brain both analyzing the sensations at the same time.

Finally, she heard the humans. They too were trying to be as quiet as possible but their breathing gave them away as they got closer. She could feel their fear and it made her lips peel back from her fangs in a predatory smile. Then she heard the unmistakable sound of a shell being loaded into a gun. She jumped to her feet, her wolf instincts warring with her human ones. The humans knew they were coming and they were ready for them. The Pack was in terrible danger!

Erin dropped on her then, pinning her to the dirt in a growling panting pile. Becca yipped as Erin's jaws closed carefully on the fur at her neck as if she were a puppy. Instinctively, Becca went limp instead of fighting back. There was a dead, waiting silence in the woods around them now.

Then all at once, Shelly barked and there was a surge of short howls and snarls in response. A gun went off and Erin bolted in the direction of the sound with Becca at her heels. They raced forward until Becca caught a movement from the corner of her eye. She gave a sharp warning bark and dove into the underbrush as a female human leaned around the tree and fired at them. She couldn't hear Erin over the noise of the shouting and gunfire. But she was angry now, angry enough to think about striking back, and that urge overrode her fear as she circled carefully around the tree.

Then she crept up behind the human. The human swung her head from side to side, night goggles trying to pierce the darkness to see what was out there, what might be hunting her. Becca gathered herself for a leap but Erin was there before her, knocking the woman over. Becca jumped instead for the gun and managed to pin the woman's arm down before she could bring the gun up to fire again.

In the struggle, the human's goggles came loose and slid down her nose. Becca recognized the woman from the riverbank. Erin snarled down at her, teeth bared and the woman snarled back. She flailed and kicked, her foot catching Erin in the ribs but the wolf stayed put.

From somewhere near by, there were more shots, and the woman tried to yell for help. In an instant, Erin's jaws closed around her jacket collar. Becca could see those jaws tightening, see the woman begin to gasp for air, almost see her begin to die. She yelped in horror. *No!*

The woman dropped her gun and her hands clutched feebly at the soil. Becca threw herself sideways into Erin, knocking her grip loose. The woman flailed again while both wolves were off balance. Then she rolled free and stood up.

Erin scrambled to her feet and circled in front of her with a menacing snarl. That was when Becca saw the glint of another gun emerging from the woman's sleeve. She snarled a warning to Erin and slammed into the human's legs. After that, it was all a blur of gunshots, the yowl of a wounded wolf, then the crash of underbrush as something large fled.

Then the Pack was back, silent as smoke. They circled Erin, collapsed and bleeding. Becca crouched over her, growling at anyone who came near. That was when Shelly stepped forward into the shadows and away from the moonlight. With bared teeth and a menacing lunge, she forced Becca back from Erin's side.

With what looked like a superhuman effort, she stretched and whined, her paws digging into the litter of the forest floor until they looked like fingers. Then they were fingers. Then hands. Shelly's arms emerged from their fur covering as her muzzle shrank back into her human face, though the rest of her didn't change Finally, she stood, a monstrous combination of wolf and woman.

Erin shuddered and closed her eyes as Shelly touched her side gently. But she didn't move after that and Becca made herself stop growling. This

Silver Moon

was her fault. She'd gotten Erin shot. And she'd let the human get away. A whimper tore its way up her throat.

Shelly ignored her and scooped Erin up very carefully with a barked command at the other wolves. Becca could see that Erin was changing back as she lost consciousness. Shelly didn't spare the rest of the Pack a glance before she began a swift run along the riverbank toward town, Erin cradled in her arms. Becca began to stumble after them until another wolf stopped her. Whoever she was, her fur was nearly white and she looked quite fierce in the moonlight. She bared her teeth at Becca and jerked her muzzle at the woods.

Then the white wolf trotted forward and glanced back, clearly expecting Becca to follow. After a long moment of hesitation, she did. Moments later they were running again, racing upstream to where the road crossed at the bridge. In front of them, several humans were racing for their distant van, glowing white in the moonlight. There were more shots and Becca slipped into the bushes, heart racing. She was furious now, burning with a bright savage anger.

She moved along more cautiously this time, her sense of smell telling her where the others were. They darted through the shadows, silent as air. Becca lost herself for the first time since she changed, the last shreds of her human self temporarily silenced. Now she hunted with her Pack, searching for those who would hunt them. These others, this human pack, they must be stopped before they hurt another wolf. No matter what the cost.

Chapter 5

Becca woke up in the woods at sunrise. At that moment, she had
no idea of where she was or why she was surrounded by women from the
Women's Club. Or where her clothes were.

Or why Mrs. Hui was sitting up next to her, also completely naked. The
other woman seemed pretty relaxed about it, too. And there was Gladys
waking up a few feet away, not a stitch on her either. Everyone else seemed
to be scattered around them in the same condition. What the hell were
they all doing here like this?

"Come on. We have clothes hidden near the bridge." Mrs. Hui rose and
began walking downstream as if she woke up like this every day.

Maybe she did. Becca hauled herself to her feet and followed her, trying
in vain to cover herself with her hands. After a few minutes, she gave up.
At least she was too cold to have hot flashes yet so that was something. But
what was this all about? There had to be way to ask just how often they'd
done this without actually saying what…*this* was. Somehow she couldn't
bring herself to ask if they'd all turned into wolves the night before. It had
to have been a dream.

She glanced from Gladys to Mrs. Hui and decided that the latter was
safer, what with being smaller, older and frailer looking. She also lived further away and the distance might help, if her question sounded as silly as
she suspected it did. "Have you done this before?"

Mrs. Hui raised a silver eyebrow and nodded, like that was perfectly
obvious.

That went well. Sort of. Becca decided to try again. "So do they have—
do they do…whatever this is—back home where you're from?" She asked,
this time knowing how stupid the question was even before she saw the
expression on the other woman's face.

Silver Moon

Mrs. Hui stretched and grimaced, her glance seeming mildly contemptuous to Becca's dazed eyes. "Back home where I'm from? I was born right here in the valley, so yes, we had werewolves back home." She shook her long white hair in what seemed to Becca like dismissal.

Becca looked everywhere but back at her and felt herself go red and hot. It wasn't like she knew the other woman that well, so she told herself that maybe she was misreading her response. Still, she felt like she'd been rude and she wasn't sure how to fix it.

Then she glanced down at her hands and saw something dark red under the nails. Her feeling of foolishness vanished, replaced with something far more sinister. She stopped and stared at her hands, trying desperately to remember what had happened. Parts of the night before came back to her: changing into a wolf, running through the woods, fighting the woman from the riverbank. Erin getting shot. But then there was a big blank spot after that. She clutched her head and leaned against a tree while her world spun around her and she tried to remember.

"It's a lot to take in," Mrs. Hui said from somewhere nearby. Her tone was somewhat sympathetic.

"But you did your duty to the Pack. You proved yourself, Becca. We're happy to have you with us." Gladys' voice was deeper than normal, almost a growl, but that wasn't what sent a thrill of pure horror through Becca. What had she done last night?

Then she was surrounded. Together the other women herded her up toward the bridge, their hands on her elbows or around her shoulders. When they got there, Deputy Lizzie Blackhawk was waiting for them. She was leaning against a tree, mirrored sunglasses perched near the end of her nose as they stumbled up. "Shit," Lizzie said slowly, "what did you grandmas get up to last night?"

"Show some respect!" Gladys snapped.

Lizzie's lips quirked in a small smile. "Get some clothes on before you freeze. We've got injured campers up at the hospital so you're going to have to help me come up with a story for the sheriff on this one."

Injuries? Becca's heart thudded its way up into her throat and she looked from Lizzie's face to her gun, then to her badge. Then she squared her shoulders and stepped forward. Whatever she'd done last night, she must've hurt someone. She could guess as much from the blood. She'd been brought up to be law abiding and to do right, so whatever she'd done, she needed to take responsibility for it. Even if she wasn't sure what it was.

"It was me, Deputy." She held out her hands, bloody nails pointed upwards and stared at the ground, waiting for the click of cuffs. "I did…" Here she struggled to remember before settling on, "Whatever it was."

There was a brief silence as Lizzie looked from Becca to Mrs. Hui and Gladys and the rest of the group. Mrs. Hui shrugged and started pulling clothes out of a couple of waterproof bags that she dragged from behind a tree. She handed out energy bars to the rest of the group. No one said anything. At last Lizzie said, "Okay, Miz Thornton. Why don't you put some clothes on? Then we'll talk about just what did go on last night."

Becca looked up to see if she was being laughed at but Lizzie just looked serious and a bit puzzled. Mrs. Hui walked over and handed Becca some jeans and a shirt. "These should fit. And eat this too, while you're at it. It'll help ground you." Becca picked up the energy bar, and unwrapped it. An instant later she was tearing into it, like it was meat. Meat she'd hunted herself, rich and bloody with life. She threw it down and backed away, staring at the half-eaten bar as though it might bite back.

"What the hell did I do last night?" She demanded, glaring at Mrs. Hui. That was when she noticed that she was the only one not dressed. She scrambled for the clothes folded at her feet.

"First time changing?" Lizzie asked in conversational tones, as if all of this was all perfectly normal.

"Are you one too?" Becca demanded. Her eyes narrowed in suspicion and she stepped up to look the deputy in the eyes. Only then did she realize that she was also sniffing the air for the other's scent. The realization made her jump back.

Lizzie went perfectly still under Becca's examination, for all the world, Becca thought, like she was being checked out by a wild animal or something. *Oh.*

The deputy cleared her throat once Becca stepped back. "Nope. I hope I will be one day." She grinned, a rare flash of white teeth in her brown face. "To be one of the guardian grandmothers, to protect the land and the people. It's a great honor, you know. Not many are called."

"She's right, Becca." Erin and Shelly walked slowly down from the bridge, their sudden appearance making them all jump. Erin had her arm in a cast and a sling. She swayed a bit, giving the impression that only Shelly's hand at her elbow was holding her up.

Becca stared at the two of them, a whirling storm of anger, betrayal and guilt swirling through her head and choking the words before they could cross her lips. They could have at least warned her. *And then what?* The

Silver Moon

voice of her own common sense demanded. *You'd be happier about turning into a monster on the full moon?*

Erin gave her a quiet smile and Becca felt butterflies dance in her stomach, despite everything. Right up until she said, "You did what you needed to do last night. You did what the magic called you to do: protect the town and the land."

Becca stared at her in horror. She'd killed someone, she had to have. They wouldn't keep talking about it this way if it wasn't something big and horrible. The words forced themselves from her mouth in a whisper. "Who was it?" She remembered the woman by the river and how murderous she felt last night after Erin went down. The stranger didn't seem to be a likeable kind of gal, certainly, but could she live with the other's blood on her hands?

Shelly walked up and put a sympathetic hand on her shoulder. "Look, Becca, there's always an adjustment period…"

The hot flash that swept through Becca just then was a doozy. It gave her the strength she needed to pull away, to haul her drenched and angry body up to the road and all the way into Wolf's Point. She ran like she had never run before, at least not before last night. She ran until she reached her own porch, racing through the town that she was supposedly protecting against unknown dangers. For once, she didn't care what the neighbors thought and ignored everyone in her flight.

Her borrowed clothes dripped with sweat as she shed them on her way to the shower. She would get clean of this, somehow. Unthinking, she washed her hands thoroughly, forgetting that the blood was evidence if she really wanted to confess. She scrubbed vigorously, turning her skin hot and pink under the pressure.

She had toweled off and was getting dressed again when she heard the knock at the front door. For a moment, she thought about pretending she wasn't home or ducking out the back. Instead, she forced her reluctant feet to the door. She couldn't hide forever, right? She found herself face to face with Erin through the glass inset on the front door. "Go away." She surprised herself by meaning it.

"Will you come by when you're ready to talk?" Erin asked. Her eyes were sad and she looked worn down. "Please?"

Becca nodded as if her head was on strings and Erin walked slowly away. She watched her neighbor go back to her porch. Molly was waiting for her. They went inside and Erin shut the front door.

Becca groaned. She'd have to talk to one of them sooner or later. That or leave Wolf's Point. Town was too small to avoid the whole group for long, especially when she worked for the leader of the Pack. She wondered if Pete and the kids knew about Shelly. He probably did; they didn't seem to keep many secrets from each other. And how was she supposed to act around them now?

Then it hit her: she didn't have to stay. She could leave Wolf's Point. Maybe that would get her outside the boundaries of the curse or whatever it was. If she got "called" because she lived here, why couldn't she get "uncalled" if she left? She looked around the room and dismissed her possessions with a glance. There wasn't time to pack. The moon was still pretty full tonight and she might change again. She'd seen that on TV once. She could come back for the rest or send for it when she was ready.

She raced upstairs, refusing to look around her at the shabby, worn chairs or the one photo of her and Ed that she couldn't manage to hide away or the knickknacks she'd inherited from her mother or her shelf of books. She'd think about what she wanted later, once she was safe and everything was back to normal.

An hour later, her clothes and necessities were stuffed into a bag, and she and it were stuffed into her car. She forced herself not to peel out of the driveway. Two hundred miles away should do it; that was the limit of the original ordinance. Becca guessed that outside that zone, middle-aged women were just what they seemed and monsters didn't run through the woods at night. Out there, maybe she could be boring, divorced Becca Thornton who didn't change into things she shouldn't under the moon and didn't have thoughts she shouldn't about her across the street neighbor either. Everything would go back to the way it was.

She floored the gas once she got past the sheriff's speed trap at the edge of town. No point in getting pulled over by Lizzie or one of the other deputies when she was this close to getting away. She hesitated when she hit the main road though, and paused, wondering where to go next.

Then she remembered her cousins Marybeth and Hal up in Mountainview, about four hours away. They'd been after her to come visit since the divorce, said she was welcome whenever she had time, in fact. Now, well, she had nothing but time.

Her phone chirped in her bag but she ignored it. She'd have to call Pete and Shelly from Mountainview while she was at it and spin some yarn, maybe something about a sick relative needing emergency care. They'd understand that, and it would give her an excuse if she decided not to come back. When she decided.

That just left Erin and Becca wasn't ready to think about her yet. Besides, Erin was a monster, like the rest of them, running through the woods and

Silver Moon

attacking people. But Becca was different. She was going to beat this thing. Then she'd make new friends, ones that didn't hide things from her or make her feel funny inside.

She told herself that again when she hit the next town over. And again on the road away from it as Wolf's Point dwindled in the distance. But there was a hole inside her and she ached to think about leaving her home and not coming back. It hurt more every mile she drove but she kept going, hoping that silencing her beastly alter ego would make the loss worth it.

Chapter 6

Certainly the distance from Wolf's Point didn't put a stop
to her body's other changes. Between finally getting her period, the occasional hot flash and her mood swings, menopause was going right along as
scheduled. Pity she couldn't leave that little bit of fun behind along with
the rest.

Becca sighed a lot, stopped for more water and called her cousins to let
them know she was on her way for a long delayed visit. Then she called and
left a message about a fictitious sick relative for Pete and Shelly. It wasn't
an easy lie. But she told herself that she might need a job reference later. If
she decided not to go back.

After that, she thrust all thoughts about home to the back of her mind
and concentrated on driving until she hit Mountainview. She wondered as
she drove past the "Welcome to Mountainview" sign if the other town had
taken the name after Wolf's Point gave it up. Her mood sank a little lower;
who wanted Wolf's Point's leftovers?

It was a pretty little town by some standards, touristy with the kind of
artificially quaint downtown that she always hated in towns like it. The
buildings were trimmed with plastic gingerbread and a lot of the stores
were called "Ye Olde" as part of their names. She made herself stop in front
of a diner, almost inevitably named "Aunt Mabel's."

At least it looked like any other small town diner, with the exception
of the poster on the door. Some words leapt out at her as she went in.
"Missing," it said. "Eight-year-old boy, not seen for two days. Possibly ab-
ducted." There were other things about a reward, the boy's name and his
family's contact information but she ignored them as she looked at the
boy's picture under the headline. He looked like any other kid. Only the
words made his face heartbreaking.

Silver Moon

It made her stomach turn. There were other monsters out there too, ones that she didn't keep inside or know personally. The thought didn't make her feel any better.

Neither did Aunt Mabel's greasy burger and wilted salad, but at least she wouldn't be showing up to mooch dinner as well as arriving out of the blue. She finished up and drove over to Hal and Marybeth's. They gave her a kind welcome and a hastily turned down the bed in the den, once they realized she planned on staying the night. Best of all, they asked her very few questions.

So it certainly wasn't their company that drove her out to walk in the moonlight that night. She had to promise them she'd bring her cell phone and a borrowed whistle from Marybeth. After all, you never knew what might happen and what with the Jensen boy missing and all, she really shouldn't go out for a walk alone at night at all. Becca smiled patiently through their list of concerns and went out anyway.

Still, she admitted to herself that it had been nice to have someone care about what she did. Someone besides those women from the club who she thought were her friends. Walking would ease the lump of ice in her center that was doing nothing to cool down her outsides. That was what she told herself.

She looked up at the mountains as she walked and felt something stir inside her. Whatever it was, it was calling her to run but she resisted. She didn't know the roads here. Or the neighbors. Maybe normal middle-aged women didn't run down the streets in the dark out here.

Her senses were sharper than she remembered them being, probably from the clear air. She inhaled deeply, pulling the wind inside her with its scents of woods and wild, exhaust and humans. Downtown was all too audible, though, so she walked away from it, hoping to find some peace in the fields and woods outside of town. Finally, the pull was too strong and she settled into a sedate jog past the houses and the parked cars.

As she reached the edge of town, she began to feel the moon stirring in her blood, calling up last night's wildness once more. What the hell? She was outside the limit of the ordinance and she'd turned last night. Shouldn't this be over with for this month? Was she getting bonus wolf points or something?

Glancing down, she could see that her hands didn't look right. Suppressing a wail of horror, she dove into the woods, scrambling around until she found a dark spot surrounded by bushes. There she fought her transformation until it was obvious that she was losing. Even then, she forced herself to undress and remembered to turn her phone off.

Then she reluctantly surrendered to the moon and the wild magic inside her. Once she changed, she ran all out, a lone wolf, freed from her Pack and charging through the woods until the trees blurred before her. Her path took her up the nearest mountain, farther from people and closer to the moon. For a time, she thought about nothing but the night, reveling in her speed and strength.

She was miles outside of Mountainview when she heard the sounds for the first time. Her wolf senses didn't recognize them at first but she moved toward them anyway, curiosity winning over caution. The Becca part of her brain woke up a bit as she got closer to whatever it was and tried to slow her wolf body down. Human fears warred with wolf curiosity until all of her attention was focused on the noises filtering through the woods.

Slowly, she recognized it as the voice of a small boy. There was another human with him, an adult male from his scent. But the cub—*child*, she managed to remind herself—sounded scared. Even so, there was nothing she could do except make it worse, given what she looked like now. Becca tried to turn her wolf self away to run up the mountain, far from the campsite. It wouldn't help the boy's terrors to meet a real monster.

Unbidden, a memory of the poster at the diner came back to her. Was this the same boy? She could remember his photo, back in the human portions of her memory. He was sniffling now, small sobs drifting out of the bushes and trees that still separated them. Whoever he was, he was terrified and hurting.

She couldn't just turn away. Literally. It was if she was frozen to the spot, all her instincts warring with each other until she wanted to bang her head against a tree. She wanted to help, if she could, but this was more than that. This felt more like a compulsion, a spell she couldn't ignore. The feeling escalated until she finally did what that insistent pull demanded and followed the sounds and scents.

Instinctively, she dropped into a hunting crouch and eased her way into the bushes, sliding slowly and carefully through them. The boy was silent now but she could still smell his fear. The wrongness she smelled on the man at his side made her lips lift back in a snarl. She slipped like a shadow through the trees until she could see them.

The man had hidden them under a lean-to of branches. There was no fire or other sign to mark their hiding place. It was easy to see how he'd avoided the human searchers for two days. The boy gave a small cry that was suddenly silenced and wolf-Becca growled, the sound far louder than she had intended. It was loud enough to bring the man out to look around. He hesitated, then picked up his gun and took a few steps into the woods.

Silver Moon

Becca's woods. She rustled the bushes as she backed further into the darkness, drawing the man from the clearing. Away from the moonlight, back into the darkness where he wouldn't be able to see her, where she was protected. He stepped forward once, then again.

She leapt, taking him off guard and knocking him down. He flailed backward, dropping his gun. Snarling, she bit into his struggling body as he thrashed and fought. His scent, a musk of lust and fear and pain, maddened her, made her sink her teeth in anywhere she could reach him through his heavy jacket. Her wolf-self wanted blood and wanted it now.

He twisted sharply under her, drawing a hunting knife from his belt and slashing it across her side. She yowled in pain and tore into his arm, tasting his blood. He managed to whip her head back and forth for a couple of moments, but he couldn't dislodge her. Becca dug her feet deeper into the soil and bit down with all the strength in her jaws.

The man dropped the knife and Becca turned and bit into his neck. He fell with her on top of him. Then he kicked out a few times, the breath wheezing in his throat as she felt her mouth fill with blood. After that, there was a moment of stillness for them both. She met his terrified eyes with her fiercest snarl. She could kill him now; it would be easy, justified even. But the little bit of Becca Thornton still awake in her head was fighting her.

Then he yanked suddenly away from her, reaching and seizing the knife again with his good hand. He slashed at her, grazing her good side and Becca lost herself, letting her wolf-self fight for her life. They twisted and turned, rolling on the rocky ground, as the knife sank in once, then twice. She howled in pain and fury, then struck again. This time, there no human voice in her head to stop her.

When Becca emerged again to regain control of her body, the man was still and her mouth was full of his blood. The scent of it was everywhere, pooled beneath him and coating her fur. She forced herself to make sure he was dead, prodding him with her paw and sniffing his face. Even if the legends weren't completely true, she didn't want to risk making him a werewolf.

Then she dragged herself over to the lean-to without looking back. The boy inside stared at her, his eyes so wide they were almost all white, and whimpered. For a long moment, she was torn between wanting to comfort him and wanting to eat him. The latter feeling sent a thrill of horror through her. Could she risk getting any closer to him?

But help was down the mountain. She couldn't just leave him with the corpse and she couldn't carry him as she was. Either she needed to bring him to help or bring help to him, somehow. She could not do either in her current form. Moonlight caressed her fur as if mocking her indecisiveness.

She tried to think and an idea slowly formed. Shelly had been able to partially change back in order to carry Erin to safety. If Shelly could do it, why couldn't she? She limped back into the shadows, leaving a trail of her own blood on the leaves; whatever happened, the boy shouldn't see this. At least she could feel her new body healing fast. Her wounds stopped bleeding as she sat down and she could feel itchy scabs beginning to form. If her healing continued like this, she might be able to make it down the mountain carrying the boy, despite the pain.

Becca closed her eyes and shut out the moon. She thought of quiet days and walks in the woods, of picnics and tea. Of anything except blood and running through the woods and the call of magic. Breathing carefully in and out, she tried to emulate the teacher of a long ago yoga class.

With excruciating slowness, her blood stilled and the pounding of her heart eased. She pictured herself with hands and a shorter muzzle, able to walk and run upright. Then she held her breath and tried to force her body to change. The horrible wrenching feeling that followed laid her out in the dirt, whimpering for a few minutes. But the second attempt went better. By her third try, she could stand on her hind legs, though she was still a bit shaky.

She approached the lean to cautiously, trying to shape her wolf muzzle into human speech. "Come. No hurt. Save." The words were horribly grow-ly and barely comprehensible but she hoped the boy would understand them. At least he didn't run or scream. She reached out with her clawed hands and his eyes rolled back in his head and he went limp.

That was something of a mercy, or so Becca hoped. At least he was still breathing. She picked him up and heaved him over one furry shoulder. Then she began to race down the mountain.

The trip was a blur of branches and pain and she stumbled frequently. The boy stayed unconscious. She tried to get him to drink at a stream they crossed but he wouldn't open his eyes or his mouth.

Holding the partial change was harder than she could have imagined. Her muscles felt like rivulets of lava and her nerves screamed as she exerted control. The run seemed to go on forever.

Finally, just as the moon began to set, she saw the lights of Mountainview. She dragged a final effort from her exhausted body and left the boy on the porch of a house on the outskirts of town. Then she staggered back toward where she'd left her clothes after ringing the doorbell.

Silver Moon

She found her clothes and collapsed on top of them, letting her Becca self come back. The change back happened quickly this time, at least. Later she couldn't remember getting dressed or dragging her leaden footsteps back to Hal and Marybeth's. She made it as far as the porch swing before she collapsed. The sleep that took her then was like falling into a well, deep and dark and utterly black.

Chapter 7

Marybeth and Hal woke her up when they found her on the porch. Which left her coming up with a good story, before coffee even. She didn't want them thinking she was the sort of divorced woman who spent her time in honky-tonks in hopes of finding herself another man but it was the most plausible explanation. Becca let her words spill over each other until they didn't make much sense, but the general import was clear enough.

Embarrassment drove them all inside and Hal turned on the TV while Marybeth silently handed Becca a cup of coffee. Then the news came on and everyone stopped worrying about Becca and her late night doings. The headline that the Jensen boy had been found alive was national news. Apparently the kid was still in shock and his family wasn't letting him talk to reporters yet. Becca uttered a silent prayer, hoping that he'd just think the whole thing was a really bad dream and forget about anything he'd seen.

The next headline was that his kidnapper, one James Harrison, had been found dead in the woods. His body had been badly torn up, like he'd been taken down by a pack of wild dogs. The reporters speculated on this until Becca wished the linoleum beneath her feet would open up and swallow her whole.

She opted to sneak off to the shower instead, then into the den to get some more sleep. Her dreams were full of running and blood and noise, but nothing was clear. Try as she might, she couldn't remember exactly how she'd felt when James Harrison died. It was all one big blur. In a way, that was worse than remembering. She should feel a little guilty, she was sure of it.

Her nightmares got worse over the next couple of nights, the images clearer. She attacked a faceless man, her ears filling with his screams, and then something happened to wake her up. After the third time it happened, she thought she finally got it: she was still a werewolf and moving away hadn't changed that. This meant that she could look forward to changing again next month. And next month, it might not be a child kidnapper and rapist whose throat she tore out.

Fears and all, she still tried to give Mountainview a chance, as if she really had the option to stay if she wanted to. She took long walks through the downtown and beyond. Plastic gingerbread and all, it was a pleasant little town. There were apartments she could rent and a couple of part-time jobs she could string together until she got back on her feet. People were friendly.

But it wasn't home. And she had no friends here, no—and she hated to use the word—*Pack* so there was no one for her to really talk to. Even with all that had happened, she missed them, all of them, Shelly and Erin and Pete most of all.

After a week, she loaded her bag up into her car and thanked her cousins with mixed emotions. It seemed to her that Marybeth and Hal weren't too sorry to see her go, but then, she wasn't all that sorry to be leaving either. She started down the road toward Wolf's Point.

All the while, her brain spun with the worries and fears and questions that she'd hoped to avoid. Why had the werewolf thing happened to her in the first place? She couldn't even remember a dog bite, let alone a wolf one, yet here she was, changing just like in that old Lon Chaney movie. Now she knew she couldn't outrun the curse or whatever it was but she wasn't giving up hope that there might be a cure out there, one that didn't involve a silver bullet.

But to find that out, she needed people to talk to and a town with the right resources. Surely if Shelly and the rest of the Club knew so much about turning into wolves, they would know something about not changing into one. Maybe. She tried really hard not to remember everything that had been said about magic and being called until she ran to the end of her limited information. Time enough for those conversations when she got home.

Her mood lifted with each mile closer to Wolf's Point. It wasn't like she really felt like she had much of a choice in coming back, but she couldn't help herself. At least there was the familiar to fall back on. Well, that and a sense of belonging, of rightness. It seemed right, for example, that the first thing she did when she got into town was to park near Millie's Cafe and go in for pie.

No sooner had she greeted the regulars and settled in for a giant slice of apple pie than the door swung open. Becca looked up to meet the stare of the aspiring werewolf slayer she'd met by the river, what seemed like another lifetime ago now. The other woman was pretty banged up. Her arm was in a sling and she was wearing a couple of bandages, but apart from that, she appeared to be quite alive.

Becca found herself nearly giddy with relief. Killing a stranger like Harrison was one thing. Killing someone she'd recommended Millie's pies to was quite a different matter.

As if she'd been invited, the woman walked over and dropped into the chair across from Becca. That made Becca shiver all over with all kinds of feelings she wasn't about to express in Millie's, and her sense of relief vanished. This woman had come here specifically to hunt her friends. Her, too, for that matter, not that she knew that. Now here she was acting like she owned the place.

"Looks like this town has a wolf problem, after all," her companion said by way of greeting. She gestured at herself. "Oya. Remember me: I am the wind that brings change."

Becca could feel her hackles rise. What was this, amateur drama night? "Indeed. Well, I'm Becca and I'd say I was pleased to meet you but I think you know that would be a lie. I'm sorry you don't like our woods. Or our wolves. When are you leaving town?"

Her hands were clenching the edge of the table, her nails growing longer and sinking into the wood, or so her imagination told her. She tried to make herself relax, tried to calm the surging tide of her blood. It wasn't as if she could change in broad daylight, after all. Or could she? The thought made her break out in a cold sweat.

Oya glared at her. "Somehow, I'm pretty sure you know exactly what happened the other night. My friends and I ran into some monsters in the woods. Stuart...well, they're not sure he's going to make it. And I think you told them about us." She rubbed her hand over her eyes, almost like she was wiping away a tear.

A cold chill went through Becca. Had she hurt this Stuart guy, whoever he was? Or had someone else? Another thought replaced it almost as quickly: it had been self-defense. The Pack was ambushed, fired upon. Erin had been wounded, maybe others. Whatever happened to these people, they'd had it coming.

Becca's mood switched fast enough to give her whiplash. Who was this woman to call her friends monsters? "Seems to me that when you go looking for monsters, that's all you see. And sometimes you miss much scarier things." Becca could feel her emotions swirling around like her insides were a washing machine. *Great*, she couldn't suppress the thought, *more hot flashes coming up.*

"And sometimes, it's just the monsters out there and they have to be stopped before they do any more damage." The other woman's eyes shone with a fanatic gleam, almost silver in the morning light. "That's what happens when you don't keep them under control."

"Just what is it you have against wolves anyway? Seems to me they mind their own business when you mind yours." A deep breath later and Becca had herself under control. She thought she knew what she was dealing with now. This woman, this Oya, was like one of the hellfire preachers who came through once in awhile, preaching from their big tent in the park on the edge of town. Zealots and fanatics, she'd always thought they were, and this one seemed one of a kind with them.

Oya looked down at the table, her shoulders slumping a bit with the movement. She studied the tabletop for a minute before looking back up. "It's not just any old wolf. It's the kind you've got here. Wolves like yours killed my parents." She stared back at Becca, her face gone suddenly haggard.

It struck Becca then that it wasn't so much grief as it was emptiness, a gaping chasm that had to be filled with a purpose. She almost reached out for Oya's hand on the table to try and bring some comfort, just like she would have done with any other woman. There was something about this woman that drew Becca in, some kind of kinship that she didn't quite understand but responded to nevertheless.

But her story couldn't be true, it just couldn't. Her Pack would never kill innocents, right? So maybe the parents weren't so innocent. Even so, she could hardly ask if the woman's dead family had been drug dealers or murderers or something.

Doubt gnawed at her, burrowing its way in. She tried to banish it by thinking about her friends, her Pack. If they wouldn't do something like that, Oya must be lying. Unless there were other packs. The enormity of that thought left her speechless for a couple of minutes. She hadn't even thought about there being more of their kind out there somewhere. Cold shivers danced up her arms and she rubbed at her skin feverishly. Then she noticed Oya watching her, the gleam in her eye suggesting that she knew she was getting to Becca.

Catherine Lundoff   46

A mild surge of pure annoyance swept through her, warming her right back up. She made herself think about James Harrison in the woods. Protection took many forms; if wolves like hers had killed Oya's parents, there had to be a good reason. Or maybe it was all a mistake and they'd been killed by ordinary wolves or wild dogs. She had to cling to that or turn herself in at the sheriff's office this very minute.

"I think you've got the wrong idea about the wolves here. But if you can't get past thinking of them the way you do, Wolf's Point isn't the town for you." Becca could hear the door jangling behind her as people came and went but otherwise Millie's was getting oddly quiet. It felt as if everyone there was listening in.

"You warning me out of town?" Oya's voice was nearly a growl now and Becca bit back one of her own.

Taking a deep breath, she met the other's stare. "Yep, I guess I am. I suggest you take your van and your buddies and go back to whatever role-playing crap you were doing before you appointed yourselves Buffy wannabes and came to Wolf's Point. You're not wanted or needed here."

The other woman glared at her and started to say something, then looked over Becca's shoulder and shut her mouth. Her face changed, her expression shifting in a weird way, like it was doing something it wasn't meant to do. Her eyes glowed for a minute, then she shoved her chair back and stood. "You'll pay for what happened here. And for my parents. We'll be back," she snarled as she stomped out.

Becca wondered what Oya had seen in her face that made her leave and she couldn't resist a glance around Millie's. Everyone to either side of her was eating their lunch and appeared oblivious, but behind her was a different story. Erin, Molly, Shelly, Gladys, Mrs. Hui and all the other women of a certain age from the Wolf's Point Women's Club stood behind her, watching the aspiring slayer get into her van and drive away.

It was a sight that Becca found both profoundly creepy and infinitely comforting. Shelly leaned over and squeezed her shoulder. "Welcome back." Then she and the others walked out together, all of them, except Erin who sat down in the recently vacated chair.

"Just one question," Becca said. "What are you doing when your cast comes off?"

Silver Moon

Chapter 8

Everything started out differently in her head. Becca meant to talk to Erin about the whole whitewater rafting trip idea. She knew that she wanted to say that. Then she remembered that Erin had known what was going to happen to her and hadn't said a thing to warn her ahead of time. A real friend would have done that much.

So what rolled out of her mouth was, "Why the hell didn't you tell me? Why me anyway? Don't give me any more of the whole 'the magic picks its own' crap, either." She blushed the minute the words were out of her mouth; Ed always hated it when she got angry and used words like "hell." She had rolled it around in her mouth before she said it, too, savoring it like it was a chocolate or something.

Erin flinched and studied her hands. "What exactly," she said finally, "was I supposed to say? 'Guess what, neighbor? I'm not sure, but we all think you might turn into a lady werewolf on the full moon, seeing as menopause is kicking in and this is Wolf's Point and you've got a wolfy sort of vibe. It just works that way around here for some of us. But then again, maybe you won't.' You'd have really believed that story, wouldn't you?" She scowled back at Becca.

They stared at each other across the table like strange dogs until Erin slapped her palm on the table and looked away with a frustrated sigh. "Look, I know this is all hard to take in. But I thought that since you came back—"

"That I'm okay with turning into a monster once a month? Plus an extra night, which believe me, came as a terrific bonus. That I'm okay with hurting and killing people? Okay with something like me killing some woman's parents? Yeah, it all sounds hunky dory to me. Anything else I just need to roll with?" Becca crossed her arms and battled a new hot flash.

Silver Moon

She tried not to remember the mountains and the man with his knife, tried not to feel the bloodlust that was humming along just under her skin. She could control this, she knew she could, if she only tried hard enough. A moment later, a bead of sweat trickled down her overheated forehead.

Erin looked stunned. "Huh? Who got killed? Those guys the other night had guns, Becca. They shot me, remember?" She gestured at the sling that held her injured arm with her good hand. "They would have killed all of us. And what do you mean by 'an extra night'?"

Becca took a deep breath. "What about Oya's parents? We'll get back to me in a minute."

"Who's Oya? The one who just stormed out?" Erin frowned at Becca's nod. "First of all, why do you believe her? It's not like she or the other Nesters have a corner on truth. She's new this time around but her buddies lied about us the last time they came through, tried to rile up the sheriff and a bunch of the local rednecks about the 'monsters in the woods.' It took nearly a year to get that settled down, Becca. Do you think everyone here loves us?"

"Well, you all make it seem like that, what with Lizzie Blackhawk and her whole 'honor to be called thing.'"

"Lizzie's smart. The sheriff, not so much. If he hadn't been convinced that they were just out of towners here to mess things up for a thrill, we'd have been in serious trouble. And then what would have happened with this town? The pack protects Wolf's Point and keeps it livable. I don't see you moving to Mountainview, do I?"

"I thought about it. I tried."

"Yet you're back here. It's harder to leave than that, Becca. Like it or not, you're one of us now. The magic does call its own and once it does, you're in it for the long haul." Erin blew a breath out between puffed cheeks, and seemed to blow some of her anger out with it. "But I, for one, am glad you're back." She glanced sidelong at Becca and grinned.

Becca flushed a little more. "So how did you feel about it when it happened to you? And how often did you change?"

"Ummm…just the standard once a month. Why?" Erin took a quick glance around. "On the other hand, that may have to be a topic for a different time and place. We're starting to attract a bit too much interest." Erin's voice pitched lower and Becca looked up to check out the rest of the Millie's crowd in astonishment. Sure enough, there didn't seem to be as much conversation as she expected, or quite as many familiar faces.

She had very nearly decided to change the topic, and rafting was going to be the first thing that came out of her mouth. But then she looked back into Erin's blue-gray eyes across the table and she chickened out. There was no other word for it.

What happened instead was that she agreed to come by later and help out with the yard work while her neighbor's arm healed, maybe pick up some groceries and do some cleaning and talking. Then she bolted.

Now Becca was staring down at the water rushing by under the bridge and trying to figure out where to begin sorting out her problems, there being so many to choose from. For starters, there was the whole werewolf thing. The hot flashes weren't so great either, but that wasn't all of it. The weird knot of emotion she had started to feel whenever Erin Adams was around was icing on the cake. And she wasn't sure she wanted to think about that too hard.

So for variety, she thought about Oya's story and wondered again if any of it was true. She knew she didn't want it to be but she'd never thought of herself as someone who cut and ran when she didn't want to know something. There had to be a right thing to do. Trouble was, what was it and what should she do about it?

Her cell phone buzzed and she pulled it out of her purse and looked at the number. Whoever this was, they weren't in her contact list and she didn't want to deal with them now. But then she was feeling that a lot today and it had to stop sooner or later. She let out a weary sigh and clicked the answer button. "Hello?"

There was a pause before the voice on the other end answered, "That you, Becca? It's Ed."

Becca nearly dropped the phone in the river. She thought about clicking it off instead. But curiosity won out. "Ed? You got a new number, I gather. What the hell do you want?" She pictured him fidgeting in that way that he did, moving from one foot to another while he rubbed his bald patch.

"Ummm…okay. I was hoping we could start the conversation out some place less hostile."

"I'll bet you were. I don't share the sentiment, unfortunately. Now what is it? I've got things to do."

"Well, Hal called. He mentioned you'd been visiting and that you didn't seem to be doing too well. He was worried."

"And he called you? Lotta good that'll do." Becca snorted. Here was a reasonable target for the roiling emotions that were twisting her up. It was so like Ed to be out of touch for a whole year, then assume that she needed him. "I could've been dead for the last while for all you knew, Ed Thornton. But be that as it may, I'm fine. We done now?" She made a mental note to

Silver Moon

block his calls somehow; did her phone have some kind of "auto ignore" button?

"I need to talk to you about the house. I'll be in town on Friday. Will you meet me for lunch?"

Becca's mood sank lower. "What've we got to talk about these days, oh ex-husband mine? Last I heard, you said I could keep the house. And it's not like we're buddies."

"Things change, Becca. Will you meet me on Friday?"

Becca blew a breath out between her pursed lips and tried to recover her equilibrium. What was the harm, after all? It's not like things could get that much worse. She'd just suggest some place for lunch that she never went to normally so no one she knew would get to watch the show. "All right. I suppose so. Meet me at noon at the Riverside Bar." Then she actually did click off and turn the phone off. It was fun being rude to Ed, even now. She grinned down at the water for a moment.

Then she stopped grinning and turned to head back into town. It was nearly time to get to work; all the other crap would still be there later and she could deal with it then. She hoped. She had a niggling worry about what he'd said about the house. True, he still owned half after the divorce but she'd taken over the mortgage. Wasn't possession nine-tenths of something or other?

Lizzie Blackhawk pulled up beside her in a sheriff department's car just as she started walking along the side of the road. "Miz Thornton, can you get in please? Shelly asked me to show you something; she and Pete know that you might be a bit late for work."

Becca froze. It was all very well to think about turning herself in for murder or attempted murder, but actually doing it was something else again. But she couldn't outrun the deputy's car and there wasn't anywhere to run to. Shoulders tight with apprehension, she walked over, opened the door and got in. "I suppose you know what happened the other night by now, huh?"

Lizzie waited until she buckled herself in before she pulled forward. She was headed toward the highway at the end of the bridge where they'd first seen the slayers' van. "I've got a pretty good idea. But what I know or don't know isn't our biggest problem right now."

"Will that guy, Stuart, I think she said his name was, live? The one in the hospital from the other night?"

"Yep, probably. Barring someone doing something they shouldn't with a pillow or eating him the next time he shoots at a wolf. I'm not sure what you heard but he just got chewed up kind of bad. A lot of stitches and rabies shots and he'll have some interesting scars. Maybe learn a lesson or two from it, if we're lucky, and find himself a new hobby."

Becca collapsed against the seat sighing with relief. "But you still need to book me for assault?" It sounded pretty silly after it rolled out of her mouth.

Lizzie laughed, a short dry snort of amusement. "Now how would I explain that, Miz Thornton? Man's covered with bite marks, and had his throat chewed on. Town ain't that big so most folks who know you know you don't have a dog. What exactly would I tell Sheriff Henderson?"

"If you're not taking me in, what's this trip about?"

"Shelly wants you to see something and I volunteered." Lizzie subsided into silence and turned out onto the highway.

They drove quietly for a while, Becca looking out the window and Lizzie thinking who knew what thoughts behind her mirrored shades. Finally Becca broke the silence. "How's Shelly's mom doing? She's your aunt, right?"

"My ex-husband's aunt, but close enough. Not too good. My cousins are all keeping an eye on her down at the hospice."

A spasm of pure guilt went through Becca. No wonder Shelly was at sixes and sevens. She hadn't even asked how bad her mother's health was. "Oh no! I'm so sorry!" Becca looked for other words, a better way to express her feelings, but Lizzie just nodded, her lips turning down in a slight grimace. She didn't seem to want to talk more about it so after a few tries, Becca gave up and looked back out at the road.

They were headed into the mountains, Becca realized after a moment. Lizzie was taking a road that she didn't recognize, one that wandered off the main road through the pine forests, then upward. Where were they were going?

Becca fidgeted, trying to answer her own question with landmarks, before she broke the silence with another question. "Did you mean what you said the other morning? About it being an honor to be called?"

Lizzie slipped her glasses up to rest on her glossy black hair and glanced Becca's way quickly before going back to watching the road. "I did. That's one of the reasons I got into law enforcement. I'm hoping I get called when I'm old enough. I like the idea of helping folks in trouble and righting wrongs, but I didn't want to wait. I'm not the only one around here who feels that way either, not that it's common knowledge."

Becca stared at Lizzie, trying to imagine the young women of Wolf's Point, respectable and otherwise, wanting to run through the woods on all fours, chasing who knew what, every full moon when they got to a certain

53   *Silver Moon*

age. She just couldn't wrap her brain around that picture. "Really?" She managed at last.

"Miz–"

"Call me Becca, seeing as you're not arresting me."

The younger woman hesitated a moment, as if she wasn't quite ready to know her passenger that well, then continued with a brief nod. "All right. Becca, the Pack has a long and ancient history in this valley, going back into prehistory even. The Indians and Europeans who came here originally came from different tribes, different traditions, different countries. They moved here because the magic called them, one way or another. And it changes you if it touches you."

"You can say that again. I'd be just happy with never changing that way again." Becca shuddered.

"Maybe we can fix that." Lizzie pulled into a clearing where the road ended with a track. Becca looked up the narrow pathway as it wound up the rest of the mountain. "We have to do a little hiking. I brought water."

Becca felt something build inside her as she looked upward. Whatever it was told her that there was something she needed to do and she shivered a little, nervous about what that might be. Finally, she got out of the car, her steps slow and reluctant. "Against my better judgment, lead on."

They began walking, and after a bit, climbing upward. It was a steep, dry path and Becca could feel her feet slide on the pebbles from time to time. Her shoes weren't up to this, and she worried that neither was she. She was panting already. There was some scrub brush growing here and there along the way but not much to hold on to if she slipped. It didn't seem to bother Lizzie though; she moved easily and powerfully up the trail, her muscular thighs bulging in the pants of her police uniform.

Before she could stop the thought, Becca found herself thinking that Lizzie would make a much better werewolf than she did. *Great. Werewolf insecurities. Just what I need.* She shook her head and said something else instead. "Just how far up are we going?" she gasped as Lizzie reached a ledge next to a large boulder.

"We're almost there. Stop a minute and have some water." Lizzie handed her the flask and looked back down the mountain. She crinkled her nose like she was breathing in something Becca couldn't smell. Becca studied her a moment, then collapsed on a flattish rock, water bottle held tightly in her hand. There was a light, cool breeze dancing down the mountain and she let it play with her hair and dry the sweat on her forehead.

Then she too, drank the air into her lungs, pulling the valley's different scents in with it. There was exhaust from the cars on the highway, pine and birch and soil from the woods below, early snow from some distant high peak. There was water trickling in a nearby stream and a wood fire burning somewhere further away. There were animal scents too, and part of her brain seemed to be able to sort out whether each was predator or prey. She could smell humans as well, Lizzie and herself included.

She didn't know how long she sat like that, sniffing the breeze until she could feel Lizzie stir, moving restlessly and fidgeting. Becca scrambled up. "Well, let's keep going," she said, a little surprised at how tired her voice sounded.

But Lizzie didn't go up as far as she feared. A few more yards and she turned off and walked along the ledge behind another boulder. Becca followed her through a narrow crevice between the rocks and into a large, shallow cave. Then she stood in the entrance with her mouth slightly open while she stared at the walls.

There were paintings on them, running in seemingly chronological order in a circle around the walls. The ones to her right looked the oldest, clearly done by hand with some sort of vegetable paint or something like it. They had a primitive quality to them, but there was something familiar about the shapes they depicted.

She walked closer to try and make out what that was, looking from painting to painting. Then it struck her: they all showed women transforming into wolves. It was harder to tell with the earlier paintings, but there was clearly a theme here. There were wolves with human faces, humans with wolf heads and all points in between.

Lizzie sat down on a rock at the entrance, her head bowed reverently. Becca wasn't sure, but she seemed like she might be praying. Becca began following the semicircle of paintings around the cave.

She noticed as the pictures changed mediums and styles, and stopped and wondered at the ones where the wolf-woman was clearly sacred, gleaming with her own light, as well as the ones where she was terrifying. The paintings glowed with power, pulling her in to them somehow. They ended a little short of the entrance on the cave's left side. She stopped at the last one, a graffiti artist's rendition of a woman in a hot pink suit with a wolf's head.

"My cousin did that one," Lizzie volunteered from her perch.

"I like it. It's very strong." Becca stepped back to look at it some more. Then she remembered that Shelly was Lizzie's cousin too. "Is it Shelly's painting?"

"Nope. It's Kira's work, Kira's vision of what her mom looks like when she changes. I think it's pretty cool, though the high school art teacher

Silver Moon

didn't like it when she brought the early sketches into school. I think it freaked him out."

Becca could see why. If you didn't know anything about the wolves, this would be a pretty intense drawing from a fifteen-year-old girl. She tried to imagine Shelly and Pete's taciturn daughter with her ever-present earbuds doing paintings like this. But she knew about the wolves and Becca didn't. What else hadn't she figured out yet? It all seemed to hit her at once and she caught at the bare rock for support as her knees got weak. "I think I need to go to work now."

"Have some more water and eat this first." The deputy handed her an energy bar and the water bottle before she took her own walk around the cave. The mirror sunglasses were perched on her head and as Becca eased down to sit on the rock floor, she was finally able to see the other woman's eyes. Her expression was solemn and respectful and every now and then she sighed a little or reached out to lightly touch one of the paintings.

"You come up here a lot?"

"Just once in a while. It's a sacred place and I don't belong here all the time, at least not yet."

Becca looked at one of the other paintings, one of a woman with white hair and a wolf's paws. This was her future. She wondered what happened to geriatric werewolves. Did they ever get Alzheimer's? Did they just keep changing until they couldn't change any more?

The thought depressed her and made her aware of how much the cave was starting to get under her skin. "There's something eerie about this place, like it's alive or something." Becca wondered where that notion had come from, but it was true. She could feel this place in her blood. It didn't feel like changing under the moon, but she could see how it could end up in the same place.

"Generations of wolf women and their people coming up here to paint what they see will do that to a place. I think this was the old ritual space, back before there was a Women's Club or anywhere else to meet in town. All of them came here to change when the moon was full," Lizzie's voice was filled with longing now.

"It's scary, you know, changing like that. And it hurts. And you do things you don't want to do, things you can't help." Becca gulped some more water. "I'd stop it if I could."

Something else occurred to her a moment later. She looked around at the paintings once more. "Why are they all women?"

Lizzie shrugged and pulled her glasses back down on her nose as if to block Becca and her questions and her doubts out. "They say it's how the magic works. Ask Shelly. She knows all about this kind of stuff. Let's head back. My shift starts in an hour." She didn't say another word all the way back to town.

Chapter 9

By the time the next Friday rolled around, Becca felt like she was trapped in some weird sitcom. She saw Erin and helped her out around the house, but couldn't bring herself to talk to her neighbor about anything but the weather and the blandest of town gossip. It was like her brain was boiling every time she was over there and her body kept joining in. The words just wouldn't come, what with all the turmoil.

Then to make things worse, Shelly was still gone since her mother's condition was growing worse. Becca felt horribly alone in a way that she hadn't felt since after the divorce. The only good part was that she didn't feel like she was going to turn into a wolf in broad daylight, at least for the moment. That was something.

Even so, lunch with Ed was likely to be even more of a treat than she had anticipated. Becca could feel that already. Her body seemed to be trying to melt away, which made it difficult to wait on customers and even harder to concentrate. She made two mistakes while making change and very nearly recommended that Al Watkins paint his garage hazard orange and that was just the first hour of Friday morning.

Pete stopped over in time to turn Al's colorblind attention to a more neutral color, then stood behind Becca as she rang him up. The minute the door closed after Al, he stepped to Becca's side and leaned on the counter. "You doing all right? Maybe it's time for a break."

Becca glared up at him and started to snap. But just then the bright orange hunting gear hanging above Pete's head caught her eye and the fight ran out of her. "Oh crap. I'm sorry, Pete. What between one thing and another and Ed calling about lunch today, my head's just a mess. It won't happen again."

"Wait, you're having lunch with Ed?" Pete's eyebrows rose.

Becca could almost read his thoughts. Pete's opinion of Ed had really plummeted right before the divorce when he heard about her ex cheating on her. It was nice to see that it wasn't making a comeback.

She hid a smile despite the way she was feeling and looked down at the counter. It was good to know that there were still nice guys out there. "Yeah. He wants me to meet him for lunch to talk to me about the house. Or so he says. Maybe he decided that there's something to be said for experience after all." She bared her teeth in an almost smile and Pete snorted.

"So are you going to meet him?"

"Might as well. I'm guessing he'll keep calling otherwise. Besides, I'm curious to find out what he wants."

Pete nodded. "Seems like a good idea. You going to be okay here until then?"

"Aye, aye, Captain. Everything will be shipshape for the rest of the day, before and after Ed. I promise." Becca gave him a chipper salute. She was surprised to realize she felt a bit better. Maybe she'd just needed to get it out of her system. After all, it was just lunch. How bad could it be?

She kept telling herself that as she walked down to the Riverside an hour and a half later. Her stomach was uncomfortably fluttery and she kept replaying her last fights with Ed before the divorce was finalized. Now she wished he'd left well enough alone and kept giving her the silent treatment. They were better off done.

But that just wasn't her luck. He was sitting in a booth toward the back, waving to her as she came in. She made herself keep moving, walking as if she hadn't a care in the world. He looked different somehow, even with the same old bald patch and the small paunch.

Finally, it struck her: he looked happy. He even smelled happy. She twitched a little at that thought, then decided she'd analyze that part later. His shoulders were tense, but it was clear that it was temporary, not their natural state. He realized that she was studying him and gave her an uncertain smile that crinkled the edges of his eyes.

She hadn't seen him look happy in a long time, years maybe. Maybe he was looking at her the same way. She hoped she looked happy to him, even if she wasn't right now. After all, they had loved each other once, she was sure of that much. *How did we come to this?* The thought showed up unexpectedly and sent a pang through her. Maybe it was time to bury the pain of his affair and the divorce.

"You look great, Becca." Ed said with the kind of fake enthusiasm he used to reserve for talking to elderly relatives.

Catherine Lundoff   60

Or maybe it's too soon for that. "Yeah, I'll bet. Let's get lunch ordered so I can find out what you want and we can get this over with." She ordered a salad and soup the minute the waitress showed up, deliberately hurrying Ed into ordering the first thing he saw on the menu.

"Thanks for coming down to meet me, Becca. I know this isn't easy for either of us." Ed straightened, looking more formal as he pulled a folder from his bag.

Becca raised an eyebrow and she'd tried to look cool and collected. "What, no lawyer? Last time I saw you with paperwork, you were hiding behind your cousin Pamela and her briefcase." She bit back a snarl at the memory.

"I'm hoping that won't be necessary. I think we should probably wait until lunch gets here to talk about it though. Things always go down better on a full stomach."

"Do they? Sometimes it's better to just rip the band-aid off and get it over with." She reached out and yanked the folder out from under Ed's elbow before he could react. Then she flipped it open and frowned for a minute as she tried to comprehend what she was reading. The shock froze her in place, unable to speak or even breath for a minute. Why hadn't she seen this coming? "Oh, shit. You want the house too. Destroying my life wasn't enough for you, was it?"

Ed made an unhappy noise. "It's not like that, Becca. Give me a chance to explain. Christy's pregnant and—" He saw the look on her face and stopped mid-sentence. "This is not how I planned on doing this." He rubbed his hands on his forehead and covered his eyes with them for a moment.

"Pregnant? For fifteen years you told me that you didn't want kids and I let it lie, thinking it might be for the best. Not even two years with Christy and she's already knocked up. Well, that's just great, Ed. Thanks." Becca could feel her hands trembling now, and tears of white-hot rage gathering behind her lids. How dare he do this to her now?

With a huge effort, she pushed the hurt down deep and something else welled up in its place. She remembered that she wasn't just Ed's ex-wife anymore. No, she was a powerful creature of moonlight and magic now and she would not cry in front of her louse of an ex. But she couldn't bite his face off either, unfortunately, not here in the diner anyway. No matter how much he deserved it. She felt the shadow of the wolf retreat a bit.

Even so, when she opened her eyes again, Ed gasped and turned very, very pale. Becca smiled at him and for a moment, she could feel the monster race just below her surface. It made her feel powerful, invincible even.

Silver Moon

"Okay, Ed. Let's talk about the house. You do remember that you never paid me support, right? Not even after I put you through school? That was your little gift from the judge, seeing as we didn't have children." She snarled the last word then took a deep breath. Losing herself completely would be a bad idea right now. Though there was something seriously compelling in the notion of seeing Ed's guts up close and personal.

Ed's hand on the table trembled a little and he looked away from her, but he didn't bolt for the door. She had to give him credit for that. "I don't make that much money, Becca. Not enough to provide for all of us and I have assets tied up in the house. I don't suppose you can afford to buy me out?" He glanced at her sidelong as if she might lunge across the table at any provocation.

"I work in a hardware store. What kind of money do you think I make? My savings won't cover it." Her heart twisted inside her when she realized she was telling the truth. But she loved her little house, had put her heart and soul into making it a home. Right now, it felt like was all she had left in the world and the thought of losing that last bit of her old life opened a pit inside her, one that felt like it went on forever.

"So we sell it and split the money. There'd be enough left over for you to get a retirement condo or something like that." Ed's voice trailed off again and she wondered what was looking out of her eyes now. "I'm sorry, Becca. I can't see any other way and things are different now. I have to do something. You know this was never meant to be permanent, just until you got on your feet and the market got better."

The realization that he was serious and that as co-owner, he could force her into selling sank in rapidly. All Becca's anger faded as she stared down at the documents in the folder, shuffling through them without seeing them. What was she going to do? The waitress set their food down and she stared at it blankly before looking up. "I'm sorry, I've changed my mind. Can I get these to go?" She stood up, closing Ed's folder with a snap and tucking it under her arm.

"Wait, Becca. Can't we talk about this, get it resolved?" Ed's voice was pleading now.

She remembered how he sounded when he finally confessed to her about Christy and the familiarity of his tone made her flinch. "I'll need to think about it." She grabbed her bag and went to meet the waitress at the register.

Ed followed her. "So you'll call me next week and let me know what you want to do? Just remember what the market's like right now. If we're going to sell, we've got to put it up for sale soon. You can keep the papers; I've got other copies."

Of course he did. His lawyer would have seen to that. Becca looked away and felt her head nod like it was on strings. Now all she had to do was to figure out what to do next. And how she was going to keep her home with no money to pay for it. Suddenly turning into a wolf on the full moon seemed like child's play.

Chapter 10

As luck would have it, Erin was at the store when Becca got back. Becca nearly turned around and bolted back out the door before she had time to think about how stupid that would look. "What's the matter?" Erin stepped up close, into not quite touching range.

The breath caught in Becca's throat and she looked up into her neighbor's eyes, losing herself there for a moment. Then dragged herself back out, stomach still fluttering. "I…I just can't talk about it. Not here, not now. I've got to finish my shift." She brushed past Erin and headed to the paint section, her back prickling. If she kept this up, Erin might never talk to her again. And that, come to think of it, might make her life simpler.

Shelly appeared in front of her, cutting her off before she could get up the aisle to comparative safety. Becca flinched away, startled, before she remembered her manners. "Shelly, you're back! How's your mom?"

"She's hanging in there; we can talk about that later. In the meantime, Pete told me about Ed. Why don't you come back to the office and sit for a minute? I'm guessing that you're not ready for the general public just yet. Pete'll watch the counter." She nodded to Erin over Becca's head.

Next thing Becca knew she was in the back office with the two of them. Shelly handed her a box of tissues. "Let it out. I can tell you're holding back."

Becca knew she must look pretty bad, but it wasn't like she was ready to burst into tears. Not right now. Not in front of them. It was way too humiliating. She started to muster an indignant denial, stringing together the words that would make it clear that she could take care of herself, most of the time anyway.

Then she thought about the house and broke down sobbing despite herself. "Damn it! I didn't want to do it this way," she choked out. She took a deep, tremulous breath. Then instead of pulling herself together, she buried her face in a tissue and gave a few more deep, hiccupy sobs.

She managed to stop long enough to say, "It's Ed. He wants to sell the house, my little house, because he's having babies with his damn midlife-crisis wife!" She collapsed into one of the chairs and bawled into a fistful of tissues.

Erin took Ed's folder from her lap, while Shelly rubbed her shoulders. Becca let out deep shuddering sobs, hating her loss of control almost as much as the situation. She wasn't emotional like this normally and she didn't want to start now. Stupid changes in her body, all of them.

At least she ran out of tears pretty quickly, much to her relief. Erin cleared her throat when it was obvious that Becca was paying attention to her. "We might be able to help you with this, you know. Let me look into it and stop worrying about it while we look for a way to take care of the problem."

Time stopped for an instant as Becca considered what Erin's tone of voice might mean. It seemed significant, somehow. Then she stared up at Erin in horror, Oya's story flashing through her brain. Did she really hate Ed enough to want him dead? Especially since, if the wolves of Wolf's Point went after him, she'd most likely be right there with them. Sure she was pissed off, but not really what you'd call rip-the-man's-throat-out mad.

Erin gave her a puzzled frown but it was Shelly who figured it out an instant before she did. "We're not going to eat him, you know. What do you take us for? The Pack has an emergency fund and Erin handles our books. We should be able to get you a good deal on a loan and maybe some cash down."

Becca drew a long shuddery breath. These were her friends and neighbors. Of course they weren't going to eat her ex-husband. What crazy ideas she was getting ever since she, well, started turning into a wolf. She pressed her face into her hands; maybe the Pack could recommend a good shrink too, one that specialized in dealing with this kind of thing. She found herself groaning out loud, then decided she was being silly and looked back up.

"So who's been putting these ideas into your head? I know we haven't had any time to talk about what went down when you left for Mountainview, but I think we can read between the lines." Shelly was frowning now and there was a newspaper in her hand. "What happened out there?"

Becca flinched when she saw the headline, "Suspect in boy's kidnapping attacked, killed by wild animals." For an instant, she was back on the mountain, covered with blood that glowed in the moonlight. A voice that didn't sound like hers forced the words out. "I'm sorry. But I had to. He had the little boy. And a knife. He kept stabbing me and I just wanted to stop him and save the kid."

"Do you understand why wolves usually travel in packs?" Shelly's tone had a weight to it that made it sound like the fate of the world hung on Becca's answer.

"Well, they're like dogs. They like the company, I guess, and someone to have their backs. And you're saying that I shouldn't have gone off alone." Becca scowled. "It's not like I knew this was going to happen, you know. Come to think of it, when Lizzie took me up to see those cave paintings, none of those paintings showed women-wolves in packs. They were all by themselves. You'd think they would have painted them with a pack if it was that important."

"Let's stick with the idea of what a pack does for the moment," Shelly said firmly. "You're right, you shouldn't have gone off like that. The Pack is there to help you manage changing, as much as to watch your back the rest of the time. You know you could have just as easily endangered an innocent bystander, don't you?"

"No!" Becca started, hands braced against the arms of the chair. She could feel her face flush, feel the blood thrum under her skin. She could smell the other women in the room and almost, but not quite, feel the changes start in her body. "I knew not to hurt the boy. Even as a wolf, I knew! I did what you did with Erin, Shelly. I changed partway and carried him down the mountain."

There was dead silence in the room as both Shelly and Erin stared back at her. Now that she'd stopped crying, she could see how tired Shelly looked, how uncomfortable Erin's cast appeared to be, hanging like a weight off her shoulder. Yet here she was whining about her own troubles.

Of course, they weren't looking at her like her complaining was the biggest problem. No, this was the kind of astonishment that would have greeted the announcement that she was able to turn into a wolf during the full moon, if she'd said it outside this room. She wondered what she'd done that was so weird.

Erin glanced from Shelly back to Becca. Her tone was very careful as she asked, "You were able to control your change when you were in Mountainview, Becca. Are you sure?"

"I think I'd remember something like that, don't you? I got out into the woods and I could feel myself start to change, just like at the Club. I fought it as hard as I could. I barely managed to get my clothes off and hidden before it happened." Becca shook her head as if to clear her memories.

Silver Moon

"It's pretty unusual to change more than once in a month, but it happens sometimes. It's generally a new wolf thing: you're more sensitive to the magic when it first starts happening." Shelly sounded like a schoolteacher, her voice soothing, calling Becca back to the present. "What happened when you found them?"

"Well, like I said, he went for me. He stabbed me a couple of times and it hurt like hell. We fought and I won. Then I made myself change partway so I could pick up the kid. I lost a lot of blood during the fight. But at least the whole Change thing seems to speed up healing. That's something at least. Think we could use it to fix the hot flashes too?" Becca was pretty pleased with herself for thinking that one up. Maybe the trip to the cave had been useful after all, if it inspired this kind of thinking.

Shelly was still frowning at her. Maybe it wasn't such a great idea after all. "But how'd you do it? What were you thinking about beforehand?"

"Well, I could smell how scared the boy was and I was covered with blood and everything hurt. But I knew I couldn't carry him down the mountain in my jaws, not without hurting him. So I guess I was just thinking about what needed to be done and how I could make that happen." Becca shrugged. "Did I do something special?"

Erin laughed but seemed to sober up quickly when Shelly caught her eye. "Yes," Shelly said finally. "You did something special. New wolves can't make that kind of partial change, or at least I've never heard of it happening. Not enough control. Even wolves who've been changing for a while have a hard time with it and most can't do it."

Becca tried to figure out if this was a good thing or not. Shelly didn't look mad, just surprised, so that was something. Erin, on the other hand, looked fit to burst. Her eyes were sparkling and she winked at Becca. And Becca, for a wonderment, didn't find herself blushing and avoiding eye contact. Nope, this time around, she just smiled back and wondered why this made her neighbor so happy.

"All right, Becca. I think it worked out reasonably well this time, all things considered. But I also think you got lucky. That you left to begin with is partially my fault: I haven't been able to pay the kind of attention to you that I should have because of my mom. We've talked about it and Erin's going to train you instead." Shelly stood up a little straighter and her voice left no room for argument.

Which didn't stop Becca from trying. She wasn't sure she should spend that much time around Erin. It would get weird fast. "Training? But what about her arm?"

"We'll manage," Erin said, her tone quiet and amused. "And half-controlled changes or not, there's a lot you don't know about being one of us."

There wasn't much point arguing with that. Becca reached for Ed's folder and Erin handed it back. "Stop worrying about the house. We'll make something work out."

That was enough to make Becca feel slightly more optimistic. Maybe everything would be all right. Somehow.

Erin sat down in the chair opposite while Shelly settled in on the edge of the desk. "Next topic. Lizzie said that she took you up to see the cave," Erin remarked as if she were talking about the weather.

"Yep. What does that have to do with any of this?"

"How did the cave make you feel?"

"I dunno. Kind of crackly around the edges like it was electric or something. And it was creepy, all those women changing into wolves. How come this doesn't happen to men?"

Shelly blew her breath out in a sigh, almost like she was expecting to hear something else. "It does happen to men. Just not here and not the same way it happens to us. There are two different kinds of wolves, Becca, and they change for different reasons. Erin, you'll need to cover that in your training. Do you think we're creepy too?"

Now there was a question. Becca looked from one to the other of her friends, seeing them change in her mind's eye. Shelly's eyes flickered gold for an instant and Becca decided to go with honesty. "Sometimes. I'm just not used to the idea yet. And I don't know that I ever will be. Does Pete know? And the kids, other than Kira?"

Shelly tilted her head to one side. "I don't keep secrets from Pete if I can help it. Pack business, yes, but not something like this. I was afraid I might hurt him or the kids when it first happened. Kira found out by accident. She says the other kids don't know and I'm not ready to tell them yet."

"How long have you been changing?"

"Six years." Shelly glanced at the clock and Becca followed her look. If it was a hint, it was a pretty successful one. She'd be making up a couple of hours for this paycheck at this rate.

"I should get back. Pete'll be wondering what happened to me."

Becca blew her nose and stood up, feeling better than she had since before lunch. "We can talk more about this later?"

Shelly nodded, a tired smile curling her lips. "We'll talk more very soon. I promise."

Erin cleared her throat. "Stop by after work tonight? We can get started then."

Silver Moon

Becca nodded her response and paused for the others to get up. They went on sitting there, though, like there were things they were going to talk about once she left the room. Evidently there were still some secrets she wasn't ready for. And who knew, maybe she wasn't. It already felt like a long day. So she nodded again and went out and relieved Pete at the counter, exerting all her newly discovered self-control to lose herself in paint and plumbing sales for the rest of the day.

Chapter 11

Becca tried as hard as she could to ignore all of her weirder feelings for the rest of the afternoon. She didn't think about anything that made her blush, for one thing. Well, not much, anyway. She did remember to pick up some take-out for their dinner, speaking politely and formally to Mrs. Hui, more or less as she always did. Just like they hadn't woken up together naked in the woods.

But now that she was standing on Erin's doorstep, everything she'd been trying to ignore came flooding back. Sure, it was a doorstep in front of a porch door with some peeling white paint on it, not unlike her own. The house even looked a bit like hers, except with dark green trim instead of white. There were a few other differences, too; maybe she should just stand here awhile and think about them.

Her imagination took flight, circling in all directions, noticing dozens of things she'd never noticed before. But when she thought she saw several of the neighbors change into wolves as they mowed their lawns, Becca shook her head to clear it and rang the doorbell. Whatever was waiting for her on the other side couldn't be any crazier than what was going on in her head.

Erin pulled the door open and gave her a lazy smile. "Hi there. C'mon in."

Becca followed her somersaulting stomach inside, wondering if Erin had known how long it had taken before she worked up the nerve to ring the bell. For a minute, she looked everywhere except at Erin and it was as if she was seeing her neighbor's house for the first time. Had the rug always been that pattern of dark reds and blacks? Suddenly it looked like blood spilt on the polished hardwood floor. And that framed painting of the wolves—was that their Pack? Or just regular wolves?

Erin shut the door behind her and reached down to take the bag of Chinese take-out. "Thanks for doing this. Cooking's still a chore with my arm like this." She moved the sling, the gesture startling Becca into looking straight at her.

The hallway was dim in the twilight and Erin's eyes shone silver for a moment. Becca could almost see the ghostly shape of pointed, furry ears above her short-cropped gray-brown hair. "Is it always going to be like this?" She closed her eyes and rubbed her hands over her face.

Erin patted her shoulder and herded her toward the kitchen. "You'll be sensitive to the moon phases for awhile. But it gets better with practice, I promise."

Becca groaned in disbelief as she pulled out a chair from the table and dropped into it. "This is all too much to take in at once. Why can't I just have the same kind of menopause everyone else has? Or just friggin' Ed and his lawyer trying to take my house? Instead of all of it with a topping of turning into a monster on moonlit nights." She remembered who she was talking to and her stomach twisted. "Cool, useful monsters, of course."

"Just lucky, I guess." Erin put the food on the table. "Seriously, do you think we all had it easy? Just took the whole thing in stride when we started changing? Shelly took it as a birthright, sure, but Pete was really freaked out. Gladys wouldn't talk to anyone for six months, just kept to herself and thought she was going nuts. I—" she stopped abruptly and pulled some plates out of the cabinet.

Becca got up and looked around for utensils and mugs, settling for taking the clean ones out of the drain. Erin had turned away and was looking out the window into the backyard like it was the most interesting view in the world.

Becca wondered what to do, what to say. It wasn't like she knew Erin that well. What if there was some terrible story about her change, one that would make it impossible for Becca to be friends with her? She wouldn't befriend a real monster, not now, not ever. She promised herself that, hoping she wasn't lying to herself, while she opened up the cardboard containers and waited for Erin to turn around.

When she did, it was to pour out some ice water into the mugs and hand one to Becca. She still wasn't looking up when she sat down. "Look," Becca said finally, "whatever you did can't be that bad. I hope." She tried to smile like she was kidding but she could feel her lips trembling. Then she braced herself for whatever was coming next.

"I had myself committed after I changed. Spent nearly a month over at Pleasant Oaks Psychiatric in Eastfork before Shelly found about it and dragged my doped up ass out of there. She got to me just before the next full moon. Can you imagine what kind of carnage there would have been if she hadn't?" Erin shuddered. "All those helpless folks locked up with an honest to God werewolf."

"But you can control it. You wouldn't have killed any of those people," Becca said indignantly.

"Really?" Erin's eyes were definitely glinting silver now, even under the kitchen's fluorescent lights. Her face seemed to be getting longer, fuzzier while Becca watched her. Something rose in the shadows of her collar and a soft growl found its way up from Becca's throat, leaping past her lips before she could stop it. She clapped her hands to her mouth and stared at Erin, eyes wide. Erin's lip curled and she snarled back.

Becca felt herself start to respond, to change, and she jumped to her feet. "Stop it! I mean it! You made your point. You're a monster, I'm a monster. None of us can really control this, not all the time." She stood over Erin and gasped for breath as she fought against the madness swirling through her.

Erin sat back and exhaled slowly as if she was letting all the wolf go with each breath. "You just did. Control it I mean. I couldn't do that right after I first started to change. So yes, I might have killed a few of those folks up at the Oaks. It wouldn't have been anything personal, mind you. Just about being in the wrong place at the wrong time."

Becca dropped back into her chair as her legs gave out. "Why didn't you stop me from going to Mountainview?"

"Well, it wasn't like you left a note or anything. We didn't know where you'd gone. Shelly took off to check out your ex's place in between trips to check on her mom and I went through every campground in the woods around here. We made a list of anyone we knew that you knew who lived somewhere else and tried to get in touch with them. Apparently, you hadn't mentioned the Mountainview relatives to Shelly in quite a while."

"She thought I went to chew Ed's face off? Funny, that's what I thought you two meant back at the office."

"He does seem to bring that out in you. And I'm not saying he might not deserve it." Erin smiled.

Becca felt herself getting angry all over again. Why was her life the only open book around here? Stupid Ed. "Speaking of families, where's yours? Why no ex-husband, kids, parents? You never mention them."

"I killed them all during a bad moonrise a couple of years back." Erin's matter-of-fact tone froze Becca in place until she rolled her eyes. "No ex-husband. I'm a lesbian, Becca. Have been since I came out as a teenager.

Silver Moon

My last partner is living with her new wife out on the East Coast. We never had kids and my parents died a few years back."

"Oh." The word hung there between them until Becca reached out and picked up a container of Chinese food. "I'm sorry to hear that."

"Which part? Me being a dyke, breaking up with my ex or the parents?"

"Your parents, but I guess your ex too." Becca concentrated on scooping rice out of the box, focusing a bit harder than she meant to. If Erin was a lesbian and if she kept having all those weird feelings about her, did that mean that she was one too? She tried to remember everything she'd ever seen about coming out on *Oprah* while a tiny voice inside screamed, *Not that too!*

"And I've found a complete conversation killer. Look, it's not contagious. Spending time with me won't make you queer. Shelly's held up just fine despite my terribly charismatic and corrupting presence. Ditto most of the other members of the club." Erin sighed and Becca looked up.

"I guess…" Becca stumbled over the words, gauging her feelings. After all, this was hardly the craziest thing that had happened to her recently. "I guess I kinda suspected it, now that I stop and think about it. Honestly, I'm just so freaked about everything right now that it doesn't rate that highly on my personal Disastermeter."

"Do you have an actual personal Disastermeter?" Erin grinned at her.

"I do lately. So speaking of Shelly, how do you two know each other? Honestly, it's like I just met you all, which I guess is true. I feel like I've got no idea about what's going on around me."

"I was born here, right outside town and down the valley a bit. Shelly and I went to good old Howling High together. We were both on the basketball team one of the years that the girls went to State so we had a lot of time to get to know each other. I moved away for a time, then came back, then moved away again. But it's a hard place to leave, and I got pulled back in. We stayed in touch, what between one thing and another." Erin shrugged and took up a forkful of sweet-and-sour pork.

"Did you know about the wolves back then? And what's Howling High?"

"Oh, sorry. It's what the kids around here call Wolf's Point High School, kind of an in-group joke. The football team is the Timberwolves and all the other teams have wolf-related names. So yes, a few of us knew a bit about the wolves and the curse, or at least we thought we did."

"It's a curse now?"

"Think of it as a mixed blessing. We get to live in Wolf's Point as part of the Pack and we get to keep the valley's magic alive. That's the wonderful, powerful aspect of it. We also get to turn into wolves one night a month and keep doing it until we get worn out. Not to mention fighting with slayers in training and the occasional meth dealer who wants to move into the area." Erin gestured with her sling. "Now what can I tell you that will make you more comfortable with all this?"

Becca opened her mouth, then closed it again. There was so much that she wanted to know, had to know. It was hard to know where to start, even harder to concentrate on everything Erin was telling her. She tuned out for a few moments while Erin kept talking, just letting the words wash over her. Erin's voice was pleasant in her wolf-enhanced ears, neither too shrill nor earth-rumbling deep.

Then the phone rang, its chirp startlingly loud on the shelf above Becca's head. She jumped, banging her head, then almost did it again when Erin reached over her head to pick it up. She scooted her chair out of the way and tried to sit quietly, breathing in her neighbor's scent. It was a mix of laundry soap and clean skin with a hint of sweat underneath.

Becca found herself wanting to reach out and touch the faded denim of her shirt or maybe the worn fabric of her jeans. She sat on her hands instead, trying to politely ignore the conversation Erin was having about two feet away.

She started with a quick look at the walls. Erin's framed copy of the "Serenity Prayer" caught her eye. If ever there was a time to accept the things she couldn't change, this was probably it. Interesting, though; she wondered if Erin had been in a twelve-step program or just found the prayer comforting. Maybe she'd work up the nerve to ask when her neighbor got off the phone.

She glanced away from it to the calendar next to it; Amelia Earhart stared back. That figured. Becca smiled a little and found her attention wandering back to her neighbor.

She studied Erin from the corner of her eye, much the way she'd been listening to her voice. She wanted to see her neighbor whole and entire from her graying hair and long, square-jawed face down to her narrow feet sheathed in faded plaid slippers. There was a small zit on the side of her jaw and one of her front teeth was crooked. The arm without the cast had a long white scar down it.

Becca wondered how Erin stayed lean and muscular while she herself had moved into spherical softness with middle age. She envied that a bit, along with the other woman's easy, athletic movements. She'd have to ask what her neighbor did to work out once she got off the phone. With any luck, it was all due to running around as a wolf and Becca wouldn't have to

Silver Moon

add anything extreme, like marathon running or powerlifting, to her short list of hobbies.

Then Erin's voice pitched up. "What the hell? On fire?"

Becca snapped back out of her fantasies and stared anxiously at Erin while she waited for the call to end. Then Erin clicked the phone off with a brusque "We're on our way." She put the phone back in the charger and stared down at Becca. "It's the Women's Club. Shelly just got there and she says it's on fire."

Chapter 12

This time, they took Becca's car and her tires squealed as she spun them out through the streets, then onto the gravel road leading to the Women's Club. "Did Shelly say how bad it was?" Becca couldn't stop herself from asking, even though the question felt silly once she heard it out loud. *Like there's good arson.* If it was arson.

"Bad enough. Even worse if it's got anything to do with the Nesters. That would mean they suspect who the wolves are and then we're all vulnerable." Erin rubbed her hand over her eyes and stared bleakly out the window.

Now *that* was a fun thought. Becca wondered what the consequences might be for all of the Pack if everyone in town knew what was going on. A vision of silver bullets, mental wards and life in jail didn't make her feel very joyous about the future.

That in turn set her to wondering whether or not ancient magic could be cured with modern medicine. They could treat bubonic plague, why not werewolfery? Maybe they could find something to fix this before her worries came true.

That was when they came around the curve in the road and all fantasies about the future, good and bad, were erased from Becca's mind. They could see smoke billowing above the trees and every now and then a lick of flame shooting skyward into the night sky. Smoke filled the road and the clearing ahead.

When they pulled into the end of the drive, the building was a huge fireball in the clearing ahead of them. Becca could feel Erin's anger coming off her like a summer-hot sidewalk. She could feel her own rage build in answer. This was theirs, their territory, their home. If this was the work of Oya and the Nesters, it was a declaration of war.

Silver Moon

The Wolf's Point fire trucks, all two of them, were out in front of the building and the volunteer firefighters were struggling with lengths of heaving hoses and spraying water.

Becca parked the car on the road away from the main site, pulling far over to the side to make room for any more trucks and emergency vehicles that might show up. Then she and Erin piled out of the car and raced down the road as fast as they could to where Shelly and Lizzie and a bunch of other folks were shoveling dirt and sand onto the outer reaches of the fire to try and contain it.

Becca grabbed a shovel and pitched in where there was a break in the semi-circle. Behind her, Erin began filling up a couple of empty buckets from the spring, hauling them to the fire's edge one-handed. Becca could hear Sheriff Henderson on the radio somewhere nearby, calling in help from the other towns. There was a crunch of gravel on the road and then Mrs. Hui and her son and daughter joined the line. After that, another carload of women who she vaguely recognized, and another, families in tow, arrived.

Becca nodded to them and kept shoveling. Her mind kept turning back to the night that she'd changed for the first time, right here in the Women's Club. She shuddered and tried to make herself remember happier times there instead: the book clubs and the birthday parties. But it was all over-shadowed with her memory of her first change.

She still recognized that the building was more than her remembered terrors. It was, she realized for the first time, the main common meeting ground between the Pack and the normal human women of the town. Where else did they all socialize together? What were they going to do without it?

She tried not to look up, tried not to see the flames leaping treetop-high above them, rapidly eating away at the building. Looking up would just make it all seem more hopeless. As it was, she could feel the anger and anxiety rippling down the line of volunteers like a live wire. The Pack was losing its main home; she knew that in her bones, even though she'd never thought of the club that way before.

And they were losing. That much she could see when she finally did raise her eyes from the shovel, startled by the sound of the crash when the roof collapsed. The women and men wavered in their shoveling, most looking up at the building as a long shuddering sigh went through the clearing. The firefighters gave the flames one last listless spray, drowning most of them, too late. There was silence as they all looked at the pile of blackened ash, still sparking wires and tiny flames that managed to stay alive despite the wet.

Becca glanced around the group, stopping when she saw Shelly's face. In the two years that she'd known her boss, she'd always had trouble reading Shelly's thoughts from her expression. Now she shivered a bit as the wind picked up and she watched Shelly nearly glow with fury. Her eyes snapped and crackled almost as much as the dying flames and her jaw was clenched just below her thinning lips. For an instant, the wolf glowed in the air around her like a cape.

Becca broke out of the line and walked over to her. *Maybe it was an accident.* That was what she wanted to say. A rogue lightning strike or an electrical failure, something ordinary. But that felt like a lie and those words wouldn't come. They vanished utterly when Lizzie walked up with an empty gas canister in her gloved hand. She and Shelly exchanged unreadable looks and Becca shut her eyes for a moment. No accident then, and no hope of peace returning to the valley any time soon.

She wondered who had done it and where the Pack's wrath would fall. It might have been a stupid high school prank gone awry. But she couldn't imagine any of the local kids doing something like this. Of course, lately she'd been feeling like her imagination was a little limited.

"Who could have done something like this?" It was Gladys who finally broke the near silence. Even the firefighters and the radio chatter on the sheriff's car seemed muted.

Shelly looked around, her expression fierce in the dim light. "We'll find out." Her tone was so heavy with unspoken consequences that it dropped like lead into the quiet.

That was when a flash of movement out by the woods on the far side of the mound of smoldering ash caught Becca's eye. She squinted a little, trying to see through the smoke. Somebody was standing there but she had trouble seeing more than just the outline of the person's body. Then the figure stepped forward just a bit, or maybe the wind moved the leaves aside, letting the weak moonlight shine down to illuminate where he or she was standing.

Becca's stomach turned a bit as she realized that there was something familiar in the set of the watcher's shoulders and the way they stood. Her memory flashed back to Oya standing on the riverbank what seemed like ages ago and suspicion was replaced with certainty. Then there was a dim flash of white in the shadows and she realized that the watcher was smiling.

Silver Moon

The person, whoever they were, disappeared a moment after Becca noticed them, vanishing before she could point out what she'd
seen to Shelly. But the alpha was talking to the sheriff and Lizzie and
Becca didn't want to interrupt just yet. What if she was wrong about Oya?
Instead, she went to help Erin and Gladys do what little they could to put
out the last of the flames.

It was Erin who finally broke the silence. "I don't think I ever appreci-
ated this place as much as I should have." Her voice was wistful and most of
the others within earshot nodded. It was as good an obituary as any.

Becca wondered again if she should say something about her suspicions.
But if she was wrong, she might kick off some kind of full-scale war. She
wasn't sure she could live with the consequences. Then she found herself
remembering what Erin had said in the car on the way over: did the Nest
know for sure who they were? Or was this just malice and guesswork?

Finally, she just blurted out her fears in a question, "Do you think someone did this to get back at us?" Better to have the thought spoken out loud
than bottled up inside her head.

It was the sheriff who answered, his voice making her jump a little. "My
first thought was kids but this looks like quite a bit of effort went into it."
He gestured at several gas cans, three at least, lined up near the edge of the
parking lot. "You ladies got any disgruntled former members?" He scowled
when he spoke, just in case anyone might think he wasn't taking the situation seriously. Becca smothered the urge to let loose a hysterical peal of
laughter.

Lizzie moved, catching her attention. The deputy made a slight gesture with her fingers, pointing toward the woods and the place where
the watcher had been standing. But she didn't say anything. No one else

answered the sheriff's question either and the silence went on just long enough to become oppressive and sinister.

Then Shelly shook herself and sighed. "I don't think it was an internal problem, Sheriff, but I promise that the Board will be meeting tomorrow. We'll see if we can think of anyone or anything that isn't coming to mind right now and get back to you right away. Thank you for all your help." Her nod took in the firefighters as well. Her expression was bleak, hopeless even. Becca wondered if they'd lost more than they realized.

Henderson didn't look too happy either but he seemed to accept what he was given, at least for the moment. He still got the last word in. "This is an open investigation now. Ladies, if you would clear out, we'll get started roping this off. You'll be able to come back in a day or two to retrieve whatever you think is salvageable after we've pulled what we need for testing. Good night."

Clearly dismissed, the Pack began clearing out in twos and threes. Becca trailed after Erin back to her car. She buzzed inside with a combination of frustration and anger and nerves that made it hard not to speed on their drive home.

In contrast, Erin was silent, so quiet in fact that Becca thought she'd fallen asleep. It wasn't until they pulled into their street that either of them said anything aloud. "I could kill them all right now, every bloody Nester that's ever come near this town" Erin said in a conversational tone. "I need to work some of this off so I can think clearly."

Becca nodded and parked the car in front of her house. A fleeting image of Ed and his paperwork crossed her mind, but she could deal with that tomorrow. There was enough going on now as it was. They got out and she stretched carefully, listening for the sound of her joints creaking. They didn't and that gave her an idea. She took a deep breath, "Jog around the block be too much for your arm?"

Erin shook her head and they looked at each other before either moved. Becca thought about hugging her, but it seemed like it was too soon, too much. Instead they took off in unison, running stiffly through the dark streets of Wolf's Point without a single thought about what anyone else might think of them.

Shelly wasn't at the store the next day and Becca wasn't too surprised. The Board would be meeting about the club and she suspected that the Pack would be meeting after that. She pushed the thought aside for the moment and glanced at Pete.

He didn't look like he'd had much sleep either. She went into the back room first thing and made them a big pot of coffee. He smiled when she handed him a cup, then frowned like his mind was elsewhere. "I heard about the Women's Club," he rumbled finally, just as they got started with restocking. "I'm sorry I didn't get to come down and help but I had to stay home with the kids. Shelly didn't want to risk the twins out there and Kira's off at camp."

Becca thought about Howie and Marla, Pete and Shelly's eight-year old twins, who were completely fearless and endlessly inquisitive. She nodded. "Shelly dealing with the Board today?"

He nodded in his turn. Becca went on, stumbling over her words. "Is it always like this? I know you don't change so I don't mean that part—but the rest, always wondering what other people are up to, stuff burning up and getting shot at, all of this...stuff?" She finished weakly, realizing that maybe he wasn't supposed to talk to her about it. Maybe there was some kind of rule like Fight Club or something. That fear made her stop short of using the words "were" and "wolf."

Pete glanced down at her and raised an eyebrow. For a minute, she felt horrible. Had she violated some rule of werewolf etiquette? "What happens in the Pack, stays in the Pack." She imagined that as Wolf's Point's latest tourist campaign slogan and stifled a nervous giggle.

Pete looked away. "Can't talk about it much here, but no, it's not always like this. Most of the time, it's just changing and patrolling the woods and a few meetings a month. Just like Rotary or something along those lines, except for the obvious differences. Of course, every now and then, something goes bad. Then none of us gets any sleep for a while." He rubbed his eyes and stared out the front door. "But welcome to the Pack, I guess. I'd been wondering."

Becca blushed, feeling the beginnings of a flash coming on. Honestly, some days it was hard to say which change was worse. She chugged her coffee in a vicious couple of gulps, knowing it would just make her hotter and more uncomfortable. "Thanks," she said in tones rich with irony.

Customers began flooding in before she could ask anything else. Becca wasn't sure if it was a blessing or not that she didn't get more than a minute alone with Pete for the next few days. Even when they weren't busy, Shelly's mom was getting worse so Pete had to leave before close to make dinner for the kids. She got so much time alone with her thoughts that they climbed all over the place, like monkeys.

On Friday night, Becca was locking up the store and thinking about her own dinner when the space between her shoulders told her she was

Silver Moon

being watched. A quick glance around didn't show her anything out of the ordinary but the feeling lingered anyway, making her edgy. She turned and pressed her back to the door to survey the street, throwing in a glance at the rooftops for good measure.

Then she looked into the shadows of the alleyway across the street, just beyond the range of the streetlights. They were going to need to remind Barbara Jean at Pawprint Gifts to check the bulbs on the alley lights again, that much was clear. But then, Becca realized, the dark wasn't as dark for her as it had been, not since she'd begun to change.

Someone was moving in the shadows, someone who stepped forward and gestured to her. She stared at whoever it was, hoping it would turn out to be Erin. The butterflies started doing a quick tango through her insides. Perhaps they would be doing more training tonight. Then she realized how crazy that thought was: Erin wouldn't hide from her in the shadows.

But she knew someone who might. It appeared that Oya hadn't left town, not yet, though from the way the aspiring werewolf hunter was hugging the dark, she didn't want anyone else realizing that. She beckoned again, not saying a word, and Becca found herself rolling her eyes. What was with the drama? Why not just come over and say what she wanted to say? Unless of course, she had something new to hide. Like arson, perhaps.

Becca thought about ignoring her and going home to make dinner. She was really too tired to deal with this right now, especially by herself. Then she thought about calling the police but then she didn't have any real proof that the Nesters had done anything. Besides, wasn't she supposed to be all about protecting the town now? She should be able to handle one unstable woman by herself. With a sigh and something approaching a growl, she straightened her shoulders and crossed the street.

Oya smiled when she got closer. It was more like a baring of teeth, really, and Becca bared hers right back. She hoped they looked long and sharp and she exerted her imagination to make them look as scary as possible. But if it worked, Oya wasn't showing it.

Becca stopped a few feet away from the other woman. "What do you want?"

"I want to talk you. Alone. I've got something to show you that will help you and your furry friends." She made a quick movement toward her inside pocket and Becca flinched back, snarling a little. Oya tugged her jacket open and patted the pistol in her belt. "Full of silver bullets just in case. But then you can't change yet, can you?" Her tone was smug.

Becca forced herself to stand up straight and her face to slide into the blandest expression she could muster. The wolf inside her howled its rage as she locked it back down. "I don't know what you're talking about. But I bet Sheriff Henderson would love to hear about tourists running around downtown flashing their guns and threatening the locals."

"I bet the sheriff would like to hear about a lot of things, starting with some stories about what happens to people in this town who piss off its self-appointed guardians. Shall we go talk to him together?" Oya laughed and Becca knew her face had given her thoughts away. "I didn't think so. No, I've got something better: a cure. How'd you and your pals like to stop being wolves?"

Becca froze. Her emotions swirled through her, falling over each other in their haste to be felt. This couldn't be true, not coming from Oya. She hated them too much. She must mean killing them all off, that had to be it.

With her doubts, her pulse began to race. She had to do something, anything to stop this. Didn't she? She could feel her muscles begin to tighten as her body prepared her to attack. Or flee. She imagined the taste of Oya's blood on her lips and the wolf howled back into life inside her.

Oya held up her hand. "I know what you're thinking, but you're wrong. It's a real cure. Nothing more, nothing less," She smiled, a flash of delight and power this time, with little room for malice. "And we just perfected it. We're sure it works."

Becca managed to keep her mouth from flopping open but just barely. A real cure. Just like the one she'd been wondering about. She could be normal again: dull, ordinary Becca Thornton sliding slowly toward that great Good Night, surrounded by her completely normal friends. She'd buy that retirement condo, just like Ed suggested and then she'd—her thoughts churned for a moment, then settled.

What the hell was she thinking? She might lose everything, even her life. Oya had to be lying or planning something evil. Nothing good could come from the Nesters; they proved that already.

There was a vial in Oya's hand now, filled with a clear liquid that seemed to have a bubble or two floating in it. She tilted it, letting it catch what little light filtered down between the buildings so it glowed slightly in the dimness. The whole time she held it, she smiled at Becca, her eyes shining in the vial's reflection. She looked like she thought she held salvation in her hand.

Voice of common sense or not, Becca stared at the vial, mesmerized by it as much as she had been by Oya's words. Her rage ebbed as she thought

Silver Moon

instead about what the Women's Club had felt like before she changed, how it felt like a real community. She wanted that again.

Then it struck her—there was no more Women's Club and she was talking to the reason why. She could feel that in her bones. In a moment, she was furious again. "Why did you burn down the club? Seems to me that if you've got a cure for what you think ails us, you'd have brought it down there in broad daylight. You'd have talked to us instead of sneaking around like this. But this makes you look like a drug dealer. And an arsonist in the bargain."

Oya's lips twisted mockingly. "Remember my parents? Then try remembering that your people nearly killed one of my men and hurt a few of the others. You didn't think we'd let that go unpunished, did you? I wasn't certain that the club was where you were meeting now but I guessed from the crowd that showed up at the diner that it was the right place. Looks like I guessed right."

Now it was pure blind terror that filled Becca. They were all vulnerable, then. They could be blackmailed or even killed, picked off one by one in their human forms. Whatever she said next had to make this better, had to convince this woman that she was wrong. "Actually, it's just me and one or two others. The folks who showed up were just my friends, checking to see if I was okay. I'd just come back from a trip out of town." She made her face bland, imagined her tone as convincing as any church sermon.

Oya snorted. "Like I'd believe that. If it quacks like a duck, or in this case, howls like a wolf, then around here, she probably is one."

Becca cleared her throat, preparing herself for a different approach. "All right then. Let's say you're right. Let's say that you and your aspiring slayer buddies stormed into our town and burned down our werewolf clubhouse. And you've been bounding around town ever since. So we all know what you look like, what you smell like and where to find you. Even what some of you taste like." She smiled, letting her words sink in.

"I'm not scared of you," Oya's face tightened, lips thin, eyes dangerous. "If you were going to do anything, you'd have done it by now."

"Really? Have you ever wondered what it would be like to be a wolf, Oya?"

The woman flinched and Becca thought she'd found a way in. "I could make that happen for you. They say it just takes a bite or two." The wildness was riding Becca again. It scared her, but there was more, so much more than fear now.

The river, the forest, even the ground under her feet felt like a part of her. She could smell animals and trees on the wind, hear humans as far away as the outskirts of town. This was her town, her home. She would do whatever it took to protect it and to protect the Pack. Anything and everything. No price was too high.

Oya stumbled back, anger tinged with uncertainty. "You can't do that. You're human now."

"Am I? Do you really know all there is to know about it? I don't think so." Becca could feel her nails lengthening, her hands beginning to change. The air was full of tension and the promise of blood and she wanted more, so much more she could taste it. "There are so many things they don't talk about in those stories. I could cure you of being human, Oya." She could feel her face shift slightly and gave a short barking laugh.

Oya went pale as she fumbled at her belt, yanked her gun out with shaking hands and pointed it at her. "Stop it! You can't change now and I know it. Stop trying or I'll shoot you if I have to."

"No, I don't think you will." Lizzie's voice echoed in the alleyway from behind Becca and when Becca turned her head, she could see the glint of the deputy's drawn gun from the corner of her eye.

The wolf in Becca strained toward Oya, desperate to carry out her threat. *Human, human, human,* she chanted inside her head. Without realizing it, she had brought her hands up to her cheeks and was pressing her nails into her own flesh. After a few moments, the sharp sensation sank in and she dropped them back down to her sides. Then she let out a sigh and took in a deep breath, then another, trying to force the bloodlust to drain away.

"You one of them, too, little cousin? I thought you were a bit young for that," Oya sounded contemptuous now, indifferent to the gun pointed at her.

"Cousin, if I were, do you think you could stand against the two of us? Put the gun down and hand it over." Lizzie's voice was almost a purr now, thrumming through the alleyway and filling the air between them.

Cousins? Becca glanced from the deputy to the werewolf hunter and back again. Their features were a bit similar but that might have just been her imagination. But whatever the truth was, she could see that Lizzie's words had an effect on Oya. Emotions practically galloped over the other woman's face and for a terrifying moment, she thought that the hunter might pull the trigger and shoot them both.

Lizzie's face didn't change, though, and the gun didn't waver in her hand. She held out her free hand for Oya's gun. The hunter startled them both with a harsh, almost painful laugh. "Not likely, cousin. I'll keep it for my protection. And I think we're done here, unless you plan to shoot me in the back." She spun away and ran down the alley, disappearing into the night.

Silver Moon

The deputy lowered her gun. "You all right, Miz Thornton?"

"Why not shoot her? Or at least arrest her?" Becca couldn't stop herself. She was tempted to race down the alleyway herself, the way she was feeling.

"And that answers my question. C'mon, let's get you home."

Lizzie herded her out of the alley and into her car, ignoring Becca's protests.

"Is she really your cousin?"

Lizzie grimaced. "Yep. Shelly's too. It's complicated. Let's just say we more or less grew up together, though she's got a few years on me."

"How the hell am I supposed to do this whole wolf protector thing when no one ever tells me anything?" Becca pounded her fist on the dashboard, her voice rising to a shout.

"Look, there's Pack business and there's family business. I don't have much of the first part to tell and I'm not telling you the second without a damn good reason. So stop hitting my car. It won't help." Lizzie sounded as annoyed as Becca had ever heard her sound. That was enough to make her rage die down, make the wolf inside her curl up in her cave. She unclenched her fists and sat with her hands in her lap.

"All right then. What can you tell me? Is she really dangerous? Did werewolves really kill her family?"

Lizzie stomped on the brakes and whipped around to stare at Becca. "Did she actually tell you that?"

"Not exactly something I'd make up."

"Shit, shit, shit. Shelly's not going to be happy to hear about this." Lizzie was staring out the window now, like her thoughts were somewhere else. A car pulled up behind them and she pulled forward. "Man, I don't even know where to start. Is she dangerous? Well, she is now. Stay away from her, Miz Thornton. Let's just say she believes what she's saying and that's bad enough."

"She and her buddies burned down the Women's Club." Becca could feel her tone getting spiteful, childish. But if she couldn't stop Oya one way, she'd try another.

"I promise you, we're looking into that."

"Could be going a bit faster," Becca swallowed hard, trying to push away the tears of frustration that were threatening to spill down her cheeks. This was too much—why couldn't she get this damn woman out of her town, one way or another? Lizzie flinched but didn't say anything. "Well?"

"The wolves may not need proof, Miz Thornton, but the Sherriff and I do. Yes, I think they did it too but we need evidence. All I've got are some gas cans wiped clean of prints. You got anything more than an argument that pits her word against yours?" Lizzie looked tired and quietly angry but her voice was steady and firm.

Becca slumped in her seat and stared out the window. She'd get the evidence, somehow. She'd get Oya and her "cure" locked away somewhere safe where she couldn't hurt anyone in Wolf's Point. She promised herself that much. "Drop me off at Erin's, please." She was pleased at how little her voice shook.

Lizzie drove her there in silence and nodded when Becca thanked her. Becca didn't look back as she walked up the path to Erin's door. She knocked hard, the noise impossible to deny or ignore. When Erin answered the door, she looked her neighbor straight in the eye. "You're going to make me the best damn werewolf this town has ever seen."

Chapter 14

Over the next couple of evenings, Erin started with the basics. Becca learned about wolves and pack behavior, then werewolf myths and history from around the world. After that, it was differences between their kind of werewolves and regular wolves, apart from turning back into humans: the silver bullets, the faster healing and so forth.

Mostly, Becca was just relieved to find out that they didn't have to all move into one big den together. She didn't think she was ready for that. She did remember to ask some questions. Would being a werewolf actually stop the other changes she was going through? According to Erin, it wouldn't, but it would make her menopause timeline shorter. What about hormones and all the stuff regular menopausal women did? The Pack didn't seem to need estrogen but they had their own doctor if she wanted to check it out further.

The last question that she had was one that she didn't find the nerve to ask: were odd feelings about Erin part of the whole werewolf thing? It felt like asking that one would just make the dynamic strange. Or perhaps just stranger. She couldn't quite bring herself to use words like "crush," not even in her own head.

Erin took her out in the woods after every session. Becca liked the part where she got to use her new enhanced senses. And since she wasn't sleeping that well since she started changing, it was good to be able to do something besides toss and turn in sweat-soaked sheets. Erin had her exploring the wind, using it to distinguish between the scents of different animals as well as humans. She also practiced blending in with the trees and the brush, using all her senses to listen and feel what was going on around her.

Silver Moon

But what astonished her most was how quickly Erin healed. "It's one of the good parts," Erin said as she stretched her now cast-free arm before they went out on their third run.

"Good thing I stopped smoking back in my twenties," Becca wheezed her words a bit when they stopped to rest.

"Yep. It smells even worse with wolf senses." Erin grinned to take the sting from her words but Becca shrugged and laughed. It felt like they were getting more comfortable together, at least to Becca, and she thought she might get to like that. With any luck, the weird feelings would just go away on their own.

By the night of the next full moon, Becca could feel the magic in her blood long before moonrise. She was at Erin's door right after she finished dinner, even before she washed her dishes. Erin looked amused and got her to help with some chores while they waited. It was while they were straightening up the living room that Becca noticed a photo of the black Lab on the mantle. "When did you have a dog?"

Erin's face took on the saddest expression Becca had ever seen her wear. "That's Midnight. She died last year, a few months after I moved in here." Becca shifted uneasily and Erin muttered, "Of natural causes, thank you."

Oh, crap. Becca smacked her hand to her forehead. She had brought cookies over when Shelly told her that her new neighbor's dog had died. It all came back to her now: she'd been too shy to talk much to Erin and Erin was too sad to notice. She walked over and after a moment of hesitation, gave Erin a nervous hug. "I didn't mean it that way. I'm sorry."

Erin nodded and gestured at the door. It was nearly time, then. Becca shivered with something that felt like anticipation. They got into Erin's car and drove out of town, heading up into the mountains by the same route that Lizzie had driven the other day.

Once they got to the foot of the trail and parked, Erin got out and began to lope uphill in the dim light, Becca at her heels. When they reached it, the cave was even spookier when Becca saw it with the acuity of her wolf vision and she stopped at the entrance, trembling all over.

Before, it had just felt strange, like whatever it was inside the place was sleeping or out taking a walk somewhere, leaving a shadow of itself behind. Now the power was completely awake and sending prickly sensations down her arms and legs. Everything was shifting and it felt like the place could swallow her up, then spit her out as a new painting on the stone walls.

No! I'm not ready yet! She wanted to yell at it but the words wouldn't come out.

"What's the matter?" Erin paused just inside. Her eyes were starting to turn silver now and her hands were getting longer.

Becca could feel herself start to change in response to the magic's call. She was shaking all over, fighting to stop it. She managed to choke out, "This place. It's too much. I'm not ready." She backed up a few steps, only to find a crowd of women coming up the path behind her.

Shelly put her arm around her shoulders and leaned into her. Becca made herself relax a little into her warmth. It felt crowded on the ledge, like they were all much too close, but she still found some comfort in that.

Then Erin began to strip down and the others joined her. Becca tensed back up as she felt the wildness stir inside her. But she could feel her own transformation slip out of her control, taking over her body. She gave up and let Shelly tug her across the cave threshold.

No point in ruining another outfit, she thought as she began, reluctantly, to undress. The change, when it really hit, was even more intense in the cave. It hurt less than the last time but the stretching and sensory overload still dropped her to her shaking knees. Her heart was racing so fast she thought it would jump out of her body and her skin superheated as the fur began to sprout from it.

When she could look up, she could see everything now, all the wall paintings in sharp relief, the other women, every pinecone on every tree outside. Smells and sounds warred for her attention until she tried to bury her head in her paws.

The cave whirled around her in an ocean of sensations. She could hear somebody whimpering, a high-pitched sound of disorientation and terror. She cut it off abruptly when she realized the sound was coming from her own jaws but she couldn't stop her body from shaking in pure panic.

Then Becca felt a furry body press itself against her. Then another one on her other side. Soon she was surrounded by wolves, each leaning gently into her and each other like a warm, living carpet of fur. Their scents and small sounds, the racing of their hearts and rise and fall of their breathing, gave Becca an anchor.

Her own breathing slowed and the urge to howl and claw her way out of the cave gradually disappeared. The wolf part of her brain rose into slow dominance. She was part of a Pack and that Pack would protect her. The feeling was intensely soothing and comforting. Sleepily, she wondered if the Becca part of her had ever felt that way with other humans.

A few more moments passed before Shelly rose from Becca's side. She stood at the cave's entrance and sniffed the air. All around Becca, the other wolves began to sit up. Becca could smell it too, whatever it was, as she

Silver Moon

joined the others at the entrance. There was something out there in the woods, something with a human smell of burnt metal and harsh chemicals. It smelt like it was waiting for them.

Shelly looked up the cliff toward the mountain above the cave, then she stepped out onto a trail that seemed invisible, at least to Becca's eyes. She began to climb, her paws soundless in the quiet air. One by one, the other wolves followed her up, each one slinking low with their bellies to the rocks and hiding behind whenever cover was available. It was slow going, even on four legs, but the smells of humans ebbed as they got higher, finally fading until they disappeared.

Shelly led them over the mountain and halfway down the other side. Then they began to circle back, this time in the deep cover of the woods. Becca's wolf self was intent on following the Pack, letting her other self dream in the back of her mind.

As if she was dreaming, she was swept along with no set destination, knowing only that she jogged along with the others toward the same goal, whatever it was. And that they were once again going downhill and she could smell humans again. They were farther away this time but it seemed like Shelly was bringing the Pack closer to them. She wondered why but could not rouse herself enough to stop. Shelly was alpha; whatever she planned was necessary.

Soon she led them in a run, tongues lolling out of open jaws in a collective pant. The air was full of human scent now and there were tiny, muted growls as several of them recognized the humans from the Nest. Shelly slowed down until they all stopped in some shrubs in a thicket of trees. She looked up and they all followed her gaze. There was something in the branches, some machine that turned right and left as it looked for something.

Camera. Part of Becca's brain remembered the word. She felt a pang of fear; the humans were hunting them, might even know that they were here now.

Erin nudged her shoulder and slunk forward, as the camera swung away, its seeking eye turned elsewhere. Becca followed her, though all her instincts told her to run. They slithered through the brush, pausing every few feet to watch for other cameras. There were other machines now, too, ones that looked like weapons with blinding bright lights on them.

Ahead through the trees, she could see a small campfire with some humans grouped around it. She recognized Oya and her men, though it was hard to think of them that way. Now they were just enemies of the Pack.

She and Erin froze where they were, hidden by the trees and the shadows. Even so, Becca felt horribly exposed and vulnerable. Her wolf self wanted to run and hide more than anything in the world and it was hard to fight that fear.

To make herself stay put, she studied the cameras and other machines in the trees. They turned on an arc, carefully surveying a patch of forest at a time. Some tiny creature scuttled through the brush away from them and one of the machines fired a sharp and painful light at it, blinding the wolves for a few moments.

Becca shivered. This was terrible. There had to be something they could do to stop this, her human self clamored, nearly fully awake now. Otherwise, all of them might die out here. She remembered the sense of belonging she'd felt in the cave and both of her selves, wolf and human, ached to think of losing that.

She tried to see the campsite before them with not quite human eyes. There was a fire and weapons and food, the last making her mouth water a bit. They had tents. What else? Then she saw them: two barrels, whose acrid reek blew over to their hiding spot and made her gag. Her human self roused itself enough to whisper *Gasoline* into her wolf brain.

With that came the memory of the Women's Club and the smell of burning and the cans of gas in the ashes. They must be planning to do something like that again. But what else was there to burn? And did they want to wait to find out?

Becca kept watching the machines in the trees until she knew what to do. She moved forward, ignoring Erin's frantic nip at her shoulder. As silently as she could, she slid past the arc of the first camera. Then she hid again in the shadows while she watched the moving machines, studying their patterns as if they were prey. She gauged how far she was from the barrels and her human brain told her wolf self what to do. She gathered herself for one big run that would take her through the camp to her target.

But the humans were moving around the fire now, grabbing their guns and looking out into the woods. She wondered what Shelly had planned and where the others were. Whatever they were doing, she hoped it would be a good distraction.

Then one of the men looked at a glowing machine in his hand and shouted. He pointed back into the woods, over by where she and Erin had left the rest of the Pack. The humans began to split up, pointing their guns out into the trees as they left their camp.

Silver Moon

Becca knew she had to act now before they found everyone else, before it was too late. She shot out of her hiding place and dashed around the tree where the closest camera was mounted. A thin beam of light sliced through one branch over her head, then another. It began to burn a trail in the dirt behind her as she ran. She raced toward the barrels, moving faster than she could have ever imagined her middle-aged body could move, even on four legs.

A bullet whizzed past, followed by a second and a third. The humans had seen her and were firing at her now. She dodged as best she could, then threw herself at the first of the barrels with all her strength, knocking it toward the fire. Then she slammed into the second and shoved it toward the fire too. An instant later, she gathered herself into a huge leap that would take her away from the rolling barrels and the flames and back into the safety of the woods.

A sharp pain burned its way through the fur on her shoulder and she yelped and staggered. There were more shots, then she felt a second burning sensation in her back leg. She went down with a whimper. The bullets felt like they were fusing with her blood, freezing her in place. She couldn't even move when one of the humans approached.

"Well, we got one of you anyway," Oya's voice was thick with satisfaction and bloodlust. There was a click from her gun and Becca knew she was done for. She closed her eyes, letting herself drift off as waves of pain swept through her.

Then there was an explosion of flame, and a ball of fire knocked Oya sideways. She hit the ground and rolled away with a shout, "What the hell is going on?" The air around Becca was glowing against her closed lids, the wind a hot tongue on her fur and skin. Then Oya spoke again, "Holy shit, it's you." Her voice was soft.

Then there was a vicious snarl and Becca could hear Oya go down under the weight of an angry wolf. She was shouting and the air was full of bullets. Then the thicket was a blur of wolves. There were screams from near the fire, the sound of guns firing. Then a second explosion.

Becca could feel herself being picked up by someone who smelled familiar. She couldn't feel her legs anymore. Instead, it was as if she was suspended in a black velvet pool. She sank in as whoever was carrying her started to run.

Chapter 15

Becca drifted in dreams for a lifetime. In some, she was running through the woods, naked and human, and the trees were bursting into flame around her. Burning branches hit her as she tried to claw her way to a wakefulness that never came. In others, she was a wolf, racing through open fields while humans with guns shot at her. Sometimes the Pack was with her. These were the worst since then she got to see each of them picked off by the hunters, falling one by one.

When she finally woke up, it took a moment to realize that she hadn't just awakened into the next dream. Instead, she was in a white room with white curtains. There were faded prints of flowers on the wall and a hospital smell permeated the air, making it hard to breath.

She glanced down: her left arm was bandaged from the shoulder to the wrist. From the feel of things, there was at least one more bandage around her ribs, another around her thigh, but she wasn't ready to lift the sheets to find out yet. At least, she could move her feet under the covers, and that alone was a huge relief.

She kept blinking at the room until it gradually came into focus. There was a machine beeping in the corner. The streamers of sunshine that came through the curtains made her eyes tear up. Wherever she was, she hadn't been here before. That much she was sure of.

She shifted her left foot and something rattled. Her ankle fell weird, as if there was a weight on it. Slowly, she lifted the sheets and looked down. She was wearing a heavy-duty leather cuff, one that a farmer might use to hold livestock, on her ankle. There was a chain attached to it and that was attached to something else that she couldn't see under the bed.

There were also bandages around her middle and her thigh just as she'd expected. Now that she was fully awake, there was a fierce ache that ran

Silver Moon

from her midsection down through her legs and up into her chest. She rattled the chain again in complete disbelief. "What the hell is going on?"

The door opened and a dark-skinned young woman in a blue uniform poked her head in. "Oh good, you're awake." She bustled in and began checking a machine next to the bed. Becca could read her nametag once she got closer to the bed. It said "María Hernandez." But the name didn't ring a bell. Had they taken her to a hospital outside the valley?

"Listen," Becca said, clearing her throat to get the woman's attention, "I don't mean to be troublesome, but where am I? And why the hell am I chained to this bed?" Becca chided herself silently for the "hell" but then, these were pretty extraordinary circumstances.

The nurse or whatever she was raised an eyebrow and stepped carefully back out of reach. "It's standard procedure, ma'am. Let me get Dr. Green. He can explain it better than I can and he needs to check up on you now that you're awake." She vanished out the door without, Becca couldn't help but notice, unlocking the cuff. When had she become a dangerous criminal element?

That sent her thoughts in a spiral. Had she killed someone else, maybe someone who didn't deserve it this time? But she couldn't have. They'd shot her before she could have done anything like that. She was in an agony of impatience and sheer terror by the time the doctor showed up.

When he walked in, Becca started. The studious looking youngish man with his round spectacles could have been Shelly's younger brother. She squinted against the light from the blinds behind him. He smiled, with a flash of white teeth, and she realized who he was. Shelly's cousin, Dr. David Green, had moved back to Wolf's Point from the West Coast a few months back. This must be him.

"María said you were awake." He picked up her wrist and checked her pulse, then reached toward her face. She jerked away, then forced herself to sit still while he shone a penlight into her pupils. Whatever he saw must have reassured him because he pulled a key out of his pocket and unlocked the cuff.

Becca tried to pull her newly freed foot up to check it. "Ow! Why did you chain me up like that?"

He frowned then looked puzzled. "You don't know? It's standard procedure when a Pack member comes in. Doctor Chin always did it when she ran the clinic, just as a precaution. Shelly will be in soon to explain it a little more, if you like. How are you feeling otherwise?"

Becca stared up at him. Did the whole town know that they all ran around the woods on all fours every full moon? This was getting ridiculous.

She couldn't quite bring herself to ask. Saying it out loud to anyone would make it more real than it already was.

There was a noise in the hallway just as he pulled out his cell. Sheriff Henderson strode into the room, his face set with a stern frown. Lizzie Blackhawk was on his heels, her sunglasses resting on the end of her nose. "Hello, Miz Thornton." Henderson's eyes went everywhere but to Becca's face. He fidgeted like he was embarrassed to be there. "Dr. Green." The sheriff's head bobbed in a nod like it was on strings.

He cleared his throat, his discomfort clear in the sound. "Nice to see you're awake, Miz Thornton. We're wondering if you're doing well enough to tell us what happened the other night. Between the fire and the broken cameras in the trees, it looks like you were on to something with your campers." From the way he was looking at the doctor, he seemed to be waiting for more of an answer from him than from Becca herself.

She frowned and started to give him a piece of her mind when Lizzie caught her eye. From behind the sheriff, the deputy tilted her head forward and closed her eyes like she was falling asleep. Then she looked back up and winked. Becca smothered a smile as Dr. Green answered for her. "She just woke up, Sheriff. I think we might need to give her a bit more time. Right, Ms. Thornton?"

All at once, Becca realized that she really was exhausted. She yawned, only remembering to cover her mouth at the last minute. "Honestly, Sheriff, I can't remember much right now, just an explosion and a lot of chaos. I was out for a walk when it happened. But I'll probably remember more after I get a little more sleep."

The sheriff scowled, but nodded as if this was what he had expected. "I can see that, ma'am." He sighed heavily, then seemed to start to say something else. Dr. Green cleared his throat.

Henderson looked at the wall. "I'll send Lizzie around tomorrow to collect your statement, Miz Thornton, if the doctor thinks you're ready." He shook his head. "Haven't seen this kind of craziness in this town since I was a deputy. I think we'll need to call in the State Patrol on this one," His mouth drooped, giving him the look of an old dog that had just been woken up and wanted nothing more than to lie back down again. "All right. Ma'am, Doctor." He nodded and strode out. Lizzie glanced back and gave Becca another wink and a nod as she followed him out.

Becca closed her eyes while the doctor fussed over her. It seemed like it was just five minutes later when Shelly walked in, but the light through the blinds was dimmer now. Much dimmer, so it must be almost nightfall.

Shelly frowned as she saw Becca open her eyes. She seemed to be on the brink of saying something not too pleasant from her expression.

"Well, it looks like we're on the road to recovery." Erin leaned against the open door frame. Shelly and Becca jumped at the same time, and Shelly turned on her heel to face her. Erin met Shelly's glare head on.

"You know I can't let this go." Shelly's voice had the shadow of a growl running through it. "We've got two more Nesters in the hospital as it is. I think I know what you intended to do, Becca, but sooner or later, someone's going to be wondering about some very sophisticated wolves. And every time someone starts wondering, we're in danger."

"I should have stopped her. I'm the one who's supposed to be training her. That makes this mess as much my fault as it is hers." Erin tone was neutral but Becca could see her body stiffen from across the room.

Becca cringed a bit; she might've gotten someone burned pretty badly. This wasn't the time for feeling too guilty to speak up, though. "Not that I don't love everyone talking about me like I'm not here, but it seems to me that I'm responsible for my own actions." Becca couldn't quite sit up yet, though the sharp ache had faded a lot since she'd woken up earlier. Instead she put as much weight as she could into her words even though her heart was racing in something approaching pure terror. What if they kicked her out for this?

Both women turned to look at her and she had a disturbing flash of wolf eyes in their human faces. She closed her eyes and took a deep breath. Whatever was coming next, she could handle it. Right? She forced her eyes open and looked at Shelly just in time to meet her stare head on.

Shelly's lip curled for an instant and the wolf looked out from her dark eyes. From somewhere deep inside her, Becca felt a growl building. It surged up her throat and tumbled out from between her lips before she could stop it. Shelly growled back and Erin stepped forward, moving to put herself between them like she couldn't help herself.

Becca realized what she'd done at the same instant and clapped her hands over her face. "I'm so sorry," she mumbled through her fingers. "I'm still feeling like crap and I barely know what I'm doing. I know I shouldn't have run into their camp like that but I was so worried about all of you, about the Pack. I was only thinking about stopping them." She dragged her hands down into her lap, and looked up, not quite meeting Shelly's eyes this time. "Go ahead. Tell me what happens to me now."

She could feel the tension ease from the other women like it had been uncorked. For a wild instant, she wondered what it would be like to touch Erin and feel her taut muscles relax. *Not now, not now.*

Shelly cleared her throat, "This is where we talk about why I'm the alpha. For one thing, did it occur to you that I had a plan, one that didn't involve you running wild by your lonesome and getting shot?"

Becca stared down at the blanket. "Honestly, I didn't think. I saw the lasers and the barrels and I got scared and mad. I just reacted."

Shelly nodded. "As it happens, none of the rest of us got more than a few grazes and burns. The Nesters got burned when one of the barrels blew. At this point, the Sherriff realizes that it's more than an out of control campfire so we'll have to help him find a few Nesters. As for you, here's what happens next: you don't go anywhere without one of us at your side in either form. Not work, not home, not for strolls down by the river. Are we clear?"

Becca looked up, unable to keep from frowning. The whole babysitting thing was going to get old fast. It wasn't so much that she loved being alone as it was that she was used to it. It gave her time to think about what was going on and to plan what was going to happen next—were they going to be moving in with her next?

Then she found herself wandering down a different mental path. She remembered what Oya had said the other night about her family, though it seemed like ages ago now. From the look on Shelly's face, this probably wasn't the time to ask and she buried it back down in her mind for later. It had a lot of company, right now; she wondered how she was ever going to get it all straight in her head.

She managed to croak out the one thought that was uppermost. "For how long?"

Shelly's eyes narrowed and a quiet growl filled the room. "Until I say that you get it and we can trust you to be less spontaneous. Understand?"

Erin caught Becca's eye. She had an odd, hopeful look on her face and she was clearly waiting for agreement. Her expression puzzled Becca and she looked away, instead nodding in Shelly's direction by way of agreement. What else could she do? It looked like she was going to really find out what it meant to be part of a Pack.

Silver Moon

Once she was up and moving around, she felt a bit differently. It had seemed the easiest way out, saying yes to being babysat back at the clinic when Shelly was glaring at her. It wasn't like she'd had any better ideas, at least none that would have changed her angry alpha's mind. Three days later, once Becca was feeling well enough to go back to work, it got annoying pretty fast.

She went out to go to work, Erin was there to walk her downtown. She went into the hardware store and Shelly was there. She left work, and Molly or Agnes or someone else was there to walk her home. It got so that she felt like she never had a moment to herself. That was the odd thing: right after she and Ed split, she would have given anything to have a constant companion, someone to spend time with and talk to. Even though she and Ed hadn't had that kind of relationship for years. Now, it felt like too much.

Thinking about the divorce did lead her to thinking about Ed, though. Becca went back through her mail to see if she'd missed anything. She didn't see any threatening letters from him so maybe he'd given up on the house for the moment. Or he was just waiting to spring something worse on her.

She started to try and put away a little extra, just in case. Erin had told her that the Pack had an injury fund, and that would take care of the clinic bills at least. Which wasn't to say that she wasn't worrying about paying that back too.

She meant to ask Shelly about the help with the mortgage, but she was afraid to ask about that on top of the medical bills. What if she got too expensive and the Pack kicked her out?

Not that that wouldn't have been something of a relief right at the moment. She could see Gladys watching the house from her backyard when she looked out the window. Sure, it looked like her neighbor was just feeding her cats but Becca could feel her watching all the same. This much attention was starting to feel like an itch she couldn't scratch.

When the doorbell rang, Becca had already given up on reading the romance novel that she'd picked up from the library. It was interesting just how many werewolf-themed romances they had on the shelves down there. She had made a mental note to take a closer look or maybe a sniff or two at the librarian the next time she was in.

The chime distracted her from her current activity: she'd wandered down to the basement to check the windows. It had occurred to her that if she could crawl out one of them, she might be able to get out of her yard without Gladys seeing that she was sneaking out. From there, she was pretty sure that she could work her way down to the creek and gain maybe an hour or two of freedom. It was like being a spy, without the glamorous parts. It was also completely impossible: there was no way she was getting through that window.

The doorbell rang again and she climbed down off the stepladder and made her way upstairs, a polite grumble working its way out of her mouth as she opened the door. "Coming! Yes?" The last word popped out as she opened the door.

The perfectly coiffed and made-up blonde woman on her doorstep raised an eyebrow. One corner of her lipsticked mouth quirked in what might have been a smile or a grimace depending on how you wanted to read it. "Ms. Thornton? I don't know if you remember me? Pamela Grisby, Ed's attorney." She held out a set of manicured claws.

"Let me revise my greeting to 'What the hell do you want?'" Becca could feel the growl below the grumble now. It didn't help that she wasn't made up and was wearing her grubby old sweats and sneakers, all of which had seen better days. What made it worst of all was the sinking feeling in the pit of her stomach; Ed was going to carry out his threat about the house after all. "And why are you on my porch? Don't you have demonic minions to carry out your dirty work?"

"It was on my way home. I suppose being invited in is too much to ask?" Pamela pointedly looked around the porch, glancing from the chipping paint around the door down to Becca's sweats and her lip curled a little. Becca didn't move out of the way to let her inside, not even when she stepped forward. In fact, she could feel her own lip start to curl around imaginary fangs. At least she hoped they were still imaginary.

Catherine Lundoff   104

Pamela's eyes narrowed and she extended the folder in her hand. "I expect you know what this is already. You've got thirty days to come up with financing to buy out my client. Otherwise, the two of you sell the house and divide the proceeds, just like you originally agreed to. Please bear in mind that he's within his rights and is being more than reasonable."

Becca glared at her, willing herself not to reach for the folder, willing herself to transform right then and there. She'd show Ed's attorney that she wouldn't be pushed around. How dare he try and take her home away?

But the growl faded and the wolf wouldn't come when called this time. She'd known this could happen, after all. She just hadn't planned hard enough for it.

Instead of changing, Becca could feel herself flush hot and sweaty under Pamela's cold eyes. *Damnit, not now.* But there was no stopping the flash as it came on. Any more than she could stop Ed and Pamela by not taking the folder. Another moment of struggle and she gave up, defeated. She snatched the folder from the lawyer's hands. "I notice he's still got enough money to pay your fees. Or do you do his crap work pro bono?"

Pamela drew herself up and spun around on her spiked heels. She clicked deliberately across the porch and down the steps before she looked back. "If I were you," she said sweetly, "I'd hope that I don't suggest that he take all the necessary repairs out of your half of the sale money." She clicked her way down the steps to her new sedan and screeched out of Becca's driveway.

Becca watched her drive away, swearing quietly under her breath. The flash was passing now but it felt like there might be another one coming on in a few minutes. She walked over and collapsed onto the porch swing, using Pamela's folder to fan herself as she sat down. It might as well be good for something.

Erin's appearance at the bottom of her porch steps didn't even begin to surprise her. Nor did the first words out of her mouth. "You okay? What was all that about?"

This was definitely the last straw. "You know, I'm thinking right now is not the time. Babysit me later when I'm feeling up to being polite." Becca was ashamed of herself the minute the words were out of her mouth. It wasn't like any of this was Erin's fault. But she wanted to be alone to think everything over and if she had to get that by being rude, so be it.

Erin raised an eyebrow, cocking her head to one side. "Doesn't work that way, Becca. Shelly says to watch you and make sure you don't get into trouble, we watch you and that's that. That looked like trouble but if you don't want to talk to me, that's fine. I'll get one of the others to come over and check on you. But we're here for you, like it or not."

"Lucky, lucky me." Becca was snarling and on her feet now, pacing the length of the porch like it was a cage. "Is there some point soon where you think all this 'being here for me' will turn out to do me some good? So far, I'm not seeing it." She threw the folder across the porch at the swing, scattering its contents all over the floor.

They both watched the papers slide around for a minute, then Erin reached out and started picking them up, working her way on to the porch as she reached for them. "This is about your ex and the house, isn't it?" She asked the question without looking up.

Becca nodded even though Erin wasn't actually looking at her. She was making herself stare across the street and watch her other neighbors work in their yards and walk their dogs and come home from work. Just like normal people. Just like she used to be. But she was not going to burst into tears on her own front porch, no matter what. Well, her own for a bit longer, anyway. She waited for Erin to mention the emergency fund, say that the Pack could help her. Like she'd take any more charity.

Instead, Erin just picked up the folder and stuffed the forms back into it. She had her back to Becca but her shoulders looked stiff and angry even to Becca's distracted glance. When she finally did look up, her face was completely shut down, with no expression at all to tell Becca what to do next. Erin put the folder on the swing and closed her eyes as she took in a deep breath. Then she opened her eyes and met Becca's hard gaze.

That was it. For a moment, they just stared at each other while Becca felt her stomach slowly revolve. What was she supposed to do now? It was like a challenge of some kind, but she didn't understand how she was supposed to respond.

Everything that had happened in the last few months roiled up inside her and prepared to explode out of her mouth. It had all started just like this, on her porch with this woman, and maybe this was where it would end. Erin would walk away and they'd be stiff and awkward with each other until the Nesters took the whole Pack out.

Becca took one step forward, then another. The words were at her lips but she realized that she didn't want the worst-case scenario to happen. Not this way, not now. There had to be a simple way to make all this right, to get it back to where things were before. She would look Erin right in the eye and say the right words to do that.

Instead, something clicked in her head. She wanted something new, Like she was watching from another dimension or something, she could feel herself reach out at wolf speed, faster than any woman of her vintage and condition should have been able to move. She caught Erin's face between her hands. They froze there for a moment, just looking at each other.

Then Becca kissed her. The contact of their lips sent a jolt through her, running like a current from her lips to her toes. To Becca, it felt like she was waking up from a long sleep.

That was before the accompanying feeling of sheer terror swept through her in its wake. *What am I doing? What if Erin doesn't want this?* True, Erin's hands were resting very lightly on her hips, their touch reminding her of butterfly wings, but that didn't mean she'd be okay when this stopped. That, of course, also begged the question: did she really want this or was it just the crazy emotions of the last few weeks twisting her around?

There was no way to find out except to see what happened when they stopped kissing. Becca made herself let go of Erin and step back, breaking off the kiss. This time, she shut her own eyes so she wouldn't have to make eye contact. A cool shivery feeling was working its way from Erin's fingers on her hips inward as she stood there, breathing Erin's scent in through wolf-augmented senses.

There was a pause, then Erin let go of her and stepped back herself. They stood there a moment in silence. "Okay. Wow." Erin sighed a little, then, "Becca? Are you okay?"

Becca forced her eyes open. *Stop being such a coward.* Erin looked concerned, nervous even, but not disgusted or anything like that. But even so, she was frozen to the spot and not a single word would come to her mind. Instead she made an incoherent noise and that broke the spell.

Her instincts took over, telling her to run for it. So she grabbed the folder from the swing and bolted into the house. The last vestige of her good manners made her mutter, "I'm sorry! I don't know what I'm doing right now," as she dashed past Erin and slammed the door.

Once safely inside, she collapsed against the door, holding the folder to her chest. It felt like her heart was pounding blood out through her ears. She realized how much she'd underestimated menopause; this was far, far worse than being a teenager. What was she going to do now?

Chapter 17

When the next day dawned, Becca still didn't know what to do. She'd spent the afternoon in a blur and the night in troubled dreams about Erin and wolves and Oya. Everything was blood and sex and explosions, like one of those bad movies down at the multiplex. Except she kept waking up at all the good parts, usually right before anything that might turn into sex. The fact that that part also seemed to feature Erin didn't help calm her thoughts much.

The phone rang several times and she turned the ringer off rather than answer it. She thought about burying her head under the pillows again, but gave up and took the hottest shower she could stand instead. Then she made herself get dressed and go down the hall to the kitchen, only to be greeted by a persistent knocking at her front door.

It had to be Erin. Who else would come by at eight AM on a Tuesday? She was so not ready for this. The knocking continued. Finally, she couldn't stand it anymore and peeked out around the edge of the side window blind. Pete was peering back in at her, making her jerk her head away. Flushed and hanging her head, she opened the door slowly.

"You calling in sick today, Becca? I've been trying to call but you didn't answer." Pete looked concerned, if a tad irritated. "When you didn't show up to close yesterday afternoon, we got worried."

Yesterday afternoon? Becca pressed her hands to her cheeks and stared at her boss in horror. How had she lost the entire afternoon? Oh wait, it was coming back to her. "Omigosh, Pete, I'm so sorry. Come in, come in, please. I was just getting ready. Let me get you some coffee."

He followed her down the hall into the kitchen. "How are you feeling, Becca? Shelly said that you were on the mend. Since you've been back at work the last few days, I thought everything was okay."

Silver Moon

Becca smacked the coffeepot into the faucet in her hurry to get it filled up. Then she nearly dropped the mugs pulling them out of the drain. After that, she spilled some coffee on the countertop.

Then she snuck a guilty look at Pete and found herself giggling and babbling uncontrollably. "Oh, I'm just at sixes and sevens! I'm sorry, Pete, I really am. Yes, I'm feeling better, apart from having a few screws loose. And I completely forgot about yesterday. I don't know where my head was at but there's no excuse for it." She remembered to turn the coffeemaker on and tried to force herself to relax into its familiar burble.

Pete gave her a calm half-smile. "That fool of an ex-husband of yours got anything to do with whatever's going on?" Becca nodded. "You want to talk about it?" Becca shook her head for an answer. "All right then. But feel free to bend my ear whenever you're ready."

She nodded and opened the fridge to yank some bread out of it. "Toast?" He nodded and she popped it into the toaster without further comment.

She and Pete ate breakfast in companionable silence before they walked downtown. It was odd how soothing and ordinary his presence was. For the first time in days, she didn't feel like crawling out of her own skin to escape from the rest of her life. No weird urges to kiss him, either, so that was all right.

The feeling of general goodwill and amiability faded a bit when Shelly turned up at the store but it didn't completely die out. After all, she really couldn't blame her pack alpha for sending people to watch her. No one made her run amuck in the woods, then have a tantrum and kiss her neighbor, after all. All things considered, she'd have set babysitters to watch her if she'd been in Shelly's paws…shoes.

The moment that thought sank in, it brought a wave of pure depression with it. This Pack stuff was all well and good but she was going to have her house sold out from under her unless she did something about it soon. And she'd just made a very public pass at someone she thought of as a good friend. Not that after being married to Ed, many women wouldn't consider becoming lesbians if it was an option. But what if she was just lonely? She still wasn't sure what she really wanted and that wasn't fair to Erin.

While her thoughts bounced around like she was stuck in a pinball machine, more trouble came calling in the form of Oya and one of the guys from the Nest. They didn't come strolling into the store though; apparently, that was too daring even for them. Instead, they waited outside and down the block a bit until Becca went out to pick up her lunch.

"What the hell do we have to do to get you people out of this town?" Becca snarled when she got close enough to them to speak quietly.

The guy at Oya's side snorted and she gave him a long, slow glare. He was big and pale-skinned and blond with a widow's peak that came down his forehead to form a triangle over his nearly white eyebrows. He also had silvery-gray eyes like a Husky and one of his hands was bandaged.

But it wasn't the way he looked that made her blood race and her wolf-self howl its way into wakefulness inside her head, but rather the way he smelled. She sucked in his scent, recognizing a strange and new, but not-right, not-Pack wolf smell. He smelled like magic gone bad.

Oya smiled, her eyes gleaming. "That's right. Scott was like you once, but he's been cured." She reached out and clutched Becca's arm. "Just like we can do for you. We can put all this behind us. You could be human again, normal, just like you used to be."

Becca shook Oya loose and stared harder at Scott. He stared back and she tried to read what he was thinking. Was he really cured? Did he miss being a wolf? He gave her a doggy grin in response, only just steering clear of panting. His eyes held something that seemed like anger or maybe even jealousy, belying his puppy-friendly smile. It certainly didn't look like he was ready to put anything behind him. "So where did she find you?"

Scott bared his teeth in something that wasn't a smile. "Does it matter? I can smell your fear and your questions, elder sister. Trust her: it can be better." He glanced sidelong at Oya, as if for approval.

"Elder sister?" Becca thought about biting him. With any luck, her magic would be contagious and he'd go back to being a wolf. That probably wasn't the best idea though. He smelled like a big city and she guessed that he was that other kind of wolf she'd read about. If they fought, who knew what their bites might do to each other? She shifted her attention to Oya instead.

That strangely familiar quality about the other woman was back and this time it seemed like more than was justified by their few meetings. Oya looked a bit like Lizzie in broad daylight but that wasn't the only resemblance. Now that Becca was paying attention, she could smell another whiff of wolf in the air and it wasn't coming from Scott. Her eyes narrowed. "You were one too, weren't you? How come I couldn't tell before?"

Oya laughed, the sound tinny and insincere in Becca's ears. She did notice that Oya didn't move her head back when she laughed, keeping her throat covered. Disturbed that she'd even noticed that detail, she looked away for an instant.

Oya's voice called her back. "Not talking about me in the intro sessions, I guess. Yes, I was one of them once, years ago, running around like an animal every month. Fighting ordinary, normal people I had nothing against.

Silver Moon

Then I recognized that it was wrong. Being a wolf is a disease, not a gift. Why would anyone want to turn into an animal possessed by the moon's phases? It's disgusting and wrong." Oya stepped closer. "You feel it too, don't you? You're not a killer. I can see it in your eyes."

Becca remembered watching her neighbors and longing to be normal again. It wasn't a memory she was proud of right now, but she could hardly forget something she'd wished for that very morning. Life had been so much simpler before all of this started; she missed that more than anything. To her horror, she could feel her eyes start to tear up and she shook her head angrily to clear it. Whatever Oya was offering had to be snake oil. How could she even begin to trust anything this woman had to say?

Oya stepped back, but not before she slipped something in the breast pocket of Becca's shirt. "That's my card. My cell number's on it. I suspect you'll want to get in touch with me. Call me when you're ready. Come on, Scott."

Becca snarled, "I'll never be ready for anything you have to offer!" Oya and Scott turned without another word and started walking toward the white van while she glared after them. She noticed that Scott sent a glare of his own back her way. Apparently, the cure didn't make anyone mellower.

But she didn't take Oya's card from her pocket and rip it up either. And from the set of Oya's back, the other woman knew it. Becca could feel her fists ball up, the wolf's howl echo through her head like her body. The question she'd been asking all morning was back: what was she supposed to do now?

Chapter 18

When she got back to the store, she was still shaking. She'd made herself go get a sandwich and eat some of it in hopes that it would calm her down, but it didn't help much. The whole situation felt twisted and wrong. Oya couldn't be trusted, yet something in Becca wanted the cure to be real.

Shelly was at the counter when she came in, looking her over with an odd expression on her face. Becca wondered if she'd seen her talking to Oya. That had to be it. She took the wolf by its tail, or at least that's how she tried to think about it. "Oya was waiting for me when I went outside. She says the Nesters are leaving town," she said, without introduction.

Shelly's eyebrows rose. "Who's Oya? The Nester bitch, Sara?"

"She goes by Oya now. Was Sara her name before she joined the Nesters?" For the first time, Becca wondered what the Nester's new name meant. She'd said something about a storm that brought change back at Millie's, what seemed like a decade ago. At the time, it hadn't seemed that important. Now she wished she had paid more attention.

"Oya?" Shelly snorted. "Well, I knew her as Sara Hunter. You know she's our cousin, right? And that she used to live here?"

"So she mentioned. And I know that she's a wolf. Or at least she used to be one so she had to have been in the Pack." Becca faltered a little.

Shelly's face froze like one of the mountain lakes and something raged below the surface. "That was when Margaret was alpha, back when I first started to change. Sara was the Pack beta back then but she wanted something more. Her parents died in an accident, but she blamed Margaret and the Pack for it. Used it as an excuse to attack Margaret." Shelly's shoulder twitched like she was trying to shake off a bad memory.

Silver Moon

"I don't think I've met a Margaret," Becca began, feeling her way cautiously.

"That's because Margaret's dead. We think Sara k—" Shelly stopped abruptly as a customer walked in. When Becca was done helping him, Shelly was off helping someone else. Frustrated curiosity was clawing its way through her until she very nearly called Pete up from the stockroom to take over. But that, after missing Monday afternoon, would have felt like professional suicide, so she made herself restock while she waited for the rest of the story.

And waited. The afternoon went by in a flood of customers. *Just as well,* Becca thought, *for my job security if not for my mental health.* She spent the whole time she was answering questions about paint and plumbing supplies wondering about Oya/Sara and Shelly and Margaret.

If Sara/Oya killed Margaret in some kind of sneaky way, that probably got her kicked out of the Pack. That made the most sense, given Shelly's reaction to her question. But if Sara had killed the old alpha, why wasn't she in charge now? Wasn't that how it worked? Just the thought made her stomach hurt; did that mean that Erin and Shelly might fight to the death someday? She never wanted to see that.

It didn't look like she was going to get any answers, at least not today. Shelly's sister called just as Erin strolled in the store's front door. Becca went beet-red and couldn't stop herself from making a halfhearted attempt to duck behind the counter. She scrambled around in the supply box on the top shelf to try and make it less obvious while she muttered a less than enthusiastic, "Hi there."

"Hi. I noticed that your phone seemed to be turned off so I'd thought I'd stop by to make sure everything was okay." Erin leaned against the counter, corded muscles standing out under the light tan and freckled skin of her arms.

"You must about ready to strangle me," Shelly got off the phone and groaned. "But I've got to help out with my mom again. I'll try and finish our conversation tomorrow, okay?" She patted Becca's shoulder as she shot past. "Hey, Erin. Keep an eye on things, will you?"

Erin gave her a wry half-smile. "I'll try."

Becca watched Shelly disappear and felt like she was drowning. All of a sudden, the only people in the store were her and Erin. There would be no interruption to save her now. She stared down at Erin's long fingers, almost without realizing that she was avoiding eye contact. After a minute, Erin's hands began to sway slowly back and forth on the worn surface, like she was playing with a cat.

Becca looked up when she realized that she was following them through a second pass across the counter. One corner of Erin's mouth quirked up in amusement. "Sorry. I couldn't resist. You think you're about ready to talk now?"

"Here?" Becca stared frantically at the front door as if all of Wolf's Point was about to stampede through the doors looking for remodeling supplies.

"Well, it is fifteen minutes before closing time. I can certainly wait that long. I need some stuff for my house anyway." Erin walked away and down the nearest aisle and began picking up things, looking at them as if she wasn't quite seeing them.

Becca thought about smacking her head against the counter a few times. It might help. Instead, she watched Erin. The silence went on long enough to feel her guts get all churny as well as to develop a distinct impression that she was being out of line. If she wasn't going to think about Erin *that* way, then she shouldn't be ogling her, right?

Except…when had she decided what she was going to think about Erin at all? She had a brief flash of running with her neighbor through the streets as humans, then around the mountain as wolves. The memory of the hours that they'd spent together since she'd started to change were, for the most part, pleasant. And she knew she liked Erin. Was that enough to want something more?

Fifteen minutes took an eternity, but finally, when she couldn't stand it anymore, Becca went over and locked the door and flipped the sign to "Closed." Now she just had to find the words to say whatever it was that she needed to say. When she turned around, Erin was back at the counter. "Look…" they both said at once before dropping into a tense silence.

Erin cleared her throat and tried again. "I know you're really freaked out about everything that's going on. I realize this is a lot to take in."

Becca leaned back against the door. "So that excuses me making a pass at you and running away?" She snorted. "I would have thought that I was old enough not to let my hormones run away with me, but I guess not." She crossed over to the counter and looked up at her neighbor. "What happens now?"

Erin looked baffled. "Well, what do you want to happen? I'm not going to deny that I think you're an attractive woman and that I'm interested in more then being pals but I can see where coming out as a werewolf and coming out as queer in the same three-month time period would throw a gal for a loop. I can wait for an answer."

Becca's stomach mixed itself up. This was the moment to say what she wanted, whatever that was. Instead, she barked a laugh. "Yeah, you can say that again. It's been one wild ride so far."

Erin rubbed a hand on the back of her neck and looked at the floor. Finally, she asked, almost like she wasn't ready to hear the answer, "So did you mean it?"

Becca gave her an incredulous look. "No, I go around kissing just about anyone who shows up on my front porch. Didn't the Welcome Wagon lady warn you about that when you moved in?"

Pete's sudden appearance in the storeroom doorway came as both a shock and a relief, as far as Becca was concerned. "Oops, didn't mean to interrupt. Just want to let you know that I'm on my way out, Becca. Evening, Erin." His ears, as he turned away, were the pinkest that Becca had ever seen them and she couldn't suppress a quiet snort of laughter.

"Sure thing, Pete. Thanks again for understanding. I'll get the till counted out and bring the deposit over to the bank." Becca walked behind the counter and pulled out the cash drawer as Pete vanished. Then she made herself meet Erin's gaze. "How about you help me get everything closed down here and we go for a run after I stop by the bank? Then we talk."

Erin gave her a baffled look but nodded back. She pulled the shades and ran the broom around while Becca finished counting up the money and prepped the deposit. The companionable silence felt better than the strained conversation and Becca could feel both of them start to relax. A night run would feel great after this. She could almost feel the cool air on her skin and the breeze in her hair. Everything would be clearer after that, or at least she hoped so.

"Hey, wake up in there. You about ready to go?" Erin had put the broom and pan away. She was cocking her head to one side when she asked questions again and Becca smiled at the familiar gesture.

"Yep." They slipped outside and Becca locked the door behind them. She took a deep breath of dusk-filled cool air and coughed at something else that the wind carried. She shook her head, baffled by the weird burnt smell. There was something else out there tonight and it wasn't anything she recognized.

From the way Erin was looking around, she could smell it too. She pulled her cell phone out of her pocket and started punching in a number. Becca couldn't see anything out of the ordinary except for how deserted the street was. The other stores were already closed but usually there were still people going home or at least driving past. But tonight, they seemed to be the only people in Wolf's Point.

The sense of menace or whatever it was didn't seem to be caused by anything obvious beyond the quiet. Nothing was on fire and the streets weren't crawling with armed Nesters. From behind her, she could hear Erin calling someone, her voice soft as she asked something about "patrols."

Becca hoped she was talking to Lizzie. If anyone in this town could help them deal with what was going on, it was the deputy. She smiled at the thought; a few months back and she would have thought of the sheriff first. A lot of things were changing.

Erin clicked off her phone. "Was that Lizzie?" Becca asked as they moved carefully down the street, bodies tense and alert for whatever might be coming next.

Erin shook her head but starting hunting for the deputy's number on the little screen. That was when the white van swerved around the corner, tires screeching against the pavement. Becca saw Scott, the ex-wolf, behind the wheel. His expression was cold and focused.

Adrenaline kicked in and she shoved Erin into the recessed doorway of the clothing store behind them. She let her momentum take them backward. There was a hollow smack as they hit the glass, but the window panels held.

The van raced past and one of the Nesters hung out the side and aimed a gun at them from the passenger side window. He fired and something flew toward them, then a second something as they dropped to the ground. Becca flinched and Erin covered her head as the things flew over their heads and bounced off the glass behind them. The van screeched away and Becca could feel her knees shake so hard she thought she was never getting back up. "What the hell was that?" She panted her words, her heart racing too fast to breath properly.

They both looked down at the things the Nester had shot at them: tranquilizer darts. They were filled with a clear liquid. Becca's stomach turned. Evidently they could accept Oya's "cure" on their own or she'd force them to try it.

"Keep watch." Erin stood up slowly and pulled a small plastic bag from her pocket and used it to scoop up the darts without touching them. At Becca's incredulous look, she added, "It was from my sandwich at lunch. I don't have a full forensics kit on me or anything."

Becca snorted and slid forward cautiously on her butt. She poked her nose outside the doorway for a very wary look around. The white van was nowhere in sight and the street was still deserted. She stood carefully, leaning against the window for support. Then recognized that she was sniffing the breeze too. Well, no point in not being careful.

Silver Moon

She looked down at the dart in Erin's bag and shuddered. This had gone too far. It was time to tell someone what Oya had been telling her. "I think I know what that is. It's their 'cure.'"

Erin started, looking up at her in complete astonishment. "Their cure? For what?" Realization dawned a moment later. "For us? For turning into wolves? What the hell, Becca, how long have you known this?"

"Not long." Becca could feel herself start to flush and resigned herself to another round of hot flashes. "At first, I thought it was just some crap that Oya made up. But I guess…it isn't. Or at least they think it's real." Her voice faltered as she spoke. "I met some guy named Scott with her today, the same one who was driving the van just now. He said he used to be another kind of wolf from someplace else. I'm guessing he's the bitten kind?"

"There are just us and the kind from the Lugosi movie, as far as I know. And there's a few things that make them helluva lot scarier than us, at least in my biased opinion. Transmission by biting turns out killers, Becca. Is Oya seeking you out every couple of days to play Truth or Dare or what? Why didn't you tell one of us?"

Becca rolled her eyes. "Hello? Been a bit preoccupied with other things and since I didn't believe her anyway, I haven't been exactly dwelling on it." The lie burned in her mouth. Pack law said that she needed to be truthful with other Pack members. It was one of the first things that Erin had told her. Yet here she was, breaking yet another rule. Who knew being a part-time wolf would get so complicated?

"Right." Erin was searching her phone for another number. Her expression was set and grim as she stood up.

Becca knew she was calling Shelly and a little thrill of fear went through her. How badly had she screwed up this time?

The bag of store cash banged into her leg, reminding her of more mundane concerns. Erin trailed after her as she walked the final two blocks to the bank and dropped the money in the night deposit slot. Looking at the bank reminded her that she needed to try and talk to them about refinancing her house loan. She doubted that she could do anything to stop Ed and Pamela from selling the place but she should probably try.

When Erin caught up with her, she was leaning against the bank's limestone doorway, rubbing her temples with her fingers and sighing. Becca jumped a little when Erin's hand rested lightly on her shoulder. "Sorry I jumped down your throat. I can see why you wouldn't believe her. It sounds pretty crazy."

"Unlike, say, turning into a wolf yourself?" Becca grimaced. "Shelly coming here or are we going to her?"

"We're going there. She needs to get her mom settled for the night. Molly's calling everyone else together; sounds like it'll be quite the confab." Erin tugged carefully at her arm. "Come on, I'll drive. We'll get take-out on the way and redeem ourselves in her eyes."

Silver Moon

Chapter 19

Becca followed Erin to her car and wondered what she could have done differently. What if she had gone to Shelly right after she spoke with Oya? What could the Pack have done except what they had already done? Short of killing a Nester or two, preferably Oya herself, what more could any of them do?

She mulled it over as they stopped off to pick up Mexican take-out at the place on the highway out to Shelly and Pete's place. Erin's phone beeped and she glanced down at it before she pulled out of their parking spot. "This just got bigger than I expected. Looks like Shelly's called the whole Pack and the elders and all our allies together. Hopefully, we'll be able to come up with a plan." She sighed, then hit the steering wheel hard. "I hate those damn Nesters! First the Women's Club, now all this."

Becca jumped at her unexpected vehemence and mumbled her agreement. She wondered what else had been in the club besides their meeting space. If they had any weapons besides their teeth, she hadn't seen them yet. Something like a rocket launcher could come in handy, if any of them knew how to use it. The whole thing with the Nesters got more depressing by the week, like a macrocosm version of her own life. She could feel a splitting headache coming on and rubbed her temples slowly in an effort to stave it off.

Erin drove quickly, her eyes darting to the rearview mirror with enough frequency that Becca eventually looked back herself. Erin responded to her questioning look, "Probably nothing or else it's one of us headed for Shelly's. Just unusual to see the same pair of lights out here for any length of time." Then she exhaled. "There, they turned off."

Becca could hear the relief in her voice and helped herself to a bite of burrito. Her stomach growled its enthusiasm. That must be why she was

Silver Moon

getting so shaky. She nibbled at her dinner carefully, making sure not to spill anything on Erin's faded upholstery.

Her eyes were drawn, not behind them, but upward toward the moon. It was only a half full, but its glow called an echo from her blood, making her heart pound. She wanted to follow it and howl her frustration and anxiety out in the woods somewhere.

Or maybe, just maybe, part of her wanted it all to be over with instead. Maybe she really wanted Oya's cure and that's why she hadn't said anything about it to Shelly or Erin. Maybe she just wanted a nice man and a white picket fence and none of this craziness. Her headache got worse.

They pulled up to Shelly and Pete's place, a split-level ranch on a few acres outside town. The horses were out in their pen and they nickered into the darkness while the pack of dogs that roamed the place barked greetings. Becca noticed that all of them got very submissive when Erin glanced their way, bowing their muzzles into their paws or rolling over to expose their throats and bellies. Her, they jumped on and licked. It figured.

There were a few other cars already there and several more pulled up as they walked to the front door. As people got out of their cars, the mood felt pretty serious and no one said much. Becca suspected that there wouldn't be margaritas this time around either, more's the pity.

Lizzie Blackhawk opened the front door for them, her deputy's uniform replaced with jeans and a t-shirt. Even the ever-present sunglasses were missing. At Becca's surprised look, she shrugged. "Shelly thought it was time to call in reinforcements. Unofficially, in my case."

Becca smiled, relieved that she wasn't the only one thinking along those lines. Maybe the Pack had a "Girl's Auxiliary" of some sort; Erin had mentioned something about allies. Certainly the living room and kitchen were filling up. Erin herded her into the innermost circle of chairs, clearly reserved for Pack members, and put the food on the table. Shelly was already sitting there, surrounded by people who were sitting on any surface they could find.

The sight was enough to make Becca's heart swell with relief. They weren't alone. In fact, just about everyone had brought someone else, with the exception of her and Erin. *I need to start recruiting,* she thought as she glanced from Mrs. Hui's teenaged son and daughter to Adelía's husband to the young man sitting behind Molly, his hand on her shoulder. One of the library assistants was sitting with them as well; maybe that explained the werewolf-themed books she'd been noticing.

A few more folks trickled in and Shelly stood up and stayed standing, her presence stilling the room to listening silence. "Welcome. Welcome, all of you. We have gathered here tonight, Pack and friends of the Pack, to confront a danger greater than Wolf's Point has ever known."

Becca looked around, noticing a few more familiar faces. Her original guess that half of town knew about the wolves before she did wasn't too far off. The clinic nurse nodded to her from behind Shelly. Dr. Green was at her side, his arm around an older man who she didn't recognize. Green smiled at her and after a moment, she smiled back before turning her full attention back to what Shelly was saying.

Erin handed her the baggie and Shelly continued, "What I'm holding is a bag containing darts which were fired at two of our members tonight. Becca Thornton, please stand up." Her tone made it clear that it wasn't a request.

Startled, Becca stood, her knees trembling a little. What did Shelly want her to do? "Hi." She gave the crowd a weak smile.

"Please tell us what Sara Hunter told you."

This is going to be fun. Not. Becca cleared her throat. "Well…she said that the Nesters had developed a cure. One that would make us stop being wolves." There was a shocked murmur around the inner circle and she glanced at them with a slightly cynical eye. Hadn't any of them ever thought about being normal again? That seemed unlikely. "And today, she told me that not only is she a cured wolf, but one of the Nesters with her is another kind of cured wolf." There were more shocked murmurs, this time with an undercurrent of disbelief. "He smells like a wolf still, a sick one," she added.

"Did she say why they were here?" Shelly asked the question like she already knew the answer.

"She said something about wanting to cure us all, and suggested that it would be one way or another. I thought she was crazy at first and I didn't believe her." Becca found herself shivering a little. "But I think I'm starting to. I realized today that she used to be one of us. Though I don't know how she could have changed as much as she has if that's true."

Shelly patted her shoulder and she took that as a signal to sit back down. She watched people's expressions shift back and forth between anger and flavors of disbelief, plus a few other things she couldn't read. Several hands were raised and it was clearly due to Shelly's commanding presence alone that no one was just shouting out their questions. From the corner of her eye, she saw Shelly nod, acknowledging the hands but not ready to let them speak yet.

Instead, she turned and handed the bag with the darts in it to Dr. Green. "Can you try and figure out what's in these things?" He nodded and

Silver Moon

she turned back to the rest of the room. "All right, so now we have an idea of why Sara and her people have come here. They've attacked us, they've burned down the Women's Club and now they're threatening us with annihilation. We've struck back a few times, but it's not enough to stop them. I've asked you all here tonight to talk about our next steps. Erin?"

Erin rose and moved easily to Shelly's side, managing to simultaneously tower over her and still make it clear that the other woman was in command. Becca felt an odd sensation go through her watching them. They had probably never taken a minute to wonder if there was a cure, or if such a thing was worthwhile. She felt ashamed that it had ever crossed her mind. Maybe the magic was wrong and she shouldn't have been picked. Maybe there was some other woman in the Valley who should be here instead.

Erin's voice jolted Becca out of her reverie. She had already missed the introduction, but what Erin said next sure got through. "We've got to get rid of them before they get rid of us." Did that mean what it sounded like? Becca found herself staring up at Erin, praying that she wasn't going to be told to go out and rip the throats out of some stupid would-be wolf hunters. And Oya? True, she didn't like the woman and she had ample reason to bear a grudge but that didn't mean that she was ready for more extreme measures.

What came next brought some comfort. "It's not like we can win an all-out battle with them. They've got us outgunned and I don't think we can do much about that part. So we've got to use what we have. We've got to make sure that they're not welcome. No one sells anything to them, no one tells them anything. That van of theirs suddenly doesn't run any more. Maybe there's a flood or fire at their campsite. It keeps up, anything and everything we can do short of actual bloodshed to drive them off. And in the meantime, Shelly's got some other plans that we'll be working on."

This time, there were nods around the circle. Order was being restored and uncertainty banished. Becca could feel it in her bones, feel the wolf inside stirring itself into hunting mode, ready to do whatever the Pack needed. The moment that realization sank in scared her more than anything else that had happened all day. Would she blindly follow her alpha, no matter what? She'd never been much for that kind of obedience before; just how much was this changing her?

Erin and Shelly were going around the room talking to different people now. It was clear that they were being told what their roles were. Lizzie moved over to Becca's side. "How are you feeling? I still need to get together with you to coordinate our story for the sheriff."

"Why not just tell him the truth? Seems like a big chunk of town already knows." As soon as she said it, she tried to imagine the sheriff's reaction, or the mayor's for that matter, to the notion that many of the women of a certain age running around Wolf's Point turned into wolves from time to time. It was hard to say whether or not it would be better to be believed or disbelieved at that point.

"Well, on the offhand chance that he didn't call your family to see if you could be committed, there's the greater likelihood that he'd lock you up and throw away the key. Amazing how many people around here suddenly have drugs in their car or their garage when they're starting to cause trouble." Lizzie grimaced and rubbed the bridge of her nose.

Becca sat there looking at her with her mouth hanging open for what seemed like a solid minute. "You know this and you work for him?" She finally sputtered out.

"Someone's got to keep an eye on the department and he wins elections. Besides, a lot of the time, he's right about the troublemakers. Not as often as the wolves are, mind you, but often enough. Man's just not the believing type when it comes to this sort of thing though. So that leaves you and me giving him something he can believe."

"Boy Scout reunion gone wrong?"

"Now there's a thought. Tricky to explain about the obvious gasoline burns in the woods though. However, he might go for a camping trip for potential meth heads looking to case out the area. He's already got us checking for that. We could claim you saw some stuff just before something blew up," Lizzie studied her speculatively. "Any chance he'd buy the notion that you have a thing for bad boys?"

Becca rolled her eyes as Erin appeared behind them, making them both jump. "Probably not. He's likely to have met Ed at some point. Why not fall back on the old 'kids in the woods fooling around until responsible adults stumble across them, accidents happen' version of events?"

"Because we used that the last time these clowns came to town and it didn't go over that well then." Lizzie rolled her eyes. "They're a little old for the kid defense anyway."

Becca glanced past her at the rest of the room. Shelly was back in the center of the circle, now considerably emptier. Becca realized that people must have started leaving once they had their orders. Or requests, depending on how you wanted to look at it. In fact, it was down to just the Pack and a few others, including Pete and Lizzie. She wondered what their orders were going to look like.

Silver Moon

No one had to spend much time wondering. "All right. Some of you know or at least suspect that there are ways to use the magic of the valley against intruders. And you're right. But there are a couple of problems, the first one being that we're not sure how to do it, seeing as we lost the archives when the Women's Club burned down. I've been meeting with my mom and the other elders but no one remembers all of the rituals, just bits and pieces that worked at one time or another. The second problem is the price for calling on that magic. Legend says that every wolf who did it in the past didn't live to see it work."

A cascade of whispers and muttering filled the room. Erin murmured, "Great," in a slightly sarcastic tone. Becca gave her a sidelong grimace and wondered what else had been in the "archives." Lizzie raised an eyebrow as she glanced at both of them.

Shelly drew in a breath and scanned the room. Everyone fell silent again. "I know what it sounds like, but it's an option we may need to explore. In the meantime, we need to step up our patrols. Today, we've seen that Sara and her followers are a clear danger to us no matter what form we're in. We need to know where they are and what they're doing at all times. And if there's a way to split them up, maybe scare off a few at a time."

"Guess I'm off house arrest," Becca muttered to Erin, without thinking. Her voice was louder than she'd expected and she went beet-red and clapped a hand over her mouth a second later. It wasn't soon enough to avoid Shelly's cold stare though, and she hung her head as she looked down at the rug.

"Erin will be handing out the team assignments. We patrol in pairs and stay in radio contact as much as possible. It's more reliable than cell coverage around here. See Adelía if you don't have a radio already. She and I will patrol tonight until one AM. Be careful, everyone." She nodded and was immediately surrounded by women asking questions.

Erin pulled out a clipboard. "All right, I've got Gladys and Mei on for tomorrow morning. Then it's Molly and Carly from afternoon until evening." She looked around to make sure she was being heard and caught Becca's inquiring stare. "Me and Becca tomorrow night from dark until one AM."

She kept calling out team names but by then, Becca was too flustered to hear her. Should they be out patrolling together? Wouldn't that be too distracting? She fretted so much that she very nearly forgot that before she started turning into a wolf, she'd been going to bed at ten sharp. The wee hours of the morning were starting to look pretty normal now.

At any rate, before she could ask about it, Adelía came by and handed her a radio. A few minutes of instructions on how to use it followed and then she moved on to the next team. Lizzie tapped her shoulder, "I'll come by the store tomorrow and we can talk then. I'm guessing the sheriff will want some names so you may want to pick a favorite Nester to rat out. See you then."

Becca watched her walk away and thought about secrets and lies and how many more of them she was living with lately. It wasn't as if she thought there was much point in telling the sheriff the truth, but that this didn't seem like the life she saw herself leading when she grew up. She wasn't sure what was anymore.

Erin poked her gently in the ribs. "You still with us? We need to get going. Pete and Shelly want to hit the hay for as long as they can."

Becca got up obediently, noticing for the first time that her knees had stopped hurting when she got up after sitting for awhile. It seemed like the aches and pains she'd had for the last few years were dropping away, little by little. She looked down at her body and frowned. "So…did you stop hurting, in that, you know, creaky middle-aged sort of way once you started to change?"

"Just noticed that part, huh? Yep. It's one of the best of the side effects, in my humble opinion." Erin started moving toward the door. "Funny, I figured you were going to ask about what happens when we get too old to change any more. You do realize that we're not immortal, right?"

"Ummm…" Come to think of it, why hadn't she asked that question? Probably because they'd mentioned "elders." Odd how no one ever defined who they were. Did you just wake up one day and discover that you were now an elder werewolf or what?

Becca rubbed her cheek and frowned back at Erin. Life was just one long series of questions these days. She wondered if there would have been so many if she'd stayed as she was. But then, middle-aged single divorcees who didn't transform probably had a different set of questions of their own.

"So we have elders, as you've heard us mention," Erin continued, just like she had asked the question out loud. "You probably noticed some of the women around the dining room table?" Becca nodded as if she actually had noticed and tried hard to remember. There had been a group of elderly women at the table, that much she was clear on.

Erin went on, "Those are some of them. When we get too old to change without side effects, the magic lets us go, more or less. I will say that they're the healthiest, sharpest bunch of old ladies I've ever seen, even without changing. We'll have to go by Circle House so I can introduce you to them."

Silver Moon

"Circle House?" They were outside now, and the wind was picking up. Becca thought she could smell something, just the tiniest whiff of a smell that wasn't wolf or tree or regular nighttime at Shelly and Pete's place. She turned her head first one way, then the other, sniffing.

"Circle House is just what we call it. It's up at Shady Oaks, kind of a retirement community for the Pack within a retirement community for everyone else. We'll definitely stop by later on in the week. In the meantime—what's up?" The last question was in a much lower tone of voice, one that it would have been hard for nonwolf-enhanced ears to pick up on.

"Not sure," Becca answered in the same pitch. Now she was sending all her senses out into the darkness, listening for anything out of place while she peered into the shadows beneath the trees. All of the Pack and their visitors had cleared out by now so there was a good field of sight all around the house and the yard.

Not that it helped. The light scent on the wind vanished as soon as it had appeared. She couldn't hear anything or see anything moving. *Maybe being a wolf enhances my imagination too, lucky me*, she thought. Even so, she found herself beginning a big circle that would take her around the house and yard.

Erin fell in next to her and didn't ask any questions, which Becca was glad of. It made her feel like her judgment might be worth something. Even if the Pack beta couldn't sense anything wrong, at least she was willing to trust Becca's instincts.

They slipped quietly through the shadows, avoiding the dry leaves and small breakable sticks where they could. Still, they were so noisy to Becca's wolf hearing that she held up her hand and stopped them both when they got to the trees that ringed the backyard. Her gut told her something still didn't feel right, but the harder she listened and sniffed and looked, the more normal things seemed to be.

Finally she dropped her hand with an exasperated slap against her thigh. "I'm just being a nervous Nelly, I guess. There's nothing here."

Erin caught her arm, her expression turning serious in the moonlight. "Don't ever question your instincts, Becca. If something felt wrong, it felt wrong. There could be lots of reasons for it, but your first thought was to check it out and that's the way it should be. Okay?"

Becca could feel an odd tingle run through her arm into the rest of her body. For one mad, crazy moment, she thought about kissing Erin again. Then she shook herself and nodded instead. This wasn't the time or the place. Instead, she followed Erin back to the car in silence and they drove back to town. Erin dropped her off and pulled into her own driveway.

Catherine Lundoff   128

Becca watched her go inside before she let herself into her dark little house. Maybe it was time to get a dog or a cat for company. If Shelly could manage to have pets without eating them, so could she. But then, she might not be living here that much longer, at least if Ed had his way, and it would be harder to get an apartment if she had a pet. Or so she'd heard.

Her spirits felt incredibly heavy, nearly unbearably so and she was too agitated to go to sleep. She made herself a cup of decaf tea and wondered what to do next, finally settling on sitting in front of the TV. She channel-surfed until she settled on watching late night comics. The sense of unease finally ebbed as she got sleepier. Eventually, she fell asleep on the couch, dropping into a dreamless sleep until morning.

Silver Moon

Chapter 20

Dawn woke her early enough that she made it to the store and got everything ready before the time that Pete usually showed up. It felt like an apology for her screw-up earlier in the week, or at least that's what she intended it to be. She was just turning the sign to "Open" when Molly ran up and hammered on the glass of the still-locked door. Her face was as pale as Becca had ever seen it and her eyes made her look like a horse about to bolt.

Becca yanked the door open and pulled her inside. "What is it?"

"It's Shelly. She's gone. She went out to check on the horses last night after we left and Pete fell asleep before she came back in. When he woke up, she wasn't there. He took the dogs and went looking for her but he couldn't find her." Molly stopped to gasp for air.

The Nesters. It had to be them. Becca's thoughts turned to the worst possibilities. Had they killed Shelly? She wanted to throw up just thinking about it. "Was there anything to tell what happened?" She imagined blood, bits of fabric, a trail of breadcrumb clues like on a TV show. Anything.

Molly grimaced and nodded. "There was blood, hers and someone else's. But no body so we think they've kidnapped her, whoever they are. There hasn't been a note or anything yet. Lizzie's got the whole department down there checking things out. I heard about it at the post office and I was going to call here, but I thought you should hear it directly from one of us."

"When are we meeting?" Becca's thoughts were whirling. It wasn't close enough to the full moon for Shelly to start to change, not unless that was something that came with a lot more control. So their alpha was still human for the time being, which could be good or bad depending on what the Nesters intended to do with her.

Silver Moon

"Erin's taking over until we get Shelly back. There's a meeting tonight at her house, right after dark. Just the Pack this time. Erin and I, well, we're wondering if maybe someone said something that tipped the Nesters off, maybe by accident." Molly looked kind of green around the gills.

"One of the allies, you mean?" That was an unpleasant thought. It had been kind of wonderful for a few moments last night, knowing who to trust in town. But then she couldn't imagine any of the wolves doing something like that, not even the ones she didn't know that well. Then she remembered that Oya had been a wolf once and she started to reconsider.

If any of the wolves were thinking about what a cure might mean for them… The thought popped out of the back of her brain, making her heart race. She nearly screamed, "No!" out loud before she got herself under control.

But no, that couldn't be it. The other wolves were strong, she was the only one who had doubts. Even she hadn't told Oya that they were meeting last night or anything else the Nesters could use against them. Something else occurred to her. "Maybe they already knew. Oya probably already knew where Shelly lived after all. They're…they were family."

Molly shrugged. "It's possible, but Erin wants to eliminate all the possibilities. Pete said that she'd never been to the house."

Becca nodded slowly. It made sense, but then Erin had talked about seeing lights in the mirror last night too. Why assume that someone said the wrong thing when the Nesters might have just been following them? Then a thought struck her: if they could follow Erin and her to kidnap Shelly at home, she was a sitting duck if they came here while she was working at the store alone.

Molly interrupted the tumult in her head with a small cough. "Got any water?"

Becca nodded and sent her back to the office fridge while she watched the street outside. Paranoia aside, there wasn't much to see except Hal Kramer walking his dog down the street. A couple of cars pulled into the parking lot next door but she couldn't see who was getting out of them, at least not from here.

She was being ridiculous. There was no point to kidnapping her too. Who'd notice?

Kidnapping, then curing Shelly, on the other hand, might just break the Pack.

She drew in a long shuddering breath and shook her head a little. Enough of this. If Shelly was in trouble and Pete might not make it in today, she had a business to help run. It was the least she could do for them.

Molly came out of the back room drying her hands on a towel. "Pete said Kira would come down this afternoon to try and help out. He's working with the police today, but wasn't sure how long that would take." She took a closer look at Becca. "I know this is horrible, but we'll get her back. And we'll make them pay." The wolf looked out of her eyes as she spoke, glowing bright and fierce and terrifying.

For a change, it didn't make Becca flinch away. Instead, she nodded, her fears ebbing for the moment as a trickle of the wolf's strength came back to her. "Thank you for coming to tell me. I'll see you tonight."

Molly left and the first customer of the day came in. Becca managed to get through the morning in a blur of suspicion, anxiety and paint chips. Anyone who came through the door could be a Nester. She reminded herself that she'd only ever seen a couple of them, never all of them at once. Rationally, she knew that they weren't likely to come into the store but it felt like they might be capable of anything now.

As promised, Kira showed up in the afternoon and worked the register while Becca helped customers around the store. The kid had big dark circles under her red eyes and clearly hadn't slept, but she took after her mom: no incorrect change and no public breakdowns. Becca only just managed not to pat her shoulder in sympathy; something told her that might be the last straw.

Finally when it was just the two of them cleaning up, Pete came in. Both of them dashed up to him. "Any word?" Becca demanded.

"Mom?" was what rolled out of Kira's mouth. Then she burst into tears. Pete reached out and held her tight in a big hug. For a moment, Becca wished he could do the same for her, but that would be just plain inappropriate. But *nice*, she thought wistfully.

She made herself sound more adult than her thoughts. "Have the police found anything yet?"

Pete's voice was low, barely above a whisper, like he thought someone else might hear him. "The Nesters have cleared out of their campsite. Henderson couldn't find much there. Nothing to say that they did it except who else would do something like this?" His face was even more drawn than his daughter's, and that was what made Becca remember her better self.

"Look, I'll manage things up here. You and Kira go into the back and take a few minutes. There's coffee and water back there and I picked up some of the those granola nut things that you like." She took a deep breath and stopped herself short of making a shooing gesture.

Silver Moon

Pete nodded and took Kira, still weeping, into the back. The door swung open as they disappeared and Becca turned, startled. Something in her expected Oya or maybe Scott. To her overwhelming relief, it was Erin.

Just not the Erin she had come to know over the past few months. This Erin was a wolf in human form, her body moving in hunting mode. Every muscle was stretched tight and her face seemed to be transforming into her wolf's snout even though it was still broad daylight. She looked at Becca from the silver eyes of a nearly wild thing, the accountant so far in the background it looked like she wasn't coming up to the surface again.

Becca walked up to her, moving slowly with her hands held out in front of her, fingers open to show they were empty. She managed to stop herself from holding one to Erin's nose to sniff. Instead she reached for her friend's arm. "Erin? Come over here and sit for a minute." She towed Erin into the store and nudged her onto the stool behind the counter. "Are you with me?"

Erin looked at her, her expression still alien. Then she shook her head like it would rattle her thoughts into place. The wolf slipped away, bit by bit. "Oh God, Becca, I'm sorry! I lose my way sometimes, especially when I get freaked out." She leaned her face into her hands, long fingers buried in her short-cropped hair.

Becca couldn't see her face. "Hey, Erin. Look up, please." Erin threw her head back like a startled horse, the whites of her eyes showing all around the pupil. The fully human pupil. Becca relaxed a little. "Okay, honey, okay. Just sit down on the stool and take a deep breath. I don't know what to do either, except tear the place apart looking for her. We can get the posse together at the meeting." She rubbed Erin's shoulder, gingerly at first, then with greater ease as she felt the other woman's tight muscles relax a tiny bit.

"The tear-the-place-apart plan has been going forward all day and will keep going tonight, with another big round of it coming after the meeting. I was wondering if you could tell me something. Did Sara—Oya—tell you anything more about that cure of hers? Like if she had a lab or someplace they were making it?"

Becca flushed. The number, Oya's number, was still in the pocket of the shirt that she worn yesterday. It was like Erin knew it was there, somehow. Which would mean that she knew, or at least suspected, that Becca had been thinking about the cure, real or otherwise. She gave Erin a suspicious glance but the other woman's expression didn't tell her anything. Maybe she meant the question just the way it sounded.

"She didn't say anything about a lab, but she did give me her number. I think she was hoping I'd call up and want to get turned into a Nester." Becca scuffed at the mat with her shoe and studied the floor like it had answers. It took her a moment to grasp the implications of what she'd just said. What if she did what Oya was hoping for? The Nesters might tell her what they'd done with Shelly. If she was very convincing, they might tell her before anything worse happened.

She gave Erin a long, steady stare. "But I could do that, couldn't I? You want me to call her and say I want the cure, don't you?"

Erin's face lit up. "Do you think she'd go for it? If you can get close to them, maybe find out where their real base is, then we can…" Her voice trailed off. "What the hell am I saying? This is much too dangerous. I should call myself. Can you give me that number?" She straightened up and set her jaw.

"Whoa there, Nellie. I can do this. Oya already thinks she's got an in with me, that I'm vulnerable to her b.s. She'll believe me if I call and tell her this is what I think I want. She might already know or at least suspect that you've taken over for Shelly for the time being. It'd be way more dangerous for you to try it." Becca could feel herself becoming convinced. It had to be her and she could, no, *had* to do this.

Pete walked in from the back room. Erin met his anxious stare and shook her head. "Nothing yet, Pete. But we've got a plan. A couple of plans, even. We'll get them in motion and I promise I'll check in with you later on tonight." She uncoiled from the stool and went over to rest one hand on his shoulder. "We're going to get her back."

Becca could feel her insides twist when she saw the sudden wild hope on his face. What if they couldn't? They did have some kind of last resort though. What was it that Shelly had said at the meeting, something about turning the valley's magic against intruders? It sounded like someone would die trying if they had to go that route. If they could even figure out how to do it to begin with.

But she wasn't going to be the one to bring it up, not here and not now. That would only happen if she failed and she wasn't going to. Instead, she stood up. "Looks like I need make a phone call. Can you manage here, Pete?"

Chapter 21

Becca questioned her part in the plan all the way back to her place. She wasn't ready to be a double agent. What if she really did get cured and forgot all about Shelly and the Pack and everything else? Or worse, she joined the Nesters and tried to hunt her former friends down? If it could happen to Oya, it could happen to her.

But if she didn't do this, no one else would be able to. She knew that with bone-deep certainty. Oya thought she was the weak link and if that was going to help Shelly, she could go right on thinking that. All Becca had to do was to remember who she was and why she was doing what she was doing. That would have to be enough to keep her grounded.

When she got home, the mail had already come. She tossed it on the table on her way through the house. She'd look at it later; right now, she had something more important to do. She took the stairs at a dead run. Her shirt was hanging on the back of the closet door, Oya's card still visible in the pocket. She pulled it out and went downstairs to find her cell phone.

Closing her eyes for a moment, she looked for that uncertain, scared Becca who'd talked to Oya outside the store. That was someone who'd think being cured might be their best option. She just needed to sound uncertain enough to make the Nester believe that she could be persuaded.

Then she dialed the number from the card. "Hello?" she said to the first beep, then realized that she was talking to voicemail. "Hi. This is Becca Thornton. I've been thinking about what you said, about what you're offering. You were right: I do miss being normal. I…I guess I'd like to hear more." She left her number and hung up.

It seemed like an instant later that her phone chirped at her. Her heart thudded as she recognized the number. "Hello, Becca. I'm glad you called."

Silver Moon

Oya's tone was full of righteous power, joy even. It was the voice of someone who knew she held all the cards and was looking forward to winning.

It set Becca's back up right away and she had to choke back a few choice comments. At least it wasn't the voice of a woman who'd question her timing, calling right after Shelly's disappearance. Though maybe the Nester didn't think she knew about that yet. Or maybe she was deluded enough to think that it didn't matter.

"I still don't know what to think about all this. I don't know if I can trust you. I mean, I know I don't want to be a monster but maybe you're only trying to trick me. Maybe your stuff doesn't really do anything." Becca sounded whiny and wishy-washy even to her own ears. *Good, now don't overplay it.*

"There's no trick, Becca. We can make you better, make you normal just like you used to be."

However normal that was. Becca kept that thought to herself. "Well, I want proof. Right now, I've just got you and your boytoy telling me you used to be like me. You have to show me something that I can believe." She crossed her fingers, hoping this sounded right. It needed to be if she was going to find anything out about Shelly.

There was a moment of silence on the other end, like the Nester leader was thinking about what to do next. "All right, Becca. I can think of something you might believe. Are you at the store?"

"No. No, I had a headache this morning and called in sick. I'll meet you at Millie's. But just you, no one else." Hopefully, Oya wasn't wondering why she didn't invite her and her crew over for lunch or something.

"Be there in an hour." Oya clicked off and Becca's whole body sagged in temporary relief. She'd done the first part. But this was just the beginning; she had to be careful not to get too confident.

She left a message for Erin. "She's agreed to meet with me at Millie's in an hour. I don't know if you're planning on watching the place or not, but I'm going to try and find out what I can from talking to her. I'll also see if she'll take me to the rest of them. I'll leave my cell on so that Lizzie can track it or whatever it is they do with these things. Wish me luck." She hung up and went upstairs to change, her nerves jangling.

What did a werewolf secret agent wear anyway? Whatever it was, it didn't jump out at her from her usual outfits. She finally went with subdued and quiet, something that would make her blend in: beige shirt and blue jeans. A long-sleeved denim shirt completed her ensemble.

She studied herself in the mirror. Her face was still too tense, too much like she wasn't sleeping enough. But a few moments with her makeup supply and she looked a bit less haggard, so that was something. She added small gold hoop earrings and ran a comb through her hair to try and get her unruly curls under control. Then she gave herself another quick scrutiny and shrugged. She'd done what she could.

She decided to drive to Millie's since there was no point in looking hurried or nervous by showing up out of breath. It also occurred to her that she might need her car. She wondered what she was going to say, how she should sound to make Oya believe in her change of heart.

Almost every time the woman saw her, she was angry or wounded or turning back from being a wolf. Come to think of it, it was hard to imagine why the Nester leader thought she was vulnerable to persuasion. She must be sending out some confused vibes, visible only to wolf senses or something along those lines.

But perhaps starting out by asking that question was the way to go. She filed the thought away as she pulled up in Millie's parking lot. As she'd hoped, the place was crowded but not too crowded.

She walked in and grabbed a table for two in a deserted corner. If Oya brought one of her thugs, he could just stand. For the first time, it occurred to her to wonder why all the Nesters she'd seen were guys except for Oya. Not that the woman seemed to be out to develop an empowering sisterhood of ex-wolves or anything but you'd think there'd be at least one other woman in the group.

She didn't have long to ponder. Oya came through the door like she owned the place. Becca couldn't see anyone waiting outside for her, but then, that didn't mean there weren't any Nesters out there. She tried not to think about Shelly as Oya sat down; it would too easy to get angry. Instead she and Oya faced each other like wary cats.

Finally, Becca spoke first, "Well, here we are again."

Oya smiled. "It looks like things have changed quite a bit since then. But then, I knew it would. So what happened to make you reconsider?"

"And what's always made you think I might be open to it? It's not the most flattering thing anyone's ever thought about me, that I'm a pushover." Becca made herself not shout, not reach across the table to throttle this woman who was holding them all in her power.

"You're the one I see most often. But apart from that, you're a regular normal woman. Not like some of these fools who grew up here and thinks that growing fur and fangs once a month is part of their birthright." The waitress interrupted her and took their orders. Becca couldn't help but notice that Oya still liked her meat rare, whatever her current feelings about the wolves.

Silver Moon

She tried to weigh what she knew so far. Oya resented the wolves and thought she was on a mission of some sort, that much was clear. Now how did she get to more? "I heard that you grew up here, maybe used to be one of those fools yourself." She made her words a challenge. "So what made you break away? For that matter, what brought you back?"

Oya's eyes flashed for a moment, then she seemed to remember where she was and who she was talking to. She smiled, almost like she meant it. "Yes, I did grow up here. That means that I've seen firsthand what it means to have monsters running your town. I told you what they did to my family, but I can understand that when you're still one of them, that can be hard to believe. If I hadn't lived through it, I never would have believed it either."

You can say that again. Becca stopped the words before they could get past her lips, and went with her second choice, "You came back for revenge then? Is that it?"

Oya gave her an enigmatic smirk and tapped her finger on her chin.

This wasn't getting much out of the Nester, so it was time to try a different approach. She looked down at the table and rubbed her cheeks with her hands. It wasn't too hard to remember how scared she'd felt changing the first time. "I don't know what to believe. Changing is horrible…horrible. I never know what I'm going to do next or even remember most of what I did the last time. It's like being two different people or something."

Oya's breath hissed through her teeth and when Becca looked back up, the other looked sympathetic, kindly even. It was hard to reconcile her expression with what Becca already knew of her. Right now, she looked positively saintly.

She reached out and covered one of Becca's hands with her own. "I've been in the same place you're in now. Back then, there was no one to help me. I had to gather allies and find a cure on my own. This time, you've got me."

Indeed. Becca forced her mouth to tremble, just a bit. Tears would be too much, even if she could summon them. She knew that instinctively. Instead she settled for squeezing Oya's hand back, then pulling her hand away. She took a deep breath and rubbed her eyes like she was pulling herself together. Then she looked up at Oya. "I want to see your proof before this goes any further. I have to know that you can really make me better."

Oya gave her a sidelong glance, then nodded. "Okay. You'll need to come with me to see what you want to see though. Are you ready to do that now?"

Becca nodded just as the waitress arrived with their burgers. They ate them quickly and silently. Becca put money down for her tab, then after a moment, picked up Oya's as well. "After what you're willing to do for me, this is the least I can do." She smiled across the table, managing not to flinch as Oya's expression shifted to suspicious, then blank. Had she done something wrong? It was hard to tell.

They left Millie's together and walked toward the parking lot. Before Oya could open the door to the familiar white van, Becca jerked her head. "My car. I'm not ready to get in that thing yet." After a minute, Oya followed her over and got in. Becca took a deep breath. "Okay. So where am I going?"

"Head out to the highway. I'll give you more directions once we get there."

Becca pulled out, hoping that Erin was somewhere nearby and following. She was startled to see the white van pull out immediately after them. It followed them out to the highway but turned right when Oya gestured to her to turn left.

In the mirror, she could see another car follow the van. She wondered if it was someone from the Pack and her stomach churned with anxiety. It was lonely out here without back-up. She glanced at Oya. Her passenger looked more relaxed than she had back at the diner. Time to try again.

"So you said you left to find a cure, but not why you came back. Once you found what you were looking for, why return?"

Oya studied her for a moment, then looked back outside. "If you found a cure for an illness, a cure that might save people from hurting others, wouldn't you want to share it? I'm from here, Becca. I cared about this town growing up. Once I knew that the cure worked, I couldn't just abandon them."

Which would make more sense if you didn't seem to be trying to kill us most of the time. Becca frowned like she was turning over Oya's words in her mind. "I guess I can understand that. But you went about it all wrong, attacking us like that. I bet a lot of us would have been willing to listen to you if you'd just come down to the Women's Club and talked to us."

"Really?" Oya laughed. "I don't think so, Becca. Wolf's Point hasn't changed that much. The wolves who killed my parents, they're still around. As is the sheriff who looked the other way."

This time, Becca let her astonishment show. The sheriff didn't know about the wolves. So why did Oya think he was covering anything up? She wondered how to ask without sounding too incredulous.

"Turn here," Oya gestured at a side road.

Silver Moon

Becca turned the car with another glance in her mirror. Nothing back there that she could see. She was on her own. It was an empty, scary feeling. "Where are we going, anyway?"

All she could see up this way were a couple of scattered houses, and something that looked like a farm off in the distance on the lower slopes. They were going up the mountains from Wolf's Point into a part of the valley that she didn't know at all. She looked around, hoping to find enough landmarks that she could find the place again.

It seemed that her efforts hadn't gone unnoticed. "This is just a temporary base where we've been doing some of our work. We'll move out of here in a few days to a better spot." Oya jerked her head. "Pull over here. We'll need to walk the rest of the way."

Becca pulled into a mowed patch at the end of a dirt road. "Road" didn't really quite describe the overgrown trail in front of them. There was no way her car was going up there and it didn't look like the white van would have made it either. She wondered how they got in and out. Maybe there was another entrance somewhere else.

Once she got out of the car, she reluctantly followed Oya up the trail. The Nester leader didn't look back. It was as if she just expected that Becca would keep on following her wherever she went. Becca thought about tossing a pebble at her back just for the fun of it, then realized that she was onto something that might be helpful later. She pretended to stumble and trip, catching herself with her hands and making sure to rub her palm on the rock in front of her.

When they went a little further up, she caught a tree branch in her hand like she was pushing it out of the way. With any luck, she was leaving enough of her scent behind that she could find the trail again once she got away. Or the Pack could find her in case something went wrong.

They came around a curve into a clearing occupied by a big white trailer. There was a sudden sharp noise as a man in camouflage rose from behind some bushes and pointed a rifle at them. Becca flinched and growled, part of her wondering if she could move fast enough to take him out before he shot her.

Oya held up her hand. "She's with me, García. Stand down."

He lowered the rifle but kept watching Becca, suspicion clearly written on his features. "What's she doing here?" His voice had a growl buried deep inside it and Becca sniffed the air around him, carefully rubbing her nose to hide it. He smelled like Scott and looked like him too, when she met his eyes. There was something lurking there, a wolf in hiding. She could feel her lip curl over one incisor.

Oya stepped between them. "Stop it. She's come for our help, Bob. I brought her up to show her what we're doing, how we can make them all normal again. Come on, Becca."

Becca glanced at García again. He'd been in the van with Scott, she realized now. He'd been the one who'd shot at them. She wondered if Oya knew about that, wondered how much control Oya really had over these guys. García bared his teeth at her in something approaching a wolf's snarl on a human face. It was all she could do to walk past him without lunging for his throat.

But she thought about Shelly and forced herself to follow Oya up to the trailer, which sat on a ridge in the middle of the clearing. Oya rapped on the door, the three knocks clearly a signal to someone inside. After a moment, the door swung open. A burly looking man in a doctor's coat stared down at her like he was trying to decide whether or not to let them in.

He must have decided to go for it, since he stepped back as Oya moved forward. She climbed the rusting steps and Becca followed, the hairs on the back of her neck tingling. Once inside, it was clear that the Nesters had knocked out the walls to make more room; she could see the rusting bolts and stains where they used to be. The kitchen was still in place but now there was a kind of makeshift lab set up in it, with glass jars and a microscope and some kind of heating device on the countertop. Becca wished she'd paid more attention back in high school chemistry so she'd know what some of it was.

Then a movement caught her eye and she turned to see Scott strapped down on a table in one corner of the room. He stared at her and growled softly. It didn't sound like a greeting but it did help to distract her from the fact that he was naked. Becca looked over at Oya only to find the Nester watching her for her reaction. "He getting a little out of control or something?"

This time Scott snarled but went silent as Oya turned and frowned at him. "Some of us require more frequent doses of the drug than others. I only need it every six months now—" Oya smiled triumphantly—"but Scott still needs weekly doses. Eventually, that will go to a monthly dose. It depends on how long you've been changing and how much control you have."

Scott convulsed, his back bowing against the straps that held him on the table until Becca could hear them creak. His widow's peak was more pronounced now and when he looked at her, she could see the wolf in his eyes. She couldn't stop herself from glancing outside. It wasn't dark yet, let alone moonrise, so why was he starting to change? His hands were scrab-

Silver Moon

bling on the table fabric, their nails growing into claws when Becca looked down.

She grabbed a flimsy metal frame chair and held in front of her as a shield. Oya laughed. "That won't stop him if he breaks free."

Becca gave her a quick cold glance. "I just aim to slow him down long enough to even the odds. If he breaks free. Why is he changing now anyway? That a side effect of the cure?" Oya and the Nester doctor or whatever he was ignored her and she didn't ask again. She'd just have to learn what she could by watching them.

The man in the lab coat finished filling up a syringe at the counter and walked over to the table. Becca couldn't help but notice that he moved cautiously as he approached the table, turning himself sideways to make a smaller target.

They'd done this before, obviously, but then she knew that. But it didn't always work the way they planned and that was very good to know. The Nester doctor reached out to hold Scott's shoulder and she could see white scars on his arm. A few looked pretty recent. So much for the cure's being permanent.

The needle sank into Scott's neck and he screamed. He shook so hard it looked like he was having a seizure. The blood drained from his face, making him even paler and his eyes rolled back in his head. Becca thought he was going to pass out.

But after a moment, his hands began to look like hands again. He sagged back against the table, the fight draining out of him. His eyes opened and she saw the scared boy he'd been, probably back before he got bitten, staring out of them. It was almost enough to make her pity him.

Then his eyes closed and he went limp. *In more ways than one*, Becca thought as she realized that he'd had en erection when he started to change. Clearly it had been a while if she'd been able to ignore that until it went away. She shoved the thought into the back of her mind to take out and examine later.

Oya and the medic exchanged comments, their voices too low for Becca's human hearing. She took a moment to look around the trailer while she strained to listen. It didn't look like there was anything more to the place than what she could see: one room with a kitchen. Even the bathroom was open, shielded from the rest of the room by a curtain. This couldn't be where they were holding Shelly. A wave of disappointment hit her hard. But then, she'd suspected it wouldn't be that easy.

She started to walk over to the counter only to find Oya blocking her way. The Nester leader looked smug. "There. That's how the cure works. What more proof do you need?"

Am I going to make it back to town if I turn her down? Becca glanced over at Scott as if she was thinking about it. And if she wanted to be truthful with herself, she was. What would be the harm in taking one dose before the moon this month? Then she could see if it worked and if it was what she wanted. Since it had to be renewed, she could go back to changing again after that, if she didn't like it.

Scott twitched like he was dreaming and uttered a low moan. It was a creepy, mournful noise that sent chills up Becca's spine. Then again, maybe she shouldn't rush into anything. "He doesn't seem all that happy about it. I'm thinking I need to sleep on this some before I make my decision." She paused between her words, tried to make it sound like this was all freaking her out. It wasn't too far from the truth, really.

She couldn't help but notice that the doctor had positioned his massive frame between her and the door. He folded his scarred arms across his chest and looked down at her, his face expressionless. The message was clear. She glanced from him to Oya. "So I gather I'm supposed to make up my mind to take this stuff right now?"

"You've seen one of our bases and you've seen how the cure works. What more do you need, Becca? You know that you want this to end. You want to have control over your life back. Let us help you." Oya was practically purring. She reached over and rested one hand lightly on Becca's arm.

"How often would I need the shots? Weekly?" She tried to make the question sound casual but her mind was whirling. Would they make her a prisoner too, just to make sure she got regular doses?

"Weekly for the first three months, then maybe once a month for a while after that. Maybe less," Lab coat guy grumbled the first words she'd heard out of him. She noticed he was wearing camouflage under the white coat. There was some kind of patch on the front of his shirt. He didn't smell like Scott though, or even like Oya. Becca wondered how he'd fallen in with the Nesters and if it could be useful somehow.

"I have to keep working. I can't just leave everything and go all commando like you guys." She couldn't say where that phrase had come from when it popped out of her mouth but she decided to follow the trail where it led. "I wouldn't want to be a burden on your group either. Maybe I can just come back here once a week or you could find me in town or…" She found her voice trailing off.

"We'll make sure you have everything you need." Oya stepped a bit too close for Becca's comfort level. "Don't worry about that."

"As long as I'm asking questions that you'll answer, why are you the only female Nester? Are there others?" Becca stepped back again. She didn't care all that much about the response but it might buy her some time to figure a way out of this.

"You haven't met all of us, you know. There are many more Nesters than Pack members. We just haven't come here in force yet." Oya's eyes were half-closed and she had clearly gone somewhere else for a moment. Wherever it was, it gave her a glow that she hadn't had before.

She was also lying about something; Becca could feel the big guy shift uneasily, like he wanted to contradict her. Oya might believe what she was saying, but he didn't. "That's reassuring. But I thought you were going to persuade us, not make us to take your cure." Becca's voice shook and she shuddered a little.

"If persuasion won't work, we're open to using all the other methods at our disposal." Oya frowned. "Don't do this, Becca. I know you want this. Let Leroy give you the shot and we'll deal with the subsequent doses after we see how the first one goes."

"What about side effects?" Becca looked at Scott.

As if on cue, he twisted on the table, gagging as he spat something onto the floor. A moment later, a racking cough shook his body. Becca moved further out of arm's range from Oya and Leroy and backed up to the chair she'd held earlier. At least she could go out fighting.

There was a yell from outside the trailer. It was followed by a chorus of voices and a gunshot. "What the hell?" Oya dashed for one of the trailer windows while Leroy yanked off his coat. There was a good-sized pistol at his belt and he had it out of the holster faster than Becca could blink.

She had to make herself not run to the window. If the Pack had come to rescue her, she might never be able to get this close to the Nesters again. Then how were they going to get Shelly back? All the same though, a rescue would come in pretty handy right about now.

Her heart was thudding its way up her throat as Leroy freed Scott. The ex-wolf grabbed his pants and shirt and yanked them on, then he pulled his own gun out of its holster. There was another yell from outside, then two or three men's voices yelling drunkenly outside. Becca almost groaned; not a rescue after all. Probably just some lost hunters or more Nesters or something.

There was a loud bang on the side of the trailer and a cheerful whoop from outside. Oya cursed softly and walked to the door, gesturing to Leroy to follow her. The moment she opened the door, someone fell inside. "Oops, sorry about that! Wasn't paying attention to what I was doing." The dark-haired man gave them all a drunken, blissful smile.

He looked familiar. Becca squinted at him then stepped closer. He'd been with Molly at Shelly's house, she realized. There were a couple of other guys outside, all swaying a bit and wearing blaze orange. Somehow, she suspected they weren't quite as inebriated as they appeared to be. Relief washed over her. "You know what, I'm going to take the option to sleep on it after all. You gentlemen headed back to Wolf's Point, by any chance?"

The hunter gave her a wildly swinging bow, complete with flailing arms and Oya and Leroy were forced to step back. "It would be an honor to escort you, ma'am."

Becca blew out a quiet sigh of relief and nearly sprinted for the door. Oya grabbed her arms and Leroy stepped between them and the hunter. The medic kicked the door closed, knocking Molly's friend off his perch. Becca felt a sharp prick at her neck and she dropped to her knees with a groan. The trailer started to spin and go black as more yelling started up outside.

Silver Moon

Chapter 22

When she woke up, Becca was on the table where Scott had been lying. She tried flexing her arms only to find that she was now strapped in. There was a noise from the other side of the trailer, and she tried to go limp. Maybe they'd think she was still unconscious.

"She's awake," Oya's voice echoed strangely around in her head, like it was hollow. She couldn't quite remember what had happened once she had started for the door, but apparently the Nesters weren't going to let her lie around quietly while she figured it out. She opened one eye, then the other. The light was dim so it must be getting dark outside.

Oya was hanging over her. "Good. You're back with us. No one ever passed out like that after one of the shots before."

Now she remembered feeling the needle. Becca tried to summon the energy to spit at Oya. Sure, it was childish, but it might be the best opportunity she had. But her body felt like it didn't belong to her: all boneless limbs and labored breathing. And very, very dry mouth. "Some cure," she managed finally through lips gone desert-parched.

"Here." Leroy opened a water bottle and trickled some of its contents down toward her mouth. Most of it landed inside, which was good. The rest ran in rivulets down her jaw and into her collar. She shook her head in disgust and the room revolved slowly. She stopped moving.

"What are we going to do with her?" Leroy's voice was soft, as he stepped away from the table.

"She's one of us now. We'll train her up and use her against the wolves. This just shows that we're winning the war." Oya's voice echoed with anger and triumph, as if all of this should be perfectly obvious to one of her followers.

Silver Moon

"Are we? What happens if those hunters come back with more of their buddies and better guns? They were pretty pissed when they left and I don't think they bought your story about her being sick and contagious. Pete and Al went out on patrol last week and didn't come back. Stuart's arm is still messed up and most of us think he's not going to come back. And as for Scott and García, well, don't kid yourself too much about how cured they are. It's not a holy war for everyone, you know." Leroy sounded anxious and scared. It was enough to make Becca smile inside.

"Coward!" Oya hissed the word. "Do you think we've come this far to fail now? They'll stop changing, just like Scott and García did. We'll beat these bitches at their own game, then we'll stop all the others. No more monsters, remember, Leroy? That's our goal. And if you can't handle that, the door's over there."

"Yeah. Well, sometimes the monsters win." Leroy mumbled his comment, but Becca still picked it up. Did that mean that whatever they'd given her didn't mess with her wolf-augmented hearing? She sniffed the air experimentally. It didn't tell her much, just the not unexpected scents of unwashed room, sweaty restraints, some gun oil. But underneath all that, she thought she caught a whiff of wolf.

The realization thudded through her even as the scent disappeared. She tried to imagine changing, to remember running through the woods at night with the rest of the Pack, but while her brain remembered, her body did not. Instead, there was just an empty pit inside her. It felt like all wildness had gone into hibernation.

The worst of it was how alone she felt.

She could feel the tears start and she forced herself to swallow them. Oya was not going to see her cry and that was that.

It was clear that they kept arguing while she was lying there, awash in her own troubles until their raised voices finally broke into her thoughts. Then Leroy swore at Oya and there were heavy footsteps, followed by a slam as the trailer door closed behind him.

Oya's breath hissed out of her, but she seemed to remember that she wasn't alone. She appeared next to the table, her expression compassionate. "How are you feeling?" She rested one hand lightly on Becca's hair. Becca longed to bite it off.

Later. The thought popped up out of nowhere. She filed it away until she needed it and tried to focus on telling Oya what she wanted to hear. "I don't feel normal," was what she came up with. Her voice trembled with confusion as Oya's fingers began to stroke her hair.

The other woman's touch managed to be both soothing and unbearable, all at once. Becca took a deep breath and let it out in hopes that it would help her stay in control. "Why did you give me the cure, even when I said I wanted to think about it?" The whine in her voice sounded about right.

Oya smiled. "I could see that you were wavering, but I knew we could save you. And we did. We will. You'll see: it'll be better now. We'll keep helping you."

Lucky me. "When can I go home?"

Oya kept smiling. "Don't worry about a thing. Give me a minute and I'll send someone on a dinner run. You must be getting hungry by now." A final pat, and she disappeared out the door.

Becca summoned all her strength to try and break the restraints. They held. Then she tried twisting a bit on the table so she could see what was holding them closed. There was a buckle like something from a seatbelt, and another buckle on the other side. She was a lot smaller than Scott and whoever else they'd been tying down here so there was some slack in the belts. Some cautious wiggling finally let her pull a hand free.

She started to try to wriggle all the way out, then thought the better of it. Instead, she concentrated on lifting her head up and off the head-rest. Everything swam around for a few seconds until she lowered it again. Didn't look like she was quite ready for an escape attempt. That reminded her of the hunters who'd been there when Oya stuck the needle into her. What had happened to them? Leroy suggested they left but if they had come here looking for her once, they'd be back.

The door banged open again and Oya came back in, with Scott trailing at her heels. He was carrying something in a bowl in one hand and a water bottle in the other. "Here's dinner," Oya announced, as if that wasn't obvious. Becca saw Scott twitch, just a little. He set the bowl down on the countertop.

"Can we let her up? I'm not spoon-feeding her on top of everything else."

Oya looked as if she would have been just as happy to keep Becca strapped down, but after a moment, she nodded. "I think Becca might be ready to see the advantages to joining us."

Scott leaned over and unfastened her legs. "Really?" He breathed as he bent down close to enough to her ear to unfasten the strap holding down her arms. "Doesn't smell like it." Becca's lip curled over one of her incisors but she didn't growl. She wasn't sure she could right now.

But at least she was free. Scott helped her sit up, his hands rough on her arms. She swayed a little on the table, catching herself by grabbing the edge.

Silver Moon

Then she sat there for a long couple of minutes, looking down at her bare feet swinging above the grimy linoleum. Where the hell were her shoes?

A second horrible thought followed on the heels of the first. She squinted down at what she was wearing and let out a big sigh of relief when she saw a sweatshirt and sweatpants. At least it wasn't a hospital gown, open at the back to put all her cellulite on display. Clearly, things could be a lot worse. She raised her head slowly and Scott carried the bowl and the bottle over to table. He slammed them down on the metal shelf attached to the table and smiled when she flinched.

Becca looked back at him and bared her teeth. He laughed and she reached slowly and carefully for the water. It would be a while before she could manage to put any edge behind that gesture. But once she could, the Nesters were going to pay.

In the meantime, how was she going to get out of here? And as long as she was wondering about things, from what Leroy had said, it sounded like there weren't that many of them. Maybe not even enough to guard two separate camps. So where were they hiding Shelly?

She took a long drink, only remembering to wonder if they'd put more of the cure in the water after she'd swallowed. But once she'd given first the bottle, then Scott a long, suspicious look, she decided that it wasn't going to matter. It would wear off eventually for her, just like it was for Scott. She just had to wait it out. She nibbled on some cold and unappetizing chicken from the bowl.

Oya watched her eagerly, like she was some interesting new pet that the Nesters had acquired. "I knew you'd be hungry," she volunteered. A real smile darted across her face for a moment, making it light up. Laughlines crinkled around her eyes and her whole expression brightened.

Becca couldn't help thinking that she might like the Nester under other circumstances. Vastly different circumstances that she couldn't quite picture right now. Leroy opened the door and stepped inside and Oya's smile vanished like it had been erased. She didn't seem nervous about any of the men, but it looked to Becca like she thought she had to out macho them to keep them under control. Maybe she did. But it didn't rate amongst her many problems at the moment so there was no point in worrying about it.

"So did you manage to talk anyone else in Wolf's Point into trying your cure?" She had no idea if this would get anything out of them, but it was about as much sense as she could muster.

Leroy stiffened and got busy over by the counter. There was a lot of stuff to put away all of a sudden. Oya turned back to Becca and stepped closer to the table. She met Becca's stare nearly head on, but not quite. "No one else volunteered to try it, if that's what you mean."

She's lying but about which part of my question? "I don't remember volunteering either, somehow. So maybe the question is: did you make anyone else take it?" Becca could feel the tension ripple through the room now. Hopefully, it wouldn't inspire anyone to take it out on her. With any luck.

Scott's lip curled for a moment like he was going to say something but Oya caught his eye and he looked at the door. "I'll go relieve García."

"And I need a smoke." Leroy followed him out.

"Guessing that doesn't do any favors for your sense of smell," Becca murmured. All of a sudden, she was exhausted. Maybe there had been something in the food after all.

"He doesn't need a sense of smell for what he's doing. Get some sleep. The cure takes it out of you." Oya threw a blanket at her and she caught it, surprising herself with the automatic gesture. She'd never been good at catching things before. Oya didn't seem to notice. She hit the light switch on the way, dropping the trailer into darkness.

Becca collapsed back on the table. Just a little nap, then she'd see if she could sneak out. They couldn't stay awake all the time, right?

Silver Moon

Chapter 23

Whatever the noise outside was, it was enough to wake her up completely, heart pounding and all senses alert. She lay quietly in the darkness, listening as hard as she could.

And smelling. There were scents of metal and gun oil and Nesters outside. Beyond that, there were trees and mountains and small creatures scurrying through the brush, plus one or two familiar scents that her brain couldn't quite identify yet. But she felt better than she had that afternoon, almost as if she could get up and run if she had to. Becca smiled.

The sound, whatever it was, got a little louder. Becca twisted around to get under the restraints and dropped off the table into an awkward crouch on the floor. She lost her balance, barely catching herself with one hand braced on the floor, the other clutching the edge of the table. Her hands locked in place, holding her there until things stopped spinning and her heart slowed down a little.

Looking around, she could tell that her vision wasn't as good in the dark as it had been lately. The trailer was pretty dim; there wasn't enough moonlight to brighten up its gloomy insides let alone the clearing outside. Even so, she could see the countertop and the outline of the door. And the window, which was where the noise was coming from. She inched quietly across the floor toward it.

The scrap of cloth that served as a curtain moved a little, as if there was a draft in the room. Becca eased quietly over to the wall and kept creeping toward it, using the wall for support. Her hand connected with the same chair she'd thought about using as a weapon earlier and she picked it up once again, careful not to scrape the legs against the floor. Maybe she'd get to hit someone with it after all.

Silver Moon

The curtain moved again and this time, she heard a quiet click against the glass. Definitely not the wind then, not that there was much chance of that. The room swayed a little and she caught herself against the wall, nearly dropping the chair. Okay, so maybe she wasn't up to fighting anyone yet.

She stood slowly and leaned against the trailer wall. Whatever it was outside was tapping against the base of the window now, the sounds so quiet that she wondered if she would have been able to hear them before she started to change. Then the floor tilted under her feet and she shook her head to clear it. Damn Oya and her "cure."

Speaking of Oya, where was she? If Becca could hear the noises at the window, then she'd expect the other ex-wolves could hear it too. If they were quiet, did that mean that Oya and the Nesters were off somewhere else, like wherever they were holding Shelly? She thought about her alpha and shivered. If they had left this camp unguarded, they were almost certainly up to no good. Granted that was true even if they were still here. She sighed and tried to focus on the window.

It slid open with a quiet click. Then there was a long silence. Becca stretched her senses as far as they would go through the haze of the drug. A human was trying to get inside the trailer, but then she could have figured that out without any sense of smell at all.

There was more scraping outside and a hiss of breath. Then a louder sound somewhere outside, something that sounded like the heavy tread of boots on brush. That had to be a Nester.

There was dead silence from outside the window. Whoever was trying to get into the trailer clearly didn't want to attract Nester attention. *Well, the enemy of my enemy*, Becca thought and placed the chair down carefully. Holding the wall for support, she walked the last step to her goal.

By the sliver of light cast by the moon, she could see hands reaching upward to tilt the window out. They were big hands, pale, with slightly furry knuckles. There wasn't anything immediately familiar about them.

The rest of the body and the face were still hidden in shadows and bushes, or perhaps it was more aftereffects from the cure. Certainly the hands weren't very clear, even when she squinted and leaned down. There weren't too many options here: either she could scream and alert the Nesters, or she could try and help whoever it was come inside. Hoping that she wasn't making an awful mistake, Becca reached down and pulled.

And nearly got yanked out into the bushes herself. Startled, she backed away and peered down into the shadows, trying to figure out who she was looking at. The hands disappeared. Then she heard a man's shout, followed by a muffled curse from the person in the bushes. The Nesters would be here soon from the sound of it.

Becca let go of the window's edge for a moment and grabbed it again when she started to sway. If this person was here to help her, there was no way she was ready to escape yet. As softly as she could, she whispered, "I can't run yet. The drug is slowing me down." Whoever it was in the bushes was silent and very still.

Becca shrugged and turned away from the window as the sounds of men approaching got louder. Even if the mysterious hands didn't belong to a rescuer, she wouldn't let the Nesters catch them, on general principle if nothing else. She staggered over to the trailer door and threw it open. "What's a gal got to do to get some sleep around here?" She bellowed into the night. "Stop it with all the shouting!"

Scott appeared, seemingly out of nowhere. "What do you think you're doing? Why is the window open?"

"I can't get a little more air in here? Or you just afraid that I'll make a run for it?" Becca clutched at the doorframe and swayed, only slightly exaggerating. "How much running could you do after your first dose, Wolf Boy?"

Scott stepped forward, mouth twisted in a snarl. "Listen, bitch, I could…"

There was a blur as a fist met his face, seemingly out of nowhere. Oya stepped between them. Her back was turned to Becca but the set of her shoulders made it clear that she was ready for as much of a fight as Scott could offer. A low grumbling tore itself from her throat, as if it was more growl than she could hold back. Becca found herself watching for her fur to sprout and hackles to rise.

Scott stiffened and for a moment, it looked like he might take her up on it. His nostrils flared and Becca could see his hands clench into fists. His eyes seemed to flash wolf-silver for a moment, though Becca knew that was impossible. There wasn't enough moon for that and she was pretty sure no one could change after a recent dose of the drugs. But if Oya lost the fight, what would happen to her? To Shelly? She had a sinking feeling in her middle.

Then something shifted between the two adversaries, perhaps some expression on Oya's face that Becca couldn't see. Scott glared up defiantly for a few moments, then looked away. His body seemed to tremble. A moment later, his hands unclenched and his shoulders slumped, setting his jaw at a weird angle. It took Becca a second to realize that he was exposing his throat, but fighting the instinct that drove him to do it. Oya lunged, face thrust out, teeth bared in the quick glimpse that Becca caught.

Silver Moon

She stopped herself just short of his neck, and hung there a moment like she was enjoying his obvious discomfort as it turned to fear. "Don't do that again." She spoke the words with a degree of menace that made Becca shiver. Maybe she was more macho than the guys after all.

Becca wondered what she'd been like when she'd been part of the Pack, and all of a sudden it hit her. There was no way that she and Shelly could be in the same pack. She wondered how Shelly got to be alpha if she hadn't been Beta when Margaret died, and it had never occurred to her to ask. Now, Becca thought she could guess. It must have been one hell of a fight if Sara had stuck around for it.

Oya glanced away from Scott and the wolf in her eyes looked back at Becca. It sent a shiver down Becca's spine in a way that it didn't with the Pack, at least now that she was getting more used to it. Oya was one scary wolf when she changed; that much was obvious.

Then Oya turned and hit Scott in the stomach with one fist, full force, and he crumbled with a groan. Oya looked down at him for a moment, then away contemptuously. "García! Take this idiot away and dump him in your tent." The other Nester approached cautiously, his hands held low and empty. He didn't meet Oya's eyes, not even after she spoke again. "Let's make sure there isn't any more trouble tonight."

Something in the way she said it was enough to make Becca shiver even harder. Did that mean Scott's days were numbered? What about her own? Either one of them could be described as "trouble," at least the way this night was shaping up.

Oya looked at her over one shoulder. "Go back to bed. The cure will take a lot out of you for the next couple of days. I'll make sure you're not disturbed again." She turned away and followed García as he hauled the still groaning Scott toward the edge of the clearing and a distant tent.

Becca made herself close the trailer door and tried to ignore how much her hands were trembling. She fumbled at the latch in the dark, wondering if she could lock herself in. It felt loose so it was probably broken on this side of the door. But maybe she could prop the chair or something against it to block it. Then she thought about the size of Leroy and the other Nesters; it wouldn't even slow them down.

But one thing was clear: she had to get this junk out of her system and find a way to get out of here before things got worse. Maybe Erin and the others had found Shelly by now. She hoped that was true, but it seemed unlikely. Oya still seemed confident and in command. If she'd lost Shelly, it would be starting to show by now.

But there had to be a way. Becca just had to figure out how to ask the right question that would tell her where their other hideout was. Then get out of here and get back home with her answer.

But her head was hurting too much to think right now so she staggered back to the table, hoping that lying down for a few minutes would help. Everything still felt sort of odd and out of place, as if her body periodically belonged to someone else. And speaking of periods, wasn't she overdue for one? All the changing seemed to be messing with that, too and who knew what the cure would do on top of that.

She used the back of her hand to cover her eyes and groaned quietly. If she survived this, there was no telling what she'd be like when it was all said and done. She hoped for something benign but it didn't seem very likely. The way her luck had been running, she'd be transformed into some kind of completely weird new monster, neither wolf nor human.

The thought didn't make for pleasant dreams, though she did finally drop off into a restless doze. When her dreams started, they ran together like an old film reel. In one segment, she was running through the woods with the Nesters chasing after her and Oya in the lead. In another, she was chasing the Pack with the Nesters. She was the only wolf.

Each dream woke her briefly to lie staring into the dimness of the trailer for long seconds until her body dropped unwillingly back to sleep again.

The third time that she woke, she had been dreaming that she was in the Pack's cave. Magic filled the place, spilling over her in waves too powerful to ignore. She stretched her arms out like she was pulling all the power inside herself. It felt like her skin was glowing with it, like she might be able to float off the mountain. Then she looked down and saw her hands. They had become something not-human, not-wolf, unchanging and frozen in their form. The monstrousness of the transformation was enough to completely wake her up, gasping for air and grasping the table with white-knuckled fingers.

She tried to catch her breath but her heart was racing and her lungs were pulling in massive gulps of air like it was water. Water. Maybe that would help. She slid off the table and walked over to the counter, her steps steadier than they had been earlier. There had been a fridge, she was sure of it, and a faucet too.

Becca fumbled until she found the tap. She turned it and got a squeaky grind for her efforts, but nothing came out. She cursed softly and turned to the fridge. From what she'd seen of these guys so far, it probably just had beer in it. But she'd settle for that if it was cold.

Silver Moon

The fridge door opened easily enough but then she was left frozen in place, blinking at the sight inside. Trays of vials seemed to fill every shelf, each one full of a clear liquid. There were dates on the trays, though whether they were expiration dates or dosage dates, she couldn't tell. But there was enough here to dose the entire Wolf's Point Pack as well as Scott and his buddies for a couple of months at least.

She took a deep breath and started checking the dates. There seemed to be four vials missing from yesterday, at least as far as she could tell from the date system. That covered her and Scott, maybe Oya before Becca got to the camp. Who else were they giving this stuff to? Shelly?

There were also a couple of bottles of water in the door. She took one out and opened it while she studied the vials. This wasn't good. She hadn't really thought this through enough to realize that the Nesters might be close to mass-producing the stuff. Clearly, she'd have to get rid of the whole supply before she escaped. If she escaped. But that still left whatever lab they were using to create it in the first place.

Or maybe the formula was just in their heads. Her stomach churned a little at what that would mean. Wanting the Nesters to go away and leave them alone was still her goal, no matter what other Pack members might want. But what if that wasn't possible? Bloodshed had to be the last resort. She hoped.

So she was clear on what she wanted, it was just figuring out how to get there that was stumping her. Becca opened the bottle and drank slowly, letting the cold water clear her throat of the cure's after taste.

She hadn't even been aware that the stuff had a taste when she first woke up. But now that it was going away, she could feel its metallic weight on her tongue and throat. It reminded her of artificial strawberry flavoring, the really nasty kind that tasted nothing like real strawberries.

But there had been something under that. Garlic? No, that was for vampires. This was a peppery, gingery sort of taste, overlaid with several other flavors. She frowned, trying to think about what it might be and whether or not the liquid had any scent. The only way to find out was to open a vial and check, but somehow she didn't want to get any closer to the Nester cure than she needed to right now.

Instead, she walked over to the window and looked out. It was still open from earlier, which was surprising. But then with Oya fighting with Scott and who knew what else going on, it probably hadn't occurred to anyone to close it again. Dawn was beginning to break over the mountains and she took in a deep breath, her spirits rising despite her nightmares.

Then she glanced down into the bushes, wondering if she could see a trace of whoever had been there last night. A flicker of something pale caught her eye. There was a scrap of cloth tied to one of the bushes, its ends fluttering slightly in the air. She glanced around to see if there was anyone nearby. The clearing was deserted.

She reached out slowly, bracing herself on the window's metal edge, and pulled the cloth free. She palmed it and straightened up, fast enough that the movement made her head swim. Her knees buckled a little until she caught her breath. Then the momentary faintness passed.

Becca stepped back from the window. Was it too early for Oya to come and check on her? She shoved the cloth into her pocket until she got back to the table. Then she stretched out on her side, her back to the door so she could feign sleep if anyone looked in.

With trembling fingers, she pulled the cloth from her pocket and squinted at in the early morning light. There seemed to be something on it, lines of symbols that weren't quite words, or at least not any she recognized. It looked like it might be some kind of code. She brought it up a bit closer to her face and turned it back and forth to see if it looked any different from other angles.

On the third turn, she thought she recognized at least some of what she was looking at. There was a circle and a stick figure that looked like a dog, then something that might be a mountain with a dark blotch on it. Then there was a number 12. She turned it over again; the other side was blank.

Then she thought she heard something outside the door and hurriedly stuffed the message, back in her pocket. The thing that stood out was the 12. Was something going to happen at noon? Maybe. But midnight seemed more likely. If it was midnight, then the circle must be the moon.

The door opened quietly and she could smell Oya as she slipped into the room. She clamped her eyelids shut and tried to even out her breathing. Snoring might be too much but she did let her lower jaw flop open a little. She could hear Oya moving around near the countertop, then opening the fridge.

Becca tried not to hold her breath. What was the Nester leader doing? If she was going for more of the vials, who were they going to be used on? Shelly? From across the room, she could hear the clink of glass. Now she cursed the impulse that made her lie facing away from the door. She might have been able to see what was going on otherwise.

Oya paused and Becca concentrated on breathing and keeping her muscles relaxed. *Get kidnapped by werewolf hunters. It's cheaper than yoga.* She suppressed a nervous giggle.

Silver Moon

There was silence from the other side of the room, then the fridge door closed. Then there were steps going back to the door and Becca heard it open and close. But some suspicion kept her limp and quiet. After a few moments, a scrape of boot on the floor made her stiffen. Was Oya testing her? She decided it was time to find out.

She rolled over with a groan as if she was just waking up, giving the room a surreptitious glance as she stretched. Oya's eyes were bright despite the dimness in the trailer, nearly glowing as the Nester leader watched her from a few feet away. Becca faked a startled jump. "What are you doing over there?"

"I didn't want to disturb you but I thought you might be waking up soon. I brought you some clean clothes. There's a shower in there and breakfast will be ready soon." Oya tossed something onto the chair and walked out.

Great. And what happens after breakfast? Arts and crafts hour is probably too much to expect. She got up slowly, expecting the room to spin again but this time everything stayed pretty steady. The shower in the tiny bathroom was the size of a postage stamp and didn't look like the Nesters made cleaning it much of a priority but it felt good to get under the lukewarm water. Once she was washed up and dressed, with the message cloth carefully transplanted to the pocket of the new pants, she took a deep breath and opened the trailer door.

Outside, the sun was just coming up. Birds were twittering sleepily in the trees. And Leroy was cooking something she couldn't identify in a pan over an open fire. Oya nodded, "There's coffee on the picnic table."

Becca walked over to the big thermos, trying to look casual as she peered around. There were a couple of guys she didn't recognize talking near the trees some distance away, but no sign of Scott. She wondered if she could smell him if she tried, but then, her sniffing around might suggest that the cure wasn't as complete as they thought. Of course, after what she'd seen of Oya and Scott last night, she wondered how complete they really believed it was anyway. Given her thoughts, it didn't surprise her that when she sipped at her coffee, it was like mud, thick and bitter.

Oya grunted something at Leroy, then moved over to stand next to Becca. Becca forced herself to hold her ground and keep looking at the clearing, deliberately not meeting the Nester's eyes, just as if she couldn't feel the other woman boring a hole in her head with her stare. From the corner of her eye, she saw Oya's lips curl in what looked like amusement.

Slowly, Becca turned her head and met the other woman's eyes, and tried to ignore the churning in her gut. "Excellent. You're already breaking free of Pack indoctrination. I should have had your full attention the minute I walked up." Oya gave her a real smile, one tinged with anticipation. "I think we'll start training today."

"Training?" Becca wondered if she could make it to the trees before they caught her. One of the men walked toward them, the rifle at his back giving her the answer to her unspoken question. She wouldn't have a chance. Not without a distraction.

Oya nodded to the new arrival. "This is Anderson." He was a big man, a good foot taller than Becca, with shoulders like a linebacker. Aside from being big, he looked like he'd been living outdoors for a long time, long enough for his skin to turn to leather. Ice-cold dark eyes met hers from a nest of wrinkles and she couldn't suppress a shudder. If Oya was one kind of alpha, Anderson was another. And it was pretty clear that he thought he was looking at a monster. She had a good idea of how he dealt with monsters.

Oya touched his arm lightly, drawing his attention away from Becca, though she kept talking to her. "Anderson found me and helped me develop the cure after I left Wolf's Point." She smiled up at him, her face lighting up for the first time since Becca had known her. Anderson didn't seem to reciprocate, as far as she could tell. But then, he was back to studying her again. Becca didn't try to meet his eyes either, settling for staring at the bridge of his nose.

"She had her shot already?" he said finally, breaking a silence that threatened to collapse under its own weight.

"Yep. I wanted to start her on training as soon as possible." Oya trilled slightly. "We'll see how she does at that, then give her another dose next week or sooner if she needs it."

"Hmmm." Anderson didn't look too pleased as he turned away, but at least he was moving away.

Becca chugged at her coffee to try and hide her sigh of relief at his departure. But now she was worried about the "sooner" part. "So what's in the stuff anyway? And what happened to only needing a shot once a week?"

Oya smiled, her eyes glinting in the light. "The formula's a secret but the part that gives it the kick is wolfsbane." She shook her head. "Before I started taking it, I always thought that those old stories were full of it. Just goes to show that our ancestors knew what they were doing."

"Somehow, I don't remember Grandma ever mentioning 'wolfsbane' as a cure for anything. It sounds like it would be fatal." Becca didn't even like using the word; it made her think of the wolf hunting video up at the Wolf Preserve, the one they showed to demonstrate that the preserve was doing

Silver Moon

essential work. She'd never be able to hear about wolf hunting or trapping the same way again.

"Well, your grandma probably had a different set of priorities than the ones around here." Oya's lips curved in a slight smirk.

Becca managed to not hiss at her. Maybe it was time to play all her cards and see what happened. "You know, you still haven't told me what happened to Shelly."

Oya gave her a sidelong look as a sly expression settled over her features. "Happened to her? Why?"

"Well, she wasn't at the store and Pete was looking for her, right? I just figured maybe you had something to do with it," Becca reached over and picked up a roll from a grimy platter that sat on the table next to the coffee. There was no butter to be seen anywhere nearby. She gnawed a small bite off the end and choked it down.

Oya was looking away, apparently at Anderson, judging from the angle. "Why do you care?"

"Well, I've known her a few years. I'd like to know that she's okay. If she's with you, that is," Becca studied Oya, noting subtle changes in body language. The other woman was trying too hard to look relaxed, innocent. There was a second when she blinked too much, another when her fingers nearly curled into a fist then were slowly stretched out.

Shelly was out here and being held somewhere nearby. That had to be it. So that just left figuring out where and how to get her rescued. Becca wasn't going to consider any other possibilities.

"She's not here so let's not worry about that right now. We need to get started on training." Oya said and walked away with a jerk of her head that indicated Becca should follow. After a moment, Becca did.

Chapter 24

By evening Becca wished she hadn't gone with Oya. Not that it had looked like she had that much choice in the matter this morning, of course. Right now, she was hoping that her shoulders would stop screaming sometime soon. And that there would be a dinner worth eating. Neither one of those things seemed likely.

Becca sat on the edge of the table and tried to stretch her arms out. A few moments of experimentation made it clear that wasn't the best idea. She gasped as a new sharp pain danced up her neck. Her state of mind wasn't improved by watching the trailer door bang open to admit Leroy and Oya. He went straight for the fridge and emerged from behind the counter with a syringe in his hand.

Oya moved over to stand very close to Becca, the muscles in her arms twitching a little, at least to Becca's addled wolf senses. It was pretty clear what was going to happen next and every cell in Becca's body screamed at her to fight or run, preferably both. The breath caught in her throat, leaving her gasping. "What the hell are you doing? You just gave me a shot!"

"There's nothing to be afraid of," Oya was nearly purring. "It looks like you needed a refresher, just to make sure it's taking."

Leroy filled the needle from the bottle in his other hand and Becca scrambled off the table, just ahead of Oya's grab for her arm. "Shit! I told you we should have strapped her in first!" Leroy snarled the words as he put the full needle back down on the counter.

"Wait a minute." Oya held up her hand. "Come on, Becca. You know you want this. The shots will make you all better. No more turning into a monster, remember? That's a good thing."

Becca panted, glancing from Leroy to Oya, then back again as she waited for them to make their move. This was just nuts. There was no way she could get away from the two of them in here and she didn't have a prayer of fighting them off. She shifted sideways, her hip hitting the chair. The window was still open, or at least it felt like there was a breeze against her back.

But Leroy was nearly at the table and Oya was beginning to circle around it. There wasn't going to be enough time to get out the window, open or not. But she had to try. Instinctively, she grabbed for the chair and hurled it at the glass. It bounced off with a loud crack and she felt a pang of pure despair.

Then part of the glass came loose and tumbled to the floor, shattering. The noise and motion made Leroy and Oya each take a step back. Becca lunged for the opening, her muscles screaming at this new effort. She clutched the window frame and started to jump out only to feel her legs get caught and held. "Oh no, you don't," Leroy muttered as he dragged her back into the trailer.

Almost on cue, Anderson charged through the door. "What the hell's going on in here?"

"Nothing!" from Oya and "Escape attempt" from Leroy, spoken at the exact same moment.

Anderson looked at Becca hanging limp in Leroy's grasp. "Told you that you should kill that one. She'll never really turn."

Oya paled, but before Becca could plead for mercy, the Nester leader stepped forward. "No. This is my fault. I was careless. She's a new wolf. You remember how hard that is." Oya's voice quivered a little. "You don't know who or what to trust. I thought we were done winning her over and we weren't."

"Which is why she gets strapped down now," Leroy grunted as he heaved Becca up on to the table. She squirmed and kicked but he was too fast for her, and the straps soon clicked in place. Becca bit her lip to keep from crying.

It didn't look like that would help anyway. The minute she was fastened down, Leroy went for the syringe. She could feel a single tear trickle down her cheek. If last night was any indication, she'd be too disoriented to try and escape tonight either, even with help. But she was damned if she was going to give them more than that tear. Grimly, she clenched her teeth together, closed her eyes and waited for the needle.

Something outside made a noise, some sound that cried out for her attention, but she made an effort to ignore it. Whatever it was, it couldn't help her now. She'd have to just figure out a way to get away from them on her own, somehow. And the easiest way to do that was to play along. Becca took a deep, shuddering breath and opened her eyes.

Oya was still standing close to her, though now she seemed to be standing between Anderson and the table. *All to the good*, Becca thought briefly, then cleared her throat. "You're right. I was overreacting. I don't like the way the cure makes me feel." She paused between her words, trying to make them sound sincere, if hesitant.

Oya glanced back and flashed her a relieved smile. She shifted slightly and Leroy stepped forward, clearly unwilling to cross between her and Anderson. Instead, he walked carefully around them to approach the table from the far side. The noise outside, when it came again a moment later, was much closer and louder this time.

Anderson scowled at the window. "Don't you set any guards on this place? Or was that assigned to one of your wolf-boys?" He tossed the words in Oya's direction, but was on his way out the door before she could respond.

Oya yanked the gun from her belt and raced after him, leaving Leroy and Becca staring after them both. After a moment, the medic shrugged and yanked up Becca's sleeve. Something inside her took over and she jerked away from his grasp, her body twisting in a fierce convulse jerk that broke her legs free of the restraints. She kicked out fiercely, forcing Leroy back. Another sharp twist and she slid down the table, out of the upper restraints as well.

When she hit the floor in a crouch, she could feel, ever so faintly, her body start to change. And a hot flash, which was almost inevitable. Leroy stepped back, putting the table between them. They stared at each other for a long couple of seconds as if they were both wondering what was going to happen next.

The gunshots outside answered that question for them. Something pinged sharply against the side of the trailer and Leroy hit the floor, rolling past the table. He disappeared behind the countertop, gun in hand, while Becca pressed herself against the wall, trying to watch the kitchen and the window at the same time. It sure wasn't midnight, so what was going on outside?

Her heart was racing, sending the blood pounding through her head as she felt a wave of heat wash over her. *Breathe*, she thought, *breathe*, forcing her body back under her own control. The wolf was still coming though. She could feel the beginnings of fur, here and there along her arms and her fingers were longer than they should have been. It wasn't too hard to figure out what would happen if Anderson came back through the door. If he thought she was a monster before, this would be her death sentence.

When she gathered herself up and jumped through the window this time, there was no one to grab her legs. The bushes outside hurt when she landed in a tangle of limbs though. Fortunately, there were more shots and a lot of yelling to cover the noise that she made. She untangled herself and rubbed at a few bleeding scratches while she looked around. It was hard to see what was going on from this angle; all the action seemed to be on the other side of the trailer.

She wondered if it was Erin, trying to rescue her. The idea gave her a momentarily warm, happy feeling until she remembered that could get Erin killed. At the same time, she couldn't imagine who else the Nesters could have pissed off around here, if whoever was firing back at them wasn't the Pack. She ventured a cautious peek out of the bushes. It didn't look like there was anyone nearby. If she ran to the nearest stand of trees, she might be able to look around and see what was going on.

Before she could think too hard about what might happen if this was a bad idea, she rolled out of the bushes and ran awkwardly across the short open stretch into the trees, keeping her head low. Something pinged by, shattering bark down on her head and she threw herself to the ground under the first tree, scrambling to get it between her and the shooters. More bullets flew by, sending a cascade of bark and twigs down on her and she bolted.

She charged almost blindly in her panic, barely noticing the trees she ducked behind or the bushes she tried to use as cover. There was more noise behind her: yelling, more shots, the sound of someone or several someones crashing into the brush. Becca kept running.

Chapter 25

Finally, the noises behind her faded away. The minute she could, she collapsed behind some rocks that provided some cover and panted, her lungs burning like they were going to jump out of her chest. The fact that she'd made it this far made her grateful that she'd gone on all those evening runs with Erin.

Erin. And the Pack. Had she left them behind in terrible danger? Or did the Nesters have other enemies? Even she felt like shooting at them right now, so it wouldn't be too surprising if someone else did too. But if the Pack had been planning to come back at midnight, maybe it was the hunters coming back with reinforcements.

Since she couldn't do anything about it on her own, she needed to get back to Wolf's Point or get to a phone and try get in touch with Erin and the rest of the Pack. When she could breathe again, she raised her head cautiously to look around and sniff the air. All of her senses seemed to be coming back to life, though still weaker than she thought they'd been before the injection. For instance, she could smell a car or truck on the highway and that couldn't be that close, could it? She kept testing the air, checking for water now as much as for pursuers.

Wherever she was, it was well outside Wolf's Point. Her panicked run had taken her up into the foothills and a little beyond. Once she poked her nose around the rocks, she realized that she could see what appeared to be a ranch in the valley as well as a glimpse of road. The scent of pine came to her on the breeze, mingled with the smell of sheep dung and she wrinkled her nose.

On the other hand, where there were sheep, there were people. People who could direct her to a phone and help. But how did she know it was

Silver Moon

safe to leave her hiding spot? What if the Nesters were just being really quiet and waiting for her? Maybe she should just hide here until full dark.

She shook her head after a moment; hiding wasn't going to help. One way or the other, she had to get back to town and let them know what was going on. She squinted up at the setting sun, trying to gauge the best direction to move in. Then she slipped out from behind the rocks, slithering on her belly as she looked around for motion, for color or anything else that would tell her whether or not she was safe.

A hawk swooped down on to the rocks above her, making her flinch. But that was it. Of course, most of the Nesters wore brown camouflage and would probably blend in with the rocks, but she decided not to think too hard about that possibility. Instead, she pulled herself up into a crouch and ran, crablike, over to a nearby boulder. One thing was certain: if she got home in one piece, she was going to need a chiropractor.

Thinking about her cozy little house made her remember Ed. And Pamela. If they'd pulled anything with the house while she was gone, she'd…she'd…deal with them when she got back. Her lip curled slowly over a dry incisor.

That helped remind her that she needed to find water soon. Very soon, from the headache that was beginning to pound in her temples. Her stomach growled along with it, reminding her to check her hands and face. At least her fingers looked normal now. It was a relief to know that she wouldn't scare anyone she came across to death. It also made the notion of hunting a rabbit and ripping into it with her fangs less appealing. She remembered the idea crossing her mind when she was running and it sent a hungry shiver up her spine.

Two more boulders and she was on her way down the mountain, moving westward. The sun had nearly set so she hoped that her wolf sight was coming back. If not, she might have to wait the night out here and hope for the best come morning. It wasn't a very appealing idea.

At least she was more surefooted now than she had usually thought of herself as being. She stepped lightly and quickly around the loose rocks and tiny shrubs until she got to the first stand of trees. Then she stopped to taste the air again. The road was more or less ahead of her, the sheep somewhere off to her right. It was hard to tell from smell alone which was the better bet for getting help and she hesitated before picking the road. With any luck, the Nesters were still too preoccupied to patrol around by van.

But she'd have to be on her guard. She kept walking, and after a few moments, was rewarded by the smell of water ahead. Crossing her fingers against giardia, she stumbled across a tiny little stream and knelt, scooping the water into her hands and gulping it down as quickly as she could. It was wonderful, cold and refreshing. She lay next to it for a couple of minutes and took a few more drinks. Then she got to her feet and kept walking.

The road was closer than she'd thought and she stumbled a little when her feet unexpectedly met the pavement. A quick glance up and down didn't show any glow of distant or even not so distant headlights. Just her luck, there also weren't any road signs visible from where she was standing, so she still had no idea of where she was.

After looking around in frustration for a few minutes, she picked the direction that she thought led away from the Nester camp and toward town and started walking along the side of the road. She tried to hug the tree line but it was hard with the ditches and roadside weeds. After ten minutes, she gave up and went out to the edge of the pavement. It was full dark now, so with any luck she'd have plenty of warning if a car was coming.

It felt like she'd been walking for hours on her achingly tired legs. The road didn't seem to be going anywhere and she had to stop and rest a few times. What if she was headed in the totally wrong direction? It was hard to smell much of anything besides asphalt. Her thoughts kept up a constant whirl of frantic motion that didn't help her headache much. Her body felt odd, too, stretched and strange, quite apart from the aches and pains.

But at least there was a not quite full moon tonight. It made her insides flutter to see it glowing over the trees, calling to her wolf self. She smiled at it like she would at seeing an old friend in an unexpected location. With moonrise, her luck seemed to be improving: up ahead, she could make out a sign, though it was still too dark to read from this distance.

Without thinking, she broke into a lope and sped over to it, only to feel a crushing sense of disappointment. Wolf's Point was still another fifteen miles away. But at least she was on the right road. That was something, though it didn't bring much comfort.

She forgot to check the road behind her when she started walking again. The headlights were bright as a sudden sunrise when they came and she leapt off the road into the ditch like a wild thing. Then she lay flat and still in the shallow puddle of water that filled it. Maybe the driver hadn't seen her or at least wouldn't get out to check.

Her heart leapt up into her ears while she listened for the approaching vehicle. Every breath she drew in seemed to choke her. With her luck, she was probably having a heart attack. She tried to center herself but the sound of the car above slowing down made that a fruitless effort.

Silver Moon

Wheels scraped on some loose gravel on the road. Whoever they were, they were stopping. Becca bit back a curse. She had no way to defend herself if it was the Nesters. They could just shoot her, dump her in the back of whatever they were driving and take off if they wanted to. The notion took her from scared to angry in less than a minute. In fact, she felt really angry. Angry enough to change. She dug her fingers into the mud beneath her to try and control it.

A car or truck door opened in the darkness above her. First there was silence. Then loud whispers. "Did you see someone? It might have been—"

"I'm not sure I saw anything. Try and call her again."

"Becca? Are you out there?"

Becca was panting in the ditch now, trying not to change. She knew that voice, didn't she? She tried to make herself listen harder, tried to pick up any familiar scents. But the last couple of days were catching up with her. She was exhausted and with that, losing control, losing her human self.

The few shreds that were staying awake tried hard to stay alert. At first, there was just the scent of swamp water, vehicle exhaust and pavement. Then, slowly, there was a whiff of something that just might be wolf. Her kind of wolves.

The whimper that tore itself out of her throat wafted up into the air over her head, followed by a soft howl that was too big for her body to contain. The ditch spun around slowly and she felt everything start to go black at the same time that someone, then more someones splashed down into the ditch around her.

"Becca! Hey, open your eyes and look at me. C'mon, hon," A familiar voice emerged from a body which smelled very familiar. Whoever it was picked her up.

"Get her to stop it. How the hell is she doing that?" The other voice sounded familiar too.

"Give her a minute, will you? We don't know what they did to her. Becca, honey, are you still with us?"

That made her force her eyes open, blinking groggily in the moonlight. Erin and Molly were looking down at her and someone else was leaning over the side of the ditch. She wasn't sure who the other person was, but it didn't matter right now. She was back among friends.

Then Erin was pulling her up onto her shoulder and dragging her up to where Molly and the other person could pull her out. Becca blinked at the surprised looking guy on the road and realized that he was holding a fur-covered hand. It took a minute more to realize that it was attached to her arm. She staggered forward, pulling free of his grasp and collapsed against the side of the truck.

Molly and Erin came up out of the ditch, and Molly reached into her pocket and pulled out an energy bar. Wordlessly, she took the wrapper off and handed it over. Becca blinked at it, then at her hand. She tried to remember what her fingers looked like over the sudden fierce, animal growls coming from her stomach. She snatched the bar from Molly's fingers and devoured it.

"Becca, are you ready to rejoin the human world? At least for the time being?" Erin was standing in front of her now, and the wolf wasn't looking out of her eyes. Molly also looked human and as near as Becca's addled senses could tell, the guy *was* human. She also recognized him as the library assistant from the meeting at Shelly's.

Wouldn't want to be the odd one out at the party, she thought, trying to piece the words together from the fuzz in her brain. She closed her eyes and squeezed her hands into fists, wincing as her claws met her palms and tried to force herself back to human.

Deep, shuddering breaths later, she looked up. They were all still staring at her. Finally, Erin said, "It's okay. Let's get you to safety and see what a night's sleep does. You drive, Carlos." She nodded to the guy and tossed him the keys from her pocket.

Then she reached out for Becca's arm in what looked like slow motion. "Lean on me. I'll help you get into the truck." Becca didn't so much lean as slump. A distant, weary portion of her brain wondered what her feet looked like, but she couldn't bring herself to look down. Instead she fell into the truck's back seat, then scrambled over to make room for Erin.

Erin slid in carefully. "Can you talk?"

Becca stared at her in amazement. Of course, she could talk. Why wouldn't she be able to talk? She reached up. Her furry hand met the fur of her elongated jawline, then followed it out to a wolf-human hybrid nose. *Oh.* She tried to form a "Yes." It came out as a guttural hiss, swiftly followed by a whimper.

"Oh, hon, it's okay." Erin enveloped her in a careful, slow-moving hug. "They used that 'cure' of theirs on you, didn't they?"

Becca nodded, trying to convey her misery with gestures. It was obvious that she wasn't communicating much beside her mood. Molly leaned back and patted her knee while Erin rubbed her shoulders. Becca sat still and tried to think soothing nonwolfy thoughts. Her body still felt weird, though a bit more menopausal human weird, rather than wolf/human hybrid weird.

Silver Moon

But the fur didn't recede much. And they were getting closer to Wolf's Point. Erin realized the problem before Becca had to try and signal her fears. "Hey Carlos, I don't think we should head through town with Becca looking like this. Our luck, someone's bound to notice and this'll be hard to explain away. Let me call Pete and tell him that we found her." Her phone beeped as Carlos pulled over.

Molly seemed to be dozing in her seat now and Becca envied her that. If she could only relax enough to sleep, she might go back to normal, whatever that was. Erin was talking to Pete on her phone, so she leaned back against the seat and closed her eyes, not really listening. It would all be okay. Now they just had to find Shelly.

Thinking about Shelly made her remember the vials. It was possible they'd used the other missing bottle on someone besides Shelly. Maybe there were more ex-wolves with them than she'd seen so far. Unless they were giving one of the ex-wolves multiple doses like they'd tried to do with her?

Erin clicked off the phone. "Pete says to bring her there. You up for a bit more driving?"

Carlos glanced back. "Sure. She doing any better?"

Erin gave Becca a long look, as if she was searching for improvements. Becca wasn't too sure she saw any but guessed that she would say something optimistic anyway. "Yep, I think she's starting to shake it off. But since we don't know how long it will take, we better get her somewhere safe and quiet to finish recovering."

Becca tried to smile at her, then thought the better of it. She reached out and very carefully squeezed Erin's hand instead. It seemed to her as if Erin was reluctant to let go after she squeezed back, but there was no way Becca was leaving her hanging on to some mutant fur-covered mitt and she tugged free. At least she had somewhere to go tonight. It didn't feel like a good time to be alone.

She let her thoughts drift a little and as Carlos headed up to Pete and Shelly's place, she fell asleep.

Chapter 26

She didn't recognize where she was when she woke up. The sensation was becoming irritatingly familiar. Light was pouring through thin curtains covered with some kind of cartoon characters. Becca squinted at them for a moment, then rolled over to look at the rest of the room.

There were posters from some band she'd never heard of, stuffed animals and a CD collection that seemed much bigger than hers. She let out a quiet sigh of relief. Wherever she was, it wasn't the Nesters' trailer so that was a good start.

Her thoughts were still a jumbled mess but she was remembering now that they'd been headed up to Pete and Shelly's place. This must be one of the kids' rooms, probably Kira's. A wave of guilt swept through her. She'd shown up at some crazy hour and wakened the whole household and then had to be carried inside, since she didn't remember walking. And then Kira had to give up her room to accommodate her on top of all that.

Clearly, the sensible thing to do was to get up, clean up and go apologize. She looked instinctively at her hands, holding them up to the window to make sure they were normal again. Her nails looked long and scraggly and there was more hair on the backs of her fingers than she remembered, but otherwise they seemed close enough to human to pass. The stuff must be working its way out of her system.

She still went to the mirror on the far side of the room to examine her face before she opened the door. What she saw there sure wasn't the same woman from a couple of months ago. For one thing, she had a jaw that was a bit longer and fuzzier than it should be. But at least it wasn't a muzzle. She also had huge circles under her eyes and a few new wrinkles.

On the other hand, though, she looked more confident and her gaze was more direct. She stood a little straighter and her complexion seemed

Silver Moon

to be clearing up. Maybe there were some good points to everything she'd been going through.

She noticed that there were some clean clothes folded up on the chair behind her. Whoever had put her to bed had taken the muddy things she'd been wearing but left her in her underwear. Even without wolf senses, she was smelling pretty ripe so she wondered who got stuck with undressing her. But there was time enough to worry about that later. Shower and clean clothes before apologies, she thought as she wrinkled her nose.

At least she was steadier on her feet than she had been when she woke up at the trailer. The floor still seemed a little uneven as she picked up the clothes and made her way to the door, but nothing that might not really be there. Of course, finding Erin on the other side when she opened it was kind of startling. "Oh! Hi!" Becca could feel herself blushing though she wasn't really sure why.

Erin smiled down at her, her expression suggesting relief as much as anything else Becca could read into it. "You're doing better, I see. I realized I forgot to leave a towel and basic toiletries with the clothes." She handed Becca a small armload of things that included a new toothbrush, still in its package. "We'll be downstairs when you're ready."

Becca watched her walk away in bemusement. She really did think of just about everything. It made for interesting thoughts while Becca showered. She had to admit, it was getting easier to get used to Erin being in her life. It took her a moment to realize that she was running her fingers over her lips and remembering their kiss. She jerked her hand away and went back to vigorous scrubbing.

The hot water had almost run out by the time she turned it off, the water trickling its way down to a mellow warmth from the steaming heat she'd started with. It was time to get out and face the music. Or at least the other wolves and Shelly's family, which amounted to the same thing. Whatever she decided to do about her feelings for Erin, they could wait for a little bit longer.

That thought was uppermost as she came down the stairs into Pete and Shelly's front room. A ring of faces peered up at her, making her start and pause momentarily. It hadn't occurred to her that she'd have an audience for breakfast. But then, it was probably easier than trying to talk to everyone individually. Maybe.

Pete walked in from the kitchen as she got to the last step and plunked a big pot of coffee down on the dining room table. There were a few platters of food, most of them half-full of what looked like different kinds of meat. Becca's mouth watered the way that it never seemed to for, say, broccoli these days.

Erin cleared her throat. "After you've grabbed some coffee and some food, Becca, I'd like you to tell us what you can about the Nesters." She turned back to the group sitting on the two sofas and said something that didn't register with Becca. The grogginess that she'd been feeling the last few days seemed to be lingering.

Instead of listening, she took stock of who was in the living room, almost like she hadn't seen them before: Molly, Pete, Mrs. Hui (one of these days she was going to have to ask what her first name was, once she worked up the nerve), Gladys, Carlos and two or three more folks whose names she couldn't remember or never knew.

She wondered where Lizzie and Adelía were and why Gladys was there. It was hard to picture her tactless and taciturn neighbor as a leader in the Pack. But so it went; at least she was reliable. She realized that she was being a little mean. The thought made her feel even guiltier and she glanced around for Kira to make her apologies for kicking her out of her room.

Erin beckoned her over, breaking into her thoughts. Becca chugged half a cup of coffee, grabbed a plate of food and took the empty seat between the couches that they'd left for her. Everyone looked expectantly at her. *They think I know where Shelly is.* The thought was like a punch to the gut, especially when she saw the hopeful look on Pete's face.

She made herself look away as she started talking. "I'm guessing you know that Oya took me with her to see the 'proof' of the Nesters' cure. So I drove her up to their camp outside town, somewhere in the foothills. I think I can find it again, though I don't know for certain. She also said there were other camps, though that might have been a lie."

Becca paused and grabbed a bite of sausage. She kept talking, even though her mouth was full. *So much for my manners.* "I made sure to rub my hands against some of the rocks and trees on the way in. I was hoping that would be enough to mark the trail." She glanced around, relieved to see some approving nods. It might be a help, if she couldn't remember the exact route.

She took them back through everything that had happened up to Leroy injecting her, including the drunken hunters. Carlos shifted a little and she realized where she'd seen him before. "That was you!" He blushed a little and looked at his feet as she caught his hand. "Thank you for trying. It wasn't your fault they dosed me anyway. Did you come back for the gunfight yesterday?"

Silver Moon

Carlos smiled a little warily. "It wasn't exactly a gunfight. A couple of us were checking out the area because we were going to go back at midnight to try to get you out. The trigger-happy Nester assholes started firing at us, so we fired a few shots back. Then they got distracted by some kind of explosion on their side and we got out of there."

Erin made an impatient face at the interruption and Becca hurried to continue with her story. "The bad part is that I never saw Shelly. I couldn't get them to tell me where they were holding her either. I'm so sorry, Pete." He rubbed one large hand over his eyes and Becca wanted to sink into the carpet.

She'd wanted to be a hero this time, she realized that now. Or at least to be the one helping her friends out instead of the other way around for a change. But more importantly, she wanted this part to be over with, for Shelly and Pete to be back at the store and her to be working and everything back more or less the way it had been.

Instead, Erin was hugging Pete and everyone was looking everywhere but at each other. Finally, Mrs. Hui broke the silence, "Do you think they were holding her somewhere nearby? You said you thought there were fewer of them than we feared."

Becca rubbed her chin in thought. "I'm not sure. I know there seemed to be more of them when we attacked the camp than there were around the trailer. But if they have a second camp somewhere else, the rest of them could have been there. I wish I knew more!" She slammed her fist against her knee as the sense of frustration overwhelmed her.

"Whoa!" Molly jumped back, staring at Becca's hand. Becca couldn't help but notice that she put her arm up in front of Carlos, like she was protecting him.

"Becca!" Erin's voice barked across the room, her tone as full alpha as Becca had ever heard it. "Get that under control."

Becca stared at the fur-covered hand on her knee like she was trying to bend spoons with her mind or something. She could feel tears welling up, then running down her face, and she rubbed her eyes angrily with her other hand. How was she supposed to stop this? Now she felt silly as well as out of control.

Erin cleared her throat and looked away. "All right. We need to figure out where Shelly is. Some of us will need to go looking for the camp where they held Becca. Maybe we can find a clue on where their other camp is. Do you think you can get the aftereffects under control in a few hours?" She leaned forward, her eyes holding Becca's once more. "I wouldn't ask this of you if we had other options."

Becca sank into her gaze, forgetting that they had an audience for just long enough to be slightly embarrassing. It was hard to find the words. "Um…I think I can. I'll try." She glared down at her errant hand as a thought struck her. "Hey, they still have my car!"

Gladys smothered a snort of a laugh and Becca glared at her. But at least she didn't growl or feel like she was going to go full were, at least not more than she already had. Maybe she could beat this in a few hours after all. The tears receded in a wave of new-found resolve.

Looking around, she realized that the group's attention had shifted. Erin was giving out assignments and she'd missed the first few. "…Molly, you go to the Nesters' site with Gladys, Mei, and Becca. Take whoever else you need. Lizzie said she'd come when we called her so make sure you get in touch with her before you get out of range."

Carlos raised his hand and Erin gave him a surprised nod in response. "Me and Jason want to go in too. You might need some cover and we could definitely provide that. Besides, we don't want to sit around worrying." He gave Molly a crooked grin.

Erin nodded slowly. "That makes sense. You can help Becca locate the camp. Pete, can you stay here and be our base again tonight? We'll all meet back here as soon as we can." At his answering grunt, she got up, brushing her pants off and grabbing her bag from behind the couch.

"Where are you going?" Becca blurted the question, wondering a second too late if Erin had already said it while she'd been daydreaming.

"I need to go talk to the Circle about how to use the valley's magic." Erin gave her a swift smile, then looked stern as she turned away.

Wait! Didn't Shelly say that was dangerous? Becca wasn't willing to ask the question out loud. After all, everything they were doing was dangerous. Besides, Erin hadn't actually said she was going to try it, just ask about it. All the same, she couldn't say that she liked the feeling she got watching Erin walk out the door.

But there was other work to do. Speaking of which, she'd had a job a few days ago. It was probably time to ask whether or not she still had one. "Pete, who's minding the store?"

"Kira. I don't think you're quite ready yet," Pete nodded at her hand, nearly, but not quite furless now.

Becca blew out her breath in frustration. She'd have to ask for a lift home, then asked to get picked up again if she didn't stay here. What was she supposed to do for the next couple of hours while she tried to get herself back to normal?

Silver Moon

Molly supplied the answer by dropping some maps and aerial photos in front of her. "Let's try and get a bead on where they're at. Here's where we picked you up…" Becca wondered briefly why she didn't ask Carlos but Molly seemed so focused, she didn't get around to asking that question.

Molly kept her so busy with planning that Becca didn't notice when most of the group left, then trickled back in a few hours later with additions. They came back with equipment: flashlights, backpacks, food packages and a several guns. "Do we really need those?" Becca asked without thinking. Everyone looked at her like she was growing fur. She checked: nothing new so far. "Never mind. I suppose we might." Which didn't make her like them any more than she usually did.

"Got the radios?" Molly took a bag from Adelía, and at her nod, started handing out what looked like walkie-talkies. That made sense, Becca realized, seeing as they'd be heading out past the town's cell-phone coverage area.

Her group headed out in three vehicles, looking for all the world, Becca thought, like one of those military convoys on TV. Except that they weren't driving jeeps or anything like that. Still, it didn't feel quite right, the way they were doing this. They should be running through the woods, hunting their prey by smell and sound and sight, guarding the valley the way the original inhabitants had intended. Guns and jeeps and GPS weren't weapons for wolves.

Of course, neither were explosives and she'd tried to use those herself against the Nesters not too long ago. It made her wonder why Oya would want to kill her one night and save her the next. A lot of what the Nester leader was doing didn't make much sense, at least not as far as she could see. But then, maybe if they could get her "uncured," she'd go back to whatever normal was for her and figure it out. That was the point where they cleared town and Molly looked to her to find the way. Becca tried to focus on that on the drive out.

Chapter 27

The trip back up seemed to go a lot slower than it had the first time. This time around, Becca was looking at every single dirt road turnoff, wondering if it was the right one or not. She thought she remembered checking the mileage when she drove Oya out here, but what if she remembered wrong?

"Here!" She said, almost without thinking. Then after the second false alarm, "No, wait. Damn, it all looks so much alike!" She could feel a flash coming on and a trickle of sweat ran down her hairline.

Molly blew her breath out into her bangs, clearly swallowing her frustration. "Okay, Becca. I'm going to pull over. How about you get out and check things out? The smells might get you to the right place sooner than looking out of a car window."

Becca nodded. It couldn't make her feel any worse than she already did about this. And the longer they took, the more likely it was that the Nesters would disappear to who knew where. If they were taking off, they might decide to hurt Shelly. She remembered the coldness in Anderson's eyes and shivered.

Molly pulled over and Becca got out and walked away from the car. Once the smell of asphalt and gas was less overwhelming, she took a deep breath, then another. She looked up the dirt road in front of them, trying to remember all the twists and turns they'd taken on the way in. Then she caught something, a scent not quite wolf, not quite human and her whole body tensed like she was going on point.

Molly was out of the car in a whirl of limbs. "You got something, don't you?" The anticipation in her voice lent weight to every word. Becca took another breath and nodded cautiously. Molly clapped her on the shoulder, "Good job!" She turned and signaled to the third car as it pulled up, gestur-

Silver Moon

ing it up to the next turn off. If they spread out the vehicles, Molly hoped they might be a little less noticeable to anyone watching.

Becca thought that any vehicles parked by the side of the road around here might tip them off. The Nesters had to be more alert than that, didn't they? But she didn't have a better idea and this could still be the wrong road. There was no way to find out except to head up there and take a look. She inhaled again, feeling the wolf stir inside her. Side effects or no side effects, someone should take the woods while the others took the road. They were less likely to be surprised that way.

She caught Molly's eye as the thought crossed her mind. The other woman gave her a surprised look, her expression shifting slightly toward what looked like fear. But if she was scared, she got it under control fast. As the group assembled around them, she gave Becca a quick nod. Then she drew everyone's attention to herself while Becca slipped away.

Mrs. Hui gave her a curious glance as she faded into the trees, then looked deliberately away. *Had to say something for Pack discipline*, Becca thought. Even if she hadn't managed to embrace it herself yet. She stepped further into the woods, letting her senses feel their way around her.

After a few minutes, she could no longer see the Pack down by the road. Then she couldn't smell them as easily. Once that happened, she stopped and began taking off her clothes. It was dusk now, and the moon in her blood told her that it wasn't full yet. But she could feel the wolf riding under her skin, looking for a way out, just as it had since she left the Nesters' camp.

Somehow, she could do this, even though it seemed impossible. *I can. I will.* Once she was naked, she stood in the trees, arms outstretched and eyes closed. She let the wind caress her skin, not caring if anyone saw her. The land washed over her in a torrent of sounds and smells, the very earth beneath her bare feet teeming with life in a way she'd not felt before. For that moment, she was one with the Valley and the magic, and it meant to make her its own.

The change, when it came on, was swift and nearly painless. She felt as if her wolf self emerged and wrapped itself around her body like a cape almost as if this was how it had always been. Becca Thornton hit the forest floor on all four paws and raced up the hill, following the general direction of the road.

Far below her, she could hear Molly and the others walking the road, their footsteps cautious on the gravel. Above her, she could smell fragments of wolf and fear and burning metal. Occasionally, there was the smell of human. But most of all, there was blood. Her Becca-self shuddered, fear-ing what she might find when she got to her destination, but it just drove her wolf body faster.

She slowed down when she got to where she'd left her car. She could see the tire tracks leading off toward the trees, but it was nowhere in sight. What had they done with it? If she'd been able to curse through her wolf muzzle, she would have done it then. Instead, she smelled something that sent her belly down into the brush.

Once there she made herself stay still while she tried to figure out what it was. It seemed like a whole hour later that she heard human voices on the trail. They were coming from somewhere up ahead of her, but what they were saying didn't seem to make much sense. She wondered if they'd seen her yet.

An eternity passed before she ventured to inch forward, then to stand up and slip as silently as she could up the hill. She could smell her own scent on the branches, then the smell of more humans, not all of them familiar. That alone was enough to send her deeper into the woods, away from the trail. She remembered to watch for the cameras in the trees this time, dodging the few she saw.

The clearing emerged in front of her and an overwhelming stench of burnt metal assailed her sensitive wolf nose. When she poked her head around a thick tree trunk, the sight of the trailer, or rather its burnt-out shell made her start back. It looked like it had been hit with an explosive of some sort, something strong enough to rip the metal apart. She could still see the bullet holes in the remaining metal. Maybe one of Carlos' bullets had hit the gas main or something.

There was a human lying in front of it. She could smell his death from her hiding spot. There seemed to be another one in the field further over. She thought she recognized Scott's white-blonde hair, but she couldn't see well enough to be sure. Her wolf senses were filled with blood and death, sending a panicked impulse through her until it was all she could do to not tear blindly through the woods.

But someone was alive and talking when she'd reached the clearing; she had to find out who it was. If she had to pick, she hoped it was Oya and not Anderson. She began circling the clearing as carefully as she could. Molly and the others would be up here soon enough. She needed to warn them about whatever they were walking into.

She slipped carefully through the trees and the brush, trying to look for cameras and survivors at the same time. It took a few minutes to locate the source of the voices, and she might have missed it if she hadn't been checking the trees. Anderson was up in one of them, his camouflage gear making

Silver Moon

him nearly invisible to human eyes in the greenery. He had a walkie-talkie held to his mouth and was speaking very softly into it.

Becca ducked behind some bushes and concentrated on listening. He seemed to be talking in some kind of code, as far as she could tell. "…take the package and drop it off. Repeat: we can't take it with us. Once the package is dropped off, meet me at the bridge. Over."

"Package?" What was he talking about? Her Becca-self screamed itself back to life. He must mean Shelly. And if they were "dropping the package off," that could only mean one thing. She slipped away from Anderson's tree and made her way toward the road as quietly as she could.

She hit the road at a dead run once she was certain Anderson couldn't see her. Whoever he was talking to had to be nearby: Adelía had said that the range on the Pack's radios was about two miles in these mountains. She couldn't imagine that the Nesters' had much stronger ones, so it stood to reason that if she could find vehicle tracks, she might be able to follow them.

Her heart was pounding as she skidded out on to the dirt. She stuck her nose into the ruts in the road and took a deep whuff of dirt and grass, wondering if this was how bloodhounds did it. Then there was a faint smell of tires, followed by the burnt butt of a cigarette, then a bit of oil. She started following the track downhill, nearly bowling Gladys over as her neighbor slipped noiselessly around a bend in the trail. They stared at each other for a moment.

Then Becca darted around the other woman, ignoring her startled gasp. Hopefully, Gladys would realize what she was doing and let Molly know that Becca was following a trail. There wasn't any time to lose.

It took a moment, then she heard the quick crackle of the walkie-talkie behind her. *The Pack is strong. They will follow,* she thought with what might have been relief had she been thinking with just her human brain. The scent trail went down and around rocks and hummocks, following the road around until it suddenly disappeared. Becca sniffed frantically. What was the point of being a werewolf if she didn't have a supernatural sense of smell?

Molly and Mrs. Hui appeared on the road behind her, their movements even quieter than Gladys'. It reminded Becca that she had no way to warn any of them about Anderson, not without changing back anyway. If she changed back, she might not be able to shift again, and the scent would be lost.

In a moment, the decision was made: Shelly was the first priority. Hopefully, Gladys and the others were being very careful. She circled the spot where the scents of man and metal seemed to disappear, each ring wider than the last.

Then she picked the trail up again on the other side of some rocks. With a quick glance back at the other Pack members, she began following it and they followed her. There was a large rock outcropping on the edge of the clearing and the trail led straight to it.

Then a quiet hiss from Molly stopped her in her tracks. There was a movement from the rocks ahead of them. She'd been so preoccupied with the scents that she hadn't noticed García keeping watch. He hadn't seen them yet, fortunately, or he'd have been firing at them.

Becca melted into the tall grass. When she looked back, Molly and Mrs. Hui were nowhere to be seen. She could smell and hear them though, and she knew they would make their own way across. She circled the clearing, hiding carefully in the Nester's blind spot.

Part of her brain wondered where they'd hidden her car and the white van. That got clearer when she got closer to the rocks: her car was covered in brush and parked off to the side. The white van was nowhere to be seen, but there were tire tracks going up a trail that had not been visible from the road.

Becca wanted to howl her joy. She had found them and now she would be able to strike back and save Shelly. She forced herself to look for García before she leapt up the trail at full wolf speed, dashing past the outcrop and into the trees on the other side. From behind her, she heard a startled curse and the click of a gun, followed by the dull sound of something or someone being hit with something. Hard. There was a sharp scent of blood on the air now, almost enough to make her turn back. But that wasn't what she wanted, not now.

She could smell something else on the breeze, too: wolf. Sick, trapped wolf, but one of her Pack, her alpha; she shot up the trail looking for Shelly. Oya stepped out of the trees in front of her, a gun in her hand but not looking in Becca's direction. Without stopping to think, Becca charged into her, knocking the Nester leader down. The Nester's rifle went flying too, and Becca pounced on it.

For an instant, she was torn between attacking Oya and finding Shelly; there would be no time to do both. Oya had rolled over and was yelling into her radio now. Becca kept running, dragging the gun in her jaws until she thought it was far enough away from Oya to drop it.

Ahead of her the white van glowed through the trees. There were two humans starting a campfire next to it, another human doing something with human food nearby. And a kneeling figure that seemed to be sitting

Silver Moon

perfectly still and watching them. A familiar scent washed over Becca and she nearly yelped with joy.

She forced the greeting back down into her throat, instead concentrating on using her momentum to swing off the trail and into the woods. Branches crackled beneath her paws before she could force herself to slow down and check for the Nesters. What if Molly and Mrs. Hui hadn't found Oya? She'd be here in a few minutes unless something stopped her. *Act now, act now*: the thought was a drumbeat keeping pace with the pounding of Becca's heart.

There was a yell from the road, back near where she had left Oya, and one of the humans next to the van got up with a curse. He walked down the road a few steps, then a couple more. Becca watched him, waiting for him to move out of sight of the others. Once he did, he was hers.

Bloodlust filled her then, driving away all conscious thought as she stalked her prey. The man was suspicious though, clearly alerted by the distant sound. His head swung from side to side and he turned, watching the woods around him. Becca's lip curled in a snarl. She would find him no matter what he did to protect himself.

She slid around him using the brush as cover. Another noise from down the road drove him forward a couple of steps. Becca struck in a whirl of teeth and claws, dragging him from the road before he had time to fire his gun. He flailed and went still as her teeth found his throat. Blood welled between her fangs as she bit down.

"Stop it." The voice came from somewhere behind her, its tone carrying the full weight of an alpha command.

But not her alpha. Becca spun around with a snarl, releasing the Nester in a bloody but still breathing heap. Erin stood there, her face expressionless. Her hands, fingers clenching, had not changed but her eyes gleamed silver. Becca backed off several paces, her throat still covered.

They stared at each other until Erin gestured her head slightly toward the white van, still visible through the trees. She knelt and took the Nester's gun before stepping carefully away through the trees. She didn't look back to see if Becca was following her.

It took a moment, a long moment of licking blood from her fangs, of imagining what it would be like to taste more before she was ready to leave the Nester. But finally Becca got up and went after Erin, shadowing her strides. She could hear more yelling from the road, then smell burning metal as a gun was fired.

Erin ducked behind a tree, then darted cautiously around it and ran toward the white van, her body bent nearly double to make herself a smaller target. Becca tore past her, nearly oblivious to the threat of the guns. Shelly's scent filled the air, calling her, driving her forward.

A moment later and Erin was running after her. Becca hit the group of Nesters around the van at full force, knocking Leroy down with a single blow. She jumped clear of him as one of the other Nesters fired at her, turning to lunge at him, snarling. He blocked her with the butt of his rifle, trying to push her into easier firing range, and she hit the ground with a yelp. Then she spun back and came at him from another direction, faster than any real wolf could have.

There were more shots all around her. The taste of blood on her fangs seemed to be casting a red haze over everything, clouding everything but the prey she wanted. She jumped, she struck, was struck in return. There was a chorus of human voices: shouting, moaning, cursing, making the clearing a cacophony.

Then there was a silence that fell so suddenly they all froze, Pack and Nesters alike. "I think that's enough." Shelly was standing next to Erin and each of them held a gun. Erin was just lowering hers, after firing the shot that caught everyone's attention. Shelly looked at Becca, "See if you can change back, hon. We'll need you for wrapping this up."

It took Becca a few moments to realize that her alpha was speaking to her now. She had orders, a direction, something she was supposed to do. The feeling made her go limp with relief, roiling rage dissipating into the earth beneath her paws.

She looked down and tried to remember what the feeble human inside her saw when she looked at her paws. Her wolf brain strained to remember; this was what she was supposed to do. She remembered walking on two legs, remembered her fur disappearing, remembered the pain of transformation. If she tried very hard, she could almost remember what it felt like to be that human. Almost.

What she couldn't seem to do was to become that other self.

Becca Thornton stood on her back legs, held out not quite human paws to her alpha and whimpered.

Silver Moon

Chapter 28

"**What are we going to** do with her?" Molly gave Becca a sidelong glance. "Is she going to be stuck like this?"

Becca thought about biting her. But that seemed like too much effort. Instead, she crouched in front of the back doors of the white van, rocking back and forth as she listened to the Nesters locked inside. They didn't sound very happy and that small satisfaction made her loll her tongue out of her mouth in a panting grin. Until she realized that she was doing it.

Then she hung her head, misery hanging off her like the clothes she was afraid that she might never wear again. Someone stepped up next to her and rested a quiet hand on her shoulder. She could smell Erin's concern, mixed with a little fear, as she stood there. "It's just that they've messed with your metabolism or something, Becca. We'll get you some help and get it out of your system. Everything will go back to normal. You'll see."

Erin's fingers stroked Becca's fur, the feeling disturbing and soothing at the same time. Human thoughts and perceptions came and went, mingling with the wolf in her brain until she wasn't sure what she felt. Part of her wanted to rip the doors off the van and make the Nesters pay for everything she was going through. The rest of her just wanted to be human again, or at least something closer to it. She felt like a bad special effect.

Shelly walked up, stopping a couple of feet away. "Do you think you can get her to Dr. Green's, Erin? Then meet us back up at the new location?" She spoke softly, like she didn't want the Nesters to hear anything from their metal prison.

New location? Becca tried to understand what that might mean. The Women's Club was long gone. They wouldn't be meeting at Shelly's house, not talking about it that way. Where else was there? A memory of old magic, of paintings and wolves and a need to change too unbearable to be

Silver Moon

ignored, washed over her. The cave! Wolf and human united inside her for a single purpose. That was where she might find peace.

But Erin was herding her toward a pickup truck, nudging her gently away from the others and the van. Gladys and Mrs. Hui were getting into the van and preparing to drive it away. Shelly and Molly and some of the other Pack members were headed down the road toward some of the other cars. *This isn't right.* The thought shot through her as if it had started in the ground under her paws and grown up through her like a vine.

She understood what she needed to do as if someone had shouted it into her ear. As the realization struck home, she took off running into the woods at top speed, ignoring Erin's shouts from behind her. She tore uphill as fast as she could, loping along on two legs, then four, as the terrain permitted it. The trees sped by in a blur as she clambered over rocks and splashed through streams. The magic was calling her now and she could follow it straight home.

The world slipped slowly into dusk as she ran, but the darkness didn't impact her hybrid wolf sight the way it had right after the injection. Her sense of smell seemed weaker though, and the human camp that she nearly stumbled into made her freeze into the shadows. Then she forced herself to breath in the scents of people and think about them as something other than prey. These were familiar smells: Wolf's Point people then, not outsiders. Her people, almost like Pack.

The knowledge that they were under Pack protection was enough to send her on her way. She slipped around them through the trees, treading light and moving almost too swiftly for any eye to catch. Then there was another crest beyond that, then more trees. She could see the mountain above the cave up ahead of her now. Her stomach grumbled with hunger now, the quick drinks she had taken from the streams she had crossed doing nothing to fill the emptiness.

But there wasn't time to hunt. She needed to be at the cave while the moon was still in the sky. Every instinct told her so. She kept running, hoping that prey would find her on the way.

She was stumbling a little when she finally reached the path to the cave. The moon hung over the trees when she got there, its not quite round shape hanging in the upper branches. She paused to looked up at it, a tiny howl failing at her parched and hungry lips. Then she scrambled on the loose rocks alongside the path as she forced her weary body upwards.

"What the hell?" The human voice was loud and sharp from the ledge just above her. Becca looked up and into the barrel of Lizzie's gun. The deputy was swearing in what sounded like two languages, one of which

Becca didn't recognize. She paused, torn between an urge to flee and her desperate desire to get to the cave.

Maybe she could tell the deputy who she was. She opened her mouth and choked out a strangled, unintelligible sound. She coughed her way around it, like it was a furball or something, trying to make it sound human. Lizzie's gun didn't waver. Instead she called over her shoulder into the cave, "Hey, Shelly. I think Becca's here but I'm not sure. Can you come out and verify that it's her?"

Becca leaned against the rocks, letting the exhaustion catch up with her. Her hand was bleeding and she licked at it, miserably. It took a moment to realize that she was licking skin, not fur. She reached up to touch her face just as Shelly appeared above her on the ledge. "Becca, come on up here."

She reached down and Becca took her hand. Between them, Shelly and Lizzie pulled her up the last few feet. Becca collapsed on the ground, panting. A water bottle appeared in front of her and she scrambled to open it, her hands trying to remember familiar gestures. She poured its contents down her parched throat before she even looked around.

Then she glanced up at Erin who was standing in the cave opening watching her. "Would've been faster to have gotten a ride with me."

Becca shrugged, not trusting herself to speak, and touched her face again. Her jaw was still too long, too fuzzy, to be human. She still hadn't completely changed back then. Her stomach growled again, making them all jump. "There's jerky in my pack," Lizzie volunteered from behind Becca.

She pulled herself up, first on four legs, then two. Then she lurched over to the small pile of packs by the entrance. What was all this stuff? She could smell all kinds of things: jerky and herbs and salt along with stuff that made no sense to her hungry brain. She ignored her questions in favor of tearing open a package of jerky and devouring it.

Erin reached down and took the pack from her as she chewed. Part of her was wondering if Erin was repulsed by the way she was eating. Becca Thornton would never have guzzled water in great slobbering gulps or clawed her way into a package of jerky like she had just done. Not under normal circumstances, anyway.

She made herself slow down and take smaller bites. She even closed her eyes and took a few deep slow breaths while she chewed. The jerky was gone far too soon, but she could feel the fierce intensity of her hunger retreat. She got back up.

Shelly was standing next to Erin and they were looking at the stuff in the packs. "Are you sure that this is what the Circle elders told you? I'm just wondering...well, hoping that there's another answer."

Silver Moon

Becca's ears pricked up. Shelly's voice was sad and she wanted to comfort her alpha somehow. The cave was lit by torches and their light travelled out far enough to outline the new shadows under Shelly's eyes, the silver in her hair. But Erin looked almost as worn out. She squeezed Shelly's shoulder lightly. "You know it has to be this way. The Pack needs you."

Something distracted Becca and she looked away from the two of them and into the cave. There was a pattern on the ground, outlined in what looked like sand. It called her, pulling her inside before she even realized that she was moving. She found herself at the edge of the pattern's outer circle without even realizing that she'd walked toward it.

Shelly and Erin were right behind her. Shelly spoke first, "No, Becca. Don't step into the pattern. We need it to tap into the magic of the valley."

Erin's voice overlapped hers. "Hey, she's changing back. Becca, hon, you with us again?"

Becca reached up and touched her face again. Everything felt normal, at least for her daytime self. Her cheekbones seemed to be popping through her skin though; she wondered if she looked as haggard as Shelly and Erin did to her. But then, it had been a rough week

She glanced from the pattern at her feet to Shelly. The Pack alpha sighed. "I guess we need to get you caught up. We couldn't find all the Nesters and Sara…Oya got away. We think they still have their lab and their so-called cure and we're down a few folks who got wounded." Shelly grimaced, her anger glowing across her features for a moment. "And if they can get their cure into the town's water supply or something along those lines, we're not sure what'll happen next…"

Erin picked up where she left off. "I spoke with the elders and this is what they thought would work to use the magic of the valley and stop the Nesters once and for all." She gave Shelly a quick glance, "They weren't too sure what was going to happen at the end of the ritual though, so I'm going to be the one to try it."

Becca frowned, "That sounds dangerous." Her voice came out as a croak but at least the sounds were making sense now. At the moment, though, that felt like the least of her worries. What would she do if something happened to Erin? Fear twisted its way through her gut when no one contradicted her.

Shelly looked like she'd aged a decade in the last minute. She looked at the pattern and didn't meet Becca's eyes. "She may not be Erin afterwards."

"Hey, maybe I won't survive it at all. Let's try and be optimistic here," Erin grinned, her smile a shadow of its former self.

"What do you mean?" Becca felt like throwing up. Or screaming and running through the place extinguishing the torches or anything else that might stop this craziness. This kind of news called for something more than just standing here, but for the life of her, she couldn't figure out where to start.

Shelly and Erin exchanged glances but Shelly spoke first, "In order to tap into the valley's magic, the magic that makes us wolves, someone has to perform some rituals, then channel the energy. It hasn't been done before in anyone living's memory. And when they did it last, they didn't write anything down. We've just got a few stories to go by. All the other information we had was at the Women's Club and you know what happened to that."

Erin stepped forward, reaching for Becca's hand. She turned her to face one of the paintings on the wall. It was one of the ones located near the entrance, showing a wolf on two legs with breasts. She was surrounded by a white glow and her arms/paws were outstretched like she was being pulled up into a spaceship or something. There was a second, much smaller drawing of the same figure in the background, running up a mountain.

"It just looks like she's going after something." Becca squinted at the wall and stepped closer.

"Well, according to the Circle, she channeled the magic and it changed her. Permanently." Erin let go of Becca's hand and was looked at the pictures too. Her face seemed distant, disconnected from what she was seeing.

No! The thought nearly tore itself out of Becca with a howl. She had to be able to stop this. Or at least to help Erin, somehow. She glanced around wildly, trying to figure out exactly what they were planning. The backpacks were inside the cave, stacked by the entrance. Based on what she'd seen of their contents, she guessed that whatever ritual they were going to try, it would be like the one from the first time she changed. But what other alternatives did they have?

Nothing jumped out at her until she looked back at the pattern. Its center called to her like it was the center of everything that was happening or going to happen. The notion hit her like an electric shock, but she wasn't sure what it meant. She peered down at floor, trying to puzzle the design out. Finally, she asked, "How does it work?"

Shelly stepped away from the packs, changing places with Erin to stand near Becca. "Well, it's like a maze, like the ones they use for meditation. Erin will need to follow the pattern through all the loops and turns. Something will happen at each of them, but we're not really sure what that'll be."

Silver Moon

"Why does it have to be Erin?" Becca could hear the desperation in her voice and barely controlled a flinch.

"Well, the legend says that it has to be the current alpha of the Pack. Since I was with the Nesters, Erin's been the alpha—" Shelly stopped abruptly, her eyes haunted.

"They used the cure on you too, didn't they?" Becca reached out and touched her shoulder gently. Shelly probably couldn't change now, not if they'd given her multiple shots, given what one dose of that crap had done to her. She would be powerless to lead as a wolf for the time being. And Erin had lost no time volunteering to sacrifice herself. That much was clear.

Becca looked from Shelly and Erin while her thoughts turned over. On the one hand, she couldn't say Erin was wrong. If this was what needed to happen, she would put herself in danger to save Shelly too. But maybe there was another way. After all, they were planning something dangerous based on hearsay and old stories and some cave art.

Cave art. That struck home and she looked around the walls from one painting to the next, studying each of them. All of them depicted a woman or a wolf or some blend of the two. Each one was shown alone, not surrounded by other wolves. Each painting was distinct from the others from different time periods as well, adding to the impression of isolation. That had to mean something, but what? Wolves weren't usually on their own.

She tried to imagine handling changing on her own with no Pack support. She'd tried it, tried to run off to Mountainview, and it cost a man his life. He didn't crop up much in her thoughts and dreams, not lately anyway, but she hadn't forgotten him either.

Given what he'd done to that little boy, she couldn't bring herself to regret his death, but maybe, just maybe, if she'd been with the Pack, she might have done something differently. There would have been someone else weighing in before it happened, at least. It might not have changed anything, but then again…

Her thoughts trailed off as she watched Erin do some more unpacking. She had a small drum, a couple of jars with white stuff in them, some feathers and a couple of other things. There was also a long, sharp knife with an ornate black handle. "What's that for?"

Erin blushed and looked down at the pack. "Well, it's not like I had a list of things to use. The valley's magic picks and chooses what it responds to and point of origin doesn't seem to enter it. I just figured that anything that worked for any of the traditions we knew might work here. From what the Circle said, intent was the main thing, and there are European traditions that call for using a knife to cut through spiritual barriers and channel energy. I figured it couldn't hurt to have it along."

"But the pattern looks almost Navajo—is it? Only this section looks more like a maze." Becca asked, the urge to ask questions rising more from a desire to delay whatever was going to happen than real curiosity. Outside, she could feel the moon rising higher in the sky, calling to her. Instinctively, she knew they'd have to do their ritual soon to be effective.

"I think so. I got part of it from a drawing that Maria, Shelly's mom, had in her files. The rest, honestly, I got from online." Erin looked up at Shelly with an apologetic grimace. "There hasn't really been time to ask what you think. Does this look crazy wrong to you?"

Shelly rubbed her hands over her face and swayed a little on her feet. "God, I wish I knew for sure. Hey, Lizzie, can we borrow you a minute?"

The deputy stepped cautiously inside the cave, glancing approvingly at Becca when she finished blinking in the torchlight. "Nice to see you back. What's up?"

"Do you remember anything Estella had to say about the old ways, how we used to do things? I can remember bits and pieces but not enough to get us much further than this." Shelly's expression was as frustrated as her voice. Her fingers flexed whenever she stretched out her hands, almost as if she was expecting her hands to change. "We lost so much when Margaret died before she could pass everything on."

Lizzie frowned down at the floor, mouth twisting in thought. "Well, nothing about a pattern that looks like this. There was that thing she used to say about walking the path with the Pack; it might have meant something along these lines. Or it might have been a strong suggestion that we not go out with the wrong sort of boys and start smoking at thirteen," Lizzie and Shelly exchanged eyerolls. Becca tried and failed to imagine either of them as teenagers.

Lizzie glanced over her shoulder toward the cave mouth and frowned. "Don't you have to do whatever you're going to do while the moon is still up? I mean no one knows for sure how they did this in the old days, right? Can you just let the magic tell you what it wants?"

"Out of the mouths of babes," Erin said with a grin. Becca noted that it was a tired and nervous one, but at least it looked like her usual smile. The one she might not have again if this worked out the way that they feared it would.

"Wait!" Becca held her hands out. She took a deep breath and closed her eyes, trying to feel the magic in the cave. Something pushed back gently against her, vanishing the moment she reached for it, like mist. She

Silver Moon

strained, reaching for whatever it was with every bit of energy she could summon. It hovered just out of range, almost taunting her.

She opened her eyes and stared at the others, frustration making her voice shake. "I think I know what we should do. It's just there, at the edge of my mind. The one thing that seems clear is that it needs to be all three of us, not just Erin."

"All three of us doing what?" Erin cocked her head slightly, her jaw seeming to elongate in the flickering light. "Walking the pattern?"

Becca gestured at the walls, cutting Erin and Shelly off before they could argue any more. "Look at them: all of them are alone. But they shouldn't be. There should be a Pack with them. Right?"

The others looked around. "It's just paintings of the alphas, Becca. More like memorials than depictions of Pack life," Shelly said, shrugging.

"It's still wrong. It's got to be. We have to do this together," Becca said, trying to feel more certain as she picked up three candles and lit them. "We need to walk the pattern together to make this work. I'm sure of it."

Erin looked at Shelly as if for guidance. Shelly gave her a long, baffled look back, then she stepped forward to the edge of the pattern on the floor. "Okay, we'll try it your way. Give me the knife. Maybe a candle, too. Then you two follow me."

Erin jumped forward. "No way! I go first. This is my responsibility. I took it on. Besides, I don't want to face Pete and Kira and the others if something happens to you." She held the knife in one trembling hand.

Shelly looked like she was going to object but after a moment, she nodded. "All right. If something goes wrong, at least maybe one of us can finish it. Lizzie, can you take the drum? You don't have to play anything special, just give us a good steady beat."

"What about guarding this place?" Lizzie looked uncomfortable and Becca couldn't blame her. If the remaining Nesters knew about the cave and attacked tonight, they'd be sitting ducks. Wolves. Whatever.

"This is more important." Shelly's lips quirked upward. "I think."

Erin let her breath out in what sounded like a sigh. "Let's get going then. I take point. Shelly, you're between us. Becca, you're last. If something happens and I tell you two to jump out of the pattern, do it. Anything goes wrong, it should only happen to me."

Becca grinned a little. They'd see if that was how it all worked out. She'd protect Erin, somehow. Even if the other woman didn't want to be protected. She handed lit candles to Shelly and Erin as Lizzie sat down near the cave entrance and started to drum. The sound rolled through the space, echoing until Becca could feel it in her bones.

Shelly murmured something that might have been a prayer or a bless-ing. Then she stepped forward and put her hand on Erin's shoulder. Erin faced the pattern, the knife in one hand, a lit taper in the other. Becca joined the line behind them, wondering nervously what was going to hap-pen next, despite her resolve.

They all stood there for a moment. Becca sent out a prayer of her own to whoever might be listening. Her stomach felt like it was filled with lead. What if doing this made all three of them change forever, not just Erin? She tried to shrug the fear away. They needed to try it and that was all there was to it.

Erin stepped forward, entering the pattern. Shelly and Becca followed her, stepping carefully so as to stay within its lines. As Becca stepped in-side the lines, she could feel the air part around her, invisible fabric spilling over her shoulders in a wave. She took another step, then another as she followed the others, her awareness narrowing to the women in front of her, the pattern under her feet and the sound of the drum.

That focus was why she banged her nose on Shelly's shoulder when her boss stopped abruptly. "Ow! Sorry about that," she murmured, some instinct telling her to keep her voice low. "What's the matter?"

"I'm not sure. Erin says she's hit a wall." Shelly murmured back without taking her eyes off Erin.

Erin had her hands in front of her, still holding the knife and the candle, but now it looked like her knuckles were braced on thin air, as if it was a glass door or window. There didn't seem to be any obvious edges to it, judging from the way that she was able to spread her arms out and still hit the barrier. She pulled her hands in and bowed her head over the candle for a moment. Becca couldn't tell if her eyes were closed or not.

Then she straightened up. "Give me your strength," she said over one shoulder.

What the hell did that mean? Becca was completely baffled. Should they push her through? Jump forward with the candles held out in some kind of Three Musketeers move?

There was a wave of *something* from Shelly, flowing more or less in Erin's direction. It smelt like wolf, whatever it was, and it settled on Erin's shoul-ders like a cloak. Becca bit her lip trying to figure out how to do it. She thought *wolf* and nearly shrieked when she saw her hands begin to length-en. Not that much wolf, then. Right. She closed her eyes and tried to push mentally in Erin's direction.

She missed the moment when Erin pointed the knife at the barrier and pushed forward with everything she had. They lurched forward and Becca

Silver Moon

nearly fell out of the pattern. She caught herself in time and looked over Erin's shoulder to see what was coming up next, but couldn't see anything except the design. They walked around the outermost part of the pattern slowly, but without incident.

Then at the second ring, there was a flash of light and Erin stumbled badly, landing on her knees in one of the pattern's twists. Shelly bent over her, holding her shoulders and steadying her from falling over the lines. Erin swayed and Becca nearly jumped forward to hold her; only Shelly's warning look held her back.

"I might have known that I'd find you here. Interesting little confab you've got going on." They all jumped as Oya's voice boomed from the cave opening. "Give me your gun, little groupie, or Cousin Shelly bites the dust." The gun trembled slightly in her hands but there was no way she could miss any of them at that range.

Lizzie cursed softly and looked like she'd like to tackle the Nester but her hands were full of the drums. Slowly, she reached up and unsnapped her holster. "What do you think you're going to do, Sara? Shoot us all and try and get out of the county alive? You know you won't make it."

Becca shuddered, hoping that Oya wouldn't take Lizzie up on the suggestion. She wondered what kind of bullets the gun would fire; did they have to be silver if they were all in human form? Would it hurt if they were? They said silver was pretty soft. She could feel Shelly tensing under her hands, clearly planning to try something. Erin was getting slowly and carefully to her feet, her boots scuffing the pattern a little but not blurring it too much.

Oya stepped closer and picked up the gun that Lizzie pushed toward her. She tucked it into her belt but kept her own gun trained on Shelly. Wherever she'd been since Becca saw her last hadn't been kind to her. There were big circles under her eyes, twigs in her unwashed hair and leaves all over her jean jacket. A cut on one hand was still bleeding and Becca could smell it from across the cave. It made her want to bite Oya more than usual.

Judging from the expression on Shelly's face, the feeling must be nearly universal. "So what do you want to do now, Sara? You're here by yourself so I'm guessing you lost your buddies along the way."

The Nester leader's breath hissed out between her teeth. "I'm Oya now. She who brings change. You will honor my warrior name by using it. Sara," she paused and nearly spat the word out, "was someone who wanted to be one of you. She's dead now."

"Sara was our grandmother's name. And you still are one of us, some-where under all the crap they've been pumping into you." Shelly stepped forward and Becca winced. The expression on Oya's face hardened.

Becca could feel Erin start to move, as if she was thinking about lung-ing forward. A horrible vision of Erin being shot again flashed through her mind and she nearly grabbed Erin's arm. But that would just draw Oya's attention. Becca didn't want to look down the barrel of that gun again. Well, any gun, truthfully. But here they were, stuck in the middle of this ritual while Oya seemed to be waiting for something. That was the only reason that Becca could think of that made her hold her fire.

She wondered what the woman was waiting for, then she remembered Anderson. If Oya was waiting on anything, it was probably him. When he showed up, he'd no doubt have a few more Nesters with him.

With that, came the realization that the moon was riding the sky over the cave, calling to her wolf self. She could feel herself responding to it. It was distracting, almost like two different people were trying to pull her in different directions. They needed to finish this now.

She closed her eyes for a moment and missed Shelly changing and Lizzie lunging for the gun. There was a shot and Erin knocked her to the floor, the impact knocking the breath out of her. She looked up to find Shelly charging Oya in wolf form, blood leaking from a hole in her ribs.

Lizzie hit the Nester from the other side as she fired again. This time the shot threw sand up in their faces as it hit the pattern, then ricocheted. The pattern. Becca glanced down at the sand rapidly getting rolled into an unidentifiable mass underneath them. Then she lurched to her feet and pulled Erin up with her. "Keep moving through it! If Shelly can catch up, she will, but we've got to finish this."

Erin looked at Shelly and Lizzie and Oya struggling near the entrance. Shelly fell back with a yelp as Oya hit her wounded side. Erin stepped forward with a growl, colliding with Becca as she blocked her progress. "If you want to help, keep moving. We've got to finish this. I can't do it on my own—I'm not alpha."

Another shot rang out and they both ducked. Becca gently shoved Erin forward, moving her past the part of the pattern that they had destroyed when they rolled on it. Part of the third loop in, and all of the smaller rings going into the center were still intact though. Erin stepped forward and it was as if walls surrounded them on both sides. Becca felt like she could reach out and touch them. She wondered if they were bullet-proof. She hoped they didn't have to find out.

Silver Moon

There was another wolflike yelp followed by a very human voice cursing from the entrance. Becca tried to move Erin along faster but it was as if the magic was slowing them down deliberately. Every step was an effort, every breath like lifting a heavy weight. The moon outside felt muted and Becca could feel the wolf inside her slide gradually into sleep. Or at least dormancy.

She could still feel the magic running through her like a current. Erin kept stepping forward, moving as if she was facing into a strong wind, with Becca's hands on her shoulders serving as anchor and link. Becca could feel the pressure too; she tried to keep her head down and her focus on where her feet were moving. It seemed to help a little.

Or at least it did until Shelly skidded across the floor, still in wolf form, and crashed into them. Becca went to her knees while Erin stumbled and swayed. Lizzie yelled something that might have been a warning and there was a giant flash, like a flame in the center of the pattern. Becca glanced toward the cave entrance and saw Anderson and several of the other Nesters coming up the path. "Run for the center!" Erin yelled pulling Becca up and steadying Shelly as she scrambled up on all fours.

And they did. It was like running up a mountain in the snow. Shelly was changing back as she ran when Becca looked back. Anderson had a rifle in his hands, aiming at them all. There were two Nesters holding Lizzie against the wall and Oya was standing now, blood running down her chin. "Look out!" Becca yelled, ducking as much as she could while still moving.

Something whizzed past her. Erin gave a groan and staggered and Becca caught her, "Erin, no!" Her foot slipped and she was horrified to see blood beginning to obscure the pattern. *Not again.*

Shelly grabbed her shoulders with newly human hands. "Keep her going. We're almost there." She pointed forward: they had the last and shortest loop in front of them. Then the center and whatever happened next.

Becca strained to lift Erin. Anderson and his men were still firing. Unless they kept moving, they were all dead. She reached down deep inside herself and heaved Erin through the last few steps. She felt a sharp pain as something hit her shoulder hard. It burned with a white-hot agony, but the three of them kept staggering forward. The cave spun around Becca now, the torchlight dimming. *This is it, then,* she thought, taking a ragged breath.

Shelly growled softly in her ear. "We are not dying here or now. Move!" The word was like a verbal shove, the full weight of an alpha command behind it. Something in Becca responded and even Erin seemed to rouse herself and scrambled the last few steps.

The center of the pattern was nearly all that remained; the rest of it was obscured with blood or wiped out by their efforts to get through it. Erin went limp and Becca placed her gently down. Then, on impulse, she reached out and grabbed Erin's hand, holding it as she stood up. Shelly gave her a quick look before Becca took her hand as well.

"Now, howl as loud as you can. Turn the wolf inside loose. We're out of time," Shelly's voice was distant, as if it was coming from much farther away than the tiny semicircle they now formed.

Sure, easy for you to say, Becca thought. She squinted out into the cave and tried to see if Lizzie was okay. Then Shelly howled and the human thoughts began to dribble out of her mind. She threw back her head and howled with her alpha. The sound seemed to rouse Erin as well, and with a weak croak, she joined them.

The current that Becca had felt in the pattern came to life, crackling around them like a force field. Shelly said something that Becca didn't quite catch, and then there was a moment where everything was completely still: Nesters, wolves, Lizzie, even the magic.

Then it exploded back to life. Shelly's head arched back and she braced her feet far apart. For a moment, a wolf's head flickered around her like old film, at least to Becca's eyes. Then it hit her too and she staggered, held upright by Shelly's support. It was like being on fire or like changing partway and being suspended between wolf and woman. Erin's hand twitched in hers as the power, whatever it was, tossed her from the floor to stand unsteadily next to them.

The cave was glowing now and it seemed to Becca that all the paintings were in motion, racing around the walls as fast as they could go. At first, they stayed on the walls, circling the cave and disappearing at one side of the entrance, reappearing on the other. They began moving faster and faster until finally the first one leapt free, followed by another. A surge of painted wolf-women in various stages of transformation moved toward the Nesters at the entrance.

One man broke and ran, but Anderson and Oya and one or two others held their ground and fired their guns. Then the paintings struck back. Becca could barely see what was happening now. The cave was full of smoke and shots being fired and the cave's magic was controlling her movements. She could feel the urge to change move from Shelly to take over her own body and she screamed in agony. It felt like the Nesters' cure was getting burned out of her veins.

It twisted its way through her for a few moments, then the pain vanished to be replaced with a full change and she dropped to all fours. Shelly

Silver Moon

was human now, she noticed as she glanced at her alpha, so that just left Erin. The magic seemed to strike at Erin just as Becca thought she would be next and Erin yowled as it ran through her. The Nester's bullets broke free of all of them and dropped to the floor.

Then, with a howl like Becca had never heard before, Erin dropped to her knees, then scrambled as they turned into paws. For a horrible moment, her face was human while her body changed as if the magic had forgotten a part of her. Becca closed her eyes for a moment and prayed to any deity that might be listening that the legend wasn't going to come true.

A scream near the entrance made her jerk her eyes open and her head around. Anderson had fallen under the weight of the paintings, but Oya… Oya was still standing and surrounded by them. They were circling her like they'd done on the walls before they got free. Becca couldn't help but think that they looked like paper dolls at the same time that her wolf nose was telling her that they were Pack.

Apparently, they looked a lot scarier up close. Oya had her face in her hands. One of the wolf-women, the one Kira had painted of Shelly, reached out and touched her head. Oya glowed for a moment, then she changed. Two of the paintings circled and blocked Becca's view. Then she was preoccupied with her own change as she was wrenched back to human.

A quick glance at Erin showed her that her friend was human once more, though still covered in blood and clearly in pain. She looked at Shelly too, just to make sure. The alpha was standing with her arms, not paws, stretched above her head, like she was giving thanks for something or calling on a power that Becca couldn't see.

Whatever that power was, it seemed to move in a wave from the three of them and the pattern toward the cave entrance and the painted women. Becca could see Anderson lying very limp and still but that was nothing compared to what happened when the paintings stopped circling Oya.

She had changed. Her eyes were still human above her fur-covered muzzle and she didn't have full wolf form yet. Instead, she swayed on her huge hind legs with forearms that were part claw, part hand. It was like something out of a bad horror movie.

She looked down, then back up at Shelly. She tried to say something but all that emerged from her muzzle was a snarling growl, followed by a doglike bark. At that moment, Becca almost felt sorry for her. Oya, still growling, broke through the circle of paintings and vanished outside. Becca could hear her crashing through the underbrush, running away from the cave and Wolf's Point.

Shelly sang a word, then two, in that language that Becca didn't understand and the paintings began to circle once more. The circle got wider and wider this time until each painting merged back with the cave wall. A moment later, they were all back on the walls and perfectly still, as if nothing had happened.

Erin passed out, her body collapsing limply against Becca's shoulder. Lizzie stood up slowly. "Holy shit, coz. That was...amazing." She ran a hand through sweat-soaked hair. Her sunglasses seemed to be missing. "Oh crap. Erin. She's still breathing, isn't she?"

Becca nodded. Her heart raced frantically as she checked Erin's pulse. But the wound in her shoulder still gushed blood and the sight filled Becca with terror. Lizzie began to cross the pattern but it was Shelly who reached down and touched Erin's shoulder. There was a spark and a smell like burning herbs and the blood slowed, then stopped.

Erin's breathing grew less frantic and Becca grinned up at Shelly. Shelly grinned back though she looked drawn and exhausted. Together they maneuvered the barely conscious Erin to her feet and moved her out of the remains of the pattern.

A sound outside made everyone except Erin flinch and look up. Lizzie dove for one of the Nester guns and spun around to face the entrance as Molly, Mrs. Hui, Gladys and the rest of the Pack scrambled up the path. "Dammit." Molly's voice echoed a little in the cave. "I told you we were going to miss all the fun."

Silver Moon

Chapter 29

In the end, they had to build a stretcher to carry Erin down the mountain. That was after they changed into the clothes that Mrs. Hui and Gladys thought to bring. Then they all filed down the trail, taking turns with the stretcher. It felt like a triumphal procession, except for Becca's fears for Erin.

But Pete and Kira and the twins were waiting for them at the bottom of the trail. Dr. Green was with them, along with some other familiar faces.

Becca let Pete enfold her in a big, fierce hug. She had never seen him look so happy before. The feeling was contagious, especially when she heard Erin's voice from behind her.

She was sitting up, her arm back in the now familiar sling as Dr. Green wrapped her shoulder, and they were talking in low voices. Becca walked over and sat down next to them. "I'll be helping Erin out with her arm this time, Doc. What do I need to do?"

Erin gave her a surprised glance followed by that slow cowboy smile that Becca realized she hadn't seen in ages. She hadn't realized how much she missed it until now. She smiled back.

She was still smiling when they got back to Wolf's Point. Molly dropped them off at Erin's place, since she'd need help getting to bed even with werewolf recuperative powers. Between them, they got her cleaned up and into bed and the couch pulled out for Becca. She didn't think she was ready for anything closer than that yet, and Erin was already asleep. She and Molly exchanged a few whispers about getting groceries the next day and fetching Becca's car back from the Nester camp, then the other woman took off, leaving her in the quiet dimness of Erin's living room.

Silver Moon

Becca thought she would never fall asleep after all the excitement, right up until the moment when she did.

The sun was high in the sky when she woke up. There wasn't any noise from overhead yet, which meant Erin was still sleeping. She got up very quietly and took a shower in the basement bathroom. After that, there was coffee to be made and breakfast to be scavenged up. She didn't want to leave Erin alone just yet so when she was done, she moved quietly up the stairs to check on her.

Erin's eyes flickered open as she came in, her body tensing for an instant, then relaxing as she recognized Becca. That just left Becca looking for something clever to say. "How are you doing? I made coffee." The last comment made Becca feel silly; after all, Erin could smell the coffee from here. But she grinned at Becca anyway and it was like a second sunrise.

Then Erin held out her good hand. "Help me up?"

It took a while, but eventually Becca got her dressed and downstairs for breakfast. Erin was already steadier on her feet and some of the scrapes and smaller wounds were well on their way to healing. They ate the breakfast that Becca threw together quietly, occasionally watching each other sidelong and smiling. It gave Becca the weirdest, most wonderful feeling.

Which disappeared when Molly showed up with two bags of groceries, then joined them for the rest of breakfast. Couldn't she eat with Carlos and....the other guy? The thought made Becca momentarily resentful until she realized that she was being childish. Erin wasn't *hers*, after all.

Finally, Molly leaned back in her chair. "Okay, we all ready to face the real world now?" Becca was baffled; hadn't they just done that? "Erin, have you told Becca yet?"

Erin clutched at her face with her good hand and groaned. "Shit. No. I forgot, what with everything else going on. Becca, first let me tell you we'll make this right. This is my fault—I dropped the ball on the problem when the Nesters got Shelly"

"Dropped what ball? What are you talking about?" Becca looked from Molly to Erin and back again. What else could there be? Then it struck her and she got up slowly and started for the front door. Erin and Molly scrambled to follow her as she flung the door open and looked across the street.

Her house was still standing so that was one worry down. But the "For Sale" sign on the lawn was new. "What the hell are they doing to my house?"

"Your husband came by with a realtor and that lawyer cousin of his right after the Nesters took you. Look, Becca, I've got some savings. And the

Pack still has money in the emergency fund. We'll make this right." Erin's voice sounded anguished and guilty.

Becca felt numb. That house was the last of her old life. It meant security and a certain degree of comfort. It had been her refuge after Ed left. "I'm going to see what he took."

She walked across the street, the other two trailing after her. She felt like she was having a bad dream, one that she couldn't wake up from. What was she supposed to do now? Molly and Erin were whispering behind her, the noise adding to her irritation. When she got up to the front door, she turned around. "I think I need to do this by myself. Give me a few minutes." She let herself in and closed them out.

It didn't feel right, shutting them out, but she ignored that feeling, buried it deep. Instead, she walked through the house looking at her books and her photos. Her furniture. She couldn't help but notice that it was a lot cleaner and that everything had been straightened up.

Then she began to notice that things were missing: a keepsake here, some extra throw pillows there. She ran through the house in a panic until she got to the basement. Someone had begun to carefully pack things up. Each box was labeled for a different room and had a list of the contents on the side. She tore one open to check and sure enough, everything was there.

In a way that hurt more than the rest of it. There was nothing that Ed wanted of their old life that he hadn't taken away already. She rubbed away an angry tear before venturing back up stairs. Then she sat down at the kitchen table with the big pile of mail that had come in since she'd been gone.

Buried in with the catalogues she didn't like and the ones she did, the bills she still needed to pay and the advertising circulars, was the official letter telling her that the house was going up for sale. There was a Post-it on it from Pamela that mentioned several attempts to contact her. It also mentioned that there was some serious interest from a buyer. There would also be some contractors stopping by to make repairs and get everything up to code.

Becca sat there and stared at the letter like it was on fire. How had this happened? *Oh yeah, crazy werewolf hunters, jackass ex-husband. It's coming back to me.* Despite everything, the thought made her laugh a little. With all she'd survived and done in the last few months, how did this compare?

There was a noise from the porch and she got up to check it out. Erin and Molly were hanging around outside, just in case she needed them. She took one more look around, then took a deep breath and went to open the

Silver Moon

door. "Looks like there's going to be some changes around here. How about you come in and help me decide what to pack?"

It was broad daylight the next time Becca Thornton studied her face in the mirror. She looked haggard and worn but the wolf wasn't staring back out of her eyes. Not yet. That would come tonight, along with the scent of trees and the wind in her fur. And the company of others just like her, all of them running free through the woods. Their woods.

The "For Sale" sign was still up on the lawn but it looked like she had a few days to finish packing and think about where she wanted to live. And about what to do about Erin.

Everyone, including Pete and Shelly, thought that she should take Erin up on her invitation to move into Erin's house. She wasn't sure that she was ready for that yet, but then she hadn't been sure that she could ever handle turning into a wolf on a regular basis either.

Maybe there would be a lot of new beginnings, rather than the finish she thought she was headed for. She picked up the phone and made a reservation for two on an upcoming whitewater-rafting trip.

Catherine Lundoff is the two-time Goldie Award-winning author of *Night's Kiss* (Lethe Press, 2009) and *Crave: Tales of Lust, Love and Longing* (Lethe Press, 2007), as well as *A Day at the Inn, A Night at the Palace and Other Stories* (Lethe Press, 2011) and *Silver Moon: A Women of Wolf's Point Novel* (Lethe Press, 2012). She is the editor of *Haunted Hearths and Sapphic Shades: Lesbian Ghost Stories* (Lethe Press, 2008), a 2010 Gaylactic Spectrum Award Best Other Work. She is also the co-editor, with JoSelle Vanderhooft, of *Hellebore and Rue: Tales of Queer Women and Magic* (Lethe Press 2011). In her other lives, she's a professional computer geek and periodically teaches writing classes at The Loft Literary Center in Minneapolis and elsewhere. She is owned by two cats and is the proud spouse of her fabulous wife.

Website: www.catherinelundoff.com

CPSIA information can be obtained at www.ICGtesting.com
Printed in the USA
LVOW041137200512

282472LV00007B/11/P

9 781590 213797